ZONE TRIP

KITTY TURNER

Thank you, Rob
Your support is the
break I've been waiting
for.
Kitty Turner

DAILY ⌂ HOUSE

Zone Trip

Daily House, LLC

Author: <u>Kitty Turner</u>

First Edition

This is a work of fiction. All of the characters, organizations, and events portrayed in this novel are either products of the author's imagination or are used fictitiously.

For Kelly

"I pledge allegiance to the illusion and to the pyramid scheme for which it stands. One species, in denial, with error and excess, by all."

— BISHOP JOEY (EDWARD HOLMES)

CONTENTS

PART I

1

FORT POINT

I would never have agreed to this if it hadn't been Leo's idea. But it was his idea, and that changed everything. A waft of alcohol and adrenaline mixed with the primordial smell of the kelp-filled ocean. Freezing water streamed from my hair and beard. Beside me, Leo whooped and shot me a thumbs-up like a raving lunatic.

Leo, Lydia, and I clung to the Rust-Oleum painted barrier chain on the Fort Point seawall. The four-story fortification loomed behind us on a stout cliff at the end of the spit of land where the Pacific Ocean became the San Francisco Bay. Reaching from its anchor at the base of the fort, the Golden Gate Bridge stood sentinel. Lighting crackled through the grid of orange girders and cables. Across the screaming mouth of water, dark thunderheads bristled over Mount Tam, crazing the dome of the moonlit sky.

My whiskey and ginger ale sat half-finished on the coffee table in my warm, dry apartment. Thanks to Leo's obsession with the Suicide Club, he dragged Lydia and me from our comfortable spot in front of Doom VR 2030 to this godforsaken place. During the original inception of that now-defunct secret society, nearly fifty years ago, the four founding members faced their deaths by challenging hurricane-force winds and waves on this exact spot. With climate change, the violence and frequency of dangerous weather had grown on the Pacific seaboard, but this storm was one for the records. This was what Leo had been waiting for.

Weather Girl sheltered herself from the worst of the hurricane. Under the streetlights set back from the walking path, toothpaste-blue braids peeked out from behind a long Nikon lens that blocked most of her face. Her cheap plastic poncho snapped a rhythm in the gusts.

Bracing for the biggest wave yet, I held fast. An anxious thought snapped my eyes in Lydia's direction. Water towered so high over us that it cast her shadow and blocked the sight of the bridge. As the tumult fell, her arms lifted to the air like wings.

What the fuck?! She let go!

When the water receded, she was gone, carried away in the surge to the gloomy, wet world below. Her shape appeared, hard to see, tossed into the cement jacks that plunged from the promenade in a sloping jumble. No beach, just sharp rocks and whirlpools.

"Lydia!" Leo shouted down the drop of the wall.

"I'm here," she called back faintly.

"Lower me!" Leo yelled.

I stared, unable to move, frozen to the spot by a shotgun blast of fear.

"Snap out of it, Evan! We don't have much time! Quick! Lower me!" Leo roared again over the wind.

My skin prickled as I willed myself into action. I used my body as a counterbalance and eased Leo down the ten-foot drop to the jagged terrain of the breakwater. Hand to wrist, his skin was slick, he slipped free of my arms, giving way just as his feet touched the ground. Leo didn't think, he just leaped from precarious foothold to foothold. My own clumsy feet would have betrayed me. I was sure of it.

Moonglow faintly illuminated the two dark figures in the rocks. I could just make out Leo standing over Lydia's prone shape. He heaved her up to her feet and I breathed a sigh of relief. At least she was able to stand. The waves came in sets. I'd been counting. Every fifth wave had crashed over the walking path and reached the wall of the fort. A telltale swell grew in the bay and rolled toward them. My neck strained as the power of my voice erupted, "Hurry up! The next one's huge!"

Weather Girl appeared at my side. She framed me in a closeup then swept the darkness below with her camera to capture the rescue.

"Get back!" I ordered.

Thankfully, she obeyed, returning to the safe circles of light at the edge of the parking lot. Weather Girl shouted something, but I couldn't hear her over the rush of blood in my ears. It flashed across my mind that she had caught my heroics on video and not the frozen state of panic from a moment before. I pushed the vanity from my thoughts.

In the last yard of the escape, Lydia disengaged herself from Leo's grip, grappled with the top of the wet wall, and swung her petite body up with little effort. Close behind, the rising whitewater lifted Leo over the embankment and onto the footpath. He grabbed me as the airless suck of the tide pulled at my clothes and body.

Weather Girl rushed forward again to help drag us out of the storm surge before the receding wave washed us back into the break. She held up her SmartCuff to show the scrolling comments and rocketing viewer count of her live stream.

"Oh my god, that was fuckin' spectacular! Are you alright—Damn, you guys are nuts. I'm sure you're really freaked, but do you think we can do an interview? Look at this. We're at nearly a million viewers."

Leo accepted a lapel mic from Weather Girl with unnatural calm. She adjusted her lens for a closeup, the wild sea and plumes of spray framed the shot.

"We don't believe that one person can dictate what another can do. It doesn't matter if he's a judge, a cop, or a tax collector. I mean, America is supposedly a democracy, but no one consulted me on whether or not I can risk my own life for my own reasons. We push boundaries. We fear nothing. To forego dignity and face one's own death means real freedom," Leo delivered with his madman's charm.

Calm descended, despite the pure chaos of the situation. We should have been killed, yet I felt electric and invincible. That was the start of it—a feeling of stepping out of time. It was a feeling I would chase for the rest of my life.

2

RAIN DOGS

I awoke in the walkup apartment above my comic book shop. Beer bottles and glasses with dregs of whiskey or clotted milk from Lydia's white Russians littered every flat surface. A trail of dried salt and seaweed dislodged from my slept-in jeans on my shuffle to the bathroom. I kicked off the ruined pants into a stiff, sandy pile of denim on the white and black checkerboard of tiles.

Under the hot spray of a shower, my leg throbbed from a missing chunk of flesh that the rusty chain had claimed during my scramble to pull Leo over the seawall. Water rinsed away the stinging and relaxed the knots in my muscles. Wincing, I inspected the wound and picked out bits of debris from the bloody cut. The dislodged iron flakes and paint chips swirled across the age-stained enamel.

I dressed for work in a black hoodie and clean pair of

Levi's, popped a couple of Tylenol, and stepped outside onto the landing. The sun had not entirely cleared the rooftops to the east. A wormy smell rose out of the overgrown backlot as I clattered down the damp, mossy stairs that crisscrossed the rear of my building to street level. As I opened the back door of Rain Dogs Comics, the usual odor of pulp paper and a faint whiff of mildew greeted me from the gloom. The tick, tick, tick from a black Kit-Cat Klock sounded louder than usual. Lydia had given me the cat clock for my birthday last year. It had a rhinestone bowtie.

I didn't bother to unlock the front door as I walked past windows that looked onto an empty street. My movement brought the vMac at the register to life. It greeted me in a series of bright tones. Yesterday's sales report hung in the air—a paltry $130. I swiped it away with a frustrated thought. In 2032, pulp comic collectors were as rare as buffalo nickels. The ones who still collected did business with me online, mostly from overseas. I considered half a dozen purchases from walk-ins a great day.

Fortunately the rental units above the shop brought in a comfortable amount of money each month. Rain Dogs had been founded by my Aunt Cloe, the only blood relation with a kindred creative soul. Before she died, we shared a geeky love of 80s and 90s art and music—David W. Mack, Tom Waits, Mudhoney, Tool, Dave McKean. Cloe sold vintage vinyl, punk ephemera, and some rare books back in the day. Two years ago, when I inherited the store and six apartments, I transitioned to graphic novels and comics. Bibliophiles were easier to get along with than music fanatics.

I closed the sales report and opened YouTube. Weather Girl's footage from last night's stunt was at the top of my video history. My weak disgust with social media always lurked in the background of my mind, but it wasn't strong enough for me to change the habit of checking the feeds first thing in the morning. Lydia, Leo, and I had watched the video repeatedly last night, but this morning's unbelievable view count prompted me to click play again.

At least I didn't look like a coward. Regardless, Leo stole the show. He was magnetic! A replay of the live comments scrolled under the video as the timecode ticked by—"idiots," "assholes," and "reckless morons" alternated with the "heroes," "sexy," and "I want to do that!" Post after post, page after page, it was a typical mixed bag of reactions.

Weather Girl had pinned Lydia's post promoting the Freeschool to the top of the comments. The school was Lydia's and Leo's side-hustle that I hosted in Rain Dogs' reading lounge. They were here most days running their sliding-scale classes. The result of Lydia's "free" advertising was over 300 emails. Fuckin' Lydia and Leo had no idea how long it took to write back to hundreds of people. This was far from the first careless post that cost me hours, but my irritation evaporated once I entered the flow of work.

Mostly, I didn't mind sharing my space with them. I enjoyed what I did for Lydia and Leo, even if keeping up with their demands, selling comics, and finishing my Masters in Computer Science equaled three full-time occupations. Leo and Lydia didn't know about my traditional college classes. Boring and useless, Leo would say. And Lydia would angrily protest the money wasted. Free education was her passion. Why pay for what's all around, Lydia always said.

She was the true leader of the Freeschool, but without Leo, she'd be teaching poetry appreciation or some vegan-feminist studies bullshit. The idiocy we got up to and the esoteric curriculum sprang from the mind of Leo, one-hundred percent. His idea of education included radical cosplay, food fights, takeovers of public spaces, amateur pornography, and general misanthropy.

Leo was just as brilliant as Lydia but in a totally different way. It almost seemed like he could read people's minds, and he used that talent to his advantage. Compact and hairy, no one ever accused Leo of being handsome, at least not in the conventional sense. Strangers described him as ugly, yet he transformed after a sentence or two. One of my favorite things was watching the resulting confusion of that metamorphosis. Though some were immune to Leo's charm, it was rare.

I finished answering the emails, posted the same general update across our social media, and updated Instagram with photos from the stunt. After checking that off my list, I added the new Freeschool classes to the website. Lydia had left a schedule of February's courses penned in nearly illegible drunken scrawl by the register.

A single customer rapped on the glass. I ignored her.

At eleven, I finally gave in and opened the front door. Water ran hard in the gutters, and downed branches littered the road, but my property appeared intact after last night's storm.

Past the "employees only" sign, Lydia still slept on an overstuffed sofa that I had salvaged from the curb on bulk trash pickup day. It was in good condition and didn't smell —a major score by my measure. Lydia had a chill, minimalist loft across town in SOMA, but she couch-surfed my break room a lot, especially after a night of drinking and a caper.

Taking care not to wake her, I crept in and watched the rise and fall of her chest. Her dark hair was piled in a messy bun held together by two Bic pens. The cut above her eyebrow looked like it needed antiseptic and a stitch or two. Just as I reached out to touch the dried blood, the brass shopkeeper's bell rang like an alarm. A moment later, Leo burst into the break room where I had been watching Lydia sleep.

"What the fuck?" Lydia said.

She craned her neck and rolled her shoulders.

"Damn, doesn't anyone knock?" she asked, eyeing me, then him.

"Grab some beers!" Leo ordered.

I hadn't had breakfast, but sure, why not. I hooked three Fat Tires from the mini-fridge and passed them around.

"Well, fuck me! Over three million views and counting. Have you seen this?" Leo waved his SmartCuff in an arc in front of my face. He had the latest tech, a V10, which featured 3D video projection. It was an unperfected technology, but impressive all the same. A ghostly image of our antics from last night seemed to hover over his wrist. Lydia took a contemplative swig from her bottle, appraising Leo with feline scrutiny over the rim of her beer.

"We need to do another stunt like last night's! Or something to top it. Viral. Fucking viral. Let's invite more people to their own suicides. What do you think?" Leo said with manic glee.

"What's the draw?" Lydia asked. "I mean, it's a big risk, but what's the reward?"

"Leo's everlasting love and acknowledgment," I said with a razor's edge.

Leo deflected the jab I aimed at his glaring need for adoration. "Yeah, my love *is* what you really want, Lydia." He blew her a kiss. "Anyway, never mind that. Let's celebrate at Wormwoods!" He stepped toward Lydia to pluck at the lapel of her vintage cardigan like he was picking a burr. Her whole demeanor melted. Leo looked at me, a half-smile ticking up one corner of his mouth.

A two-day bender wasn't going to help with the creeping deadlines for my thesis—a frustration I couldn't share with my friends. Lydia didn't seem that enthused about riding Leo's craziness out to the bar for some day drinking either. I threw her a pleading look, but she shrugged. As usual, no backup there.

On the walk, the chill wind of late January billowed the hood of my sweatshirt. A rusty, damp patchwork of leaves covered the sidewalk. Past 14th, a short zag took us across Market and into the Mission District. Drones hummed overhead. We walked by sign after sign advertising spaces for lease. Most restaurants and businesses hadn't stood a chance against the tide of mega-online retail and autonomous food delivery. Commercial spaces now held illicitly housed people and activities, the windows painted black from the inside. Bars still did a booming business though, even with the widespread popularity of designer pharma.

At the door of Wormwoods, we broke through the barrier of warmth blown from an ancient Modine that looked more like a 70s mainframe than a gas heater. Velvet-flocked wallpaper peeled in the damp. Leo mounted the stool furthest from the street and Lydia sat next to him, inching her seat closer to his side. Thick coats of glossy dark-red paint covered what I guessed had once been beautiful millwork. The bar was a single carved timber topped by a counter edged in brass. Hidden sculptures of Black Forest figures lurked beneath to gawk at patrons' knees.

I sat on the other side of Lydia. The legs of my stool wobbled on uneven planks sanded down by the shoes of countless drunks. In the barback mirror, a fierce bum stared at me. My lank, black hair covered one bloodshot eye and an unkempt beard stubbled the lower half of my face. My hood, still up, cast shadows on my cheeks. Late nights with Leo and Lydia were starting to show.

A grizzly punk behind the bar grunted at us, his hair clipped into short hog bristles. Wormwood's regular bartenders knew us, but this guy must have been a recent hire.

"Whaddaya have?"

Towering and beefy, his black leather vest showed off full sleeves of tattoos.

"Jack, neat," Leo said.

"Bloody Mary," Lydia ordered.

"I'll have Jack and ginger."

The bartender grumbled and reached into the well for mixers and garnish. He stirred horseradish, lemon juice, and Worcestershire into Lydia's glass, shooting her stink eye for the extra work. My drink tasted mossy and too sweet, but at least it chased away the fatigue from the last twenty-four hours.

"You need to clean your hoses, man," I told the barman.

He replied with a fuck off, which I totally expected. I loved San Francisco's ferocity.

"Death Wish Club?" Leo said.

"What?" I asked, puzzled.

"The new group. We'll call it the Death Wish Club."

"That will discourage people from joining," I said.

"You think Suicide Club had more curb appeal?" Leo glared at me.

Leo's obsession, the Suicide Club, had been an extreme urban exploration society that lasted from 1977 to the mid 80s. Creative differences morphed the club into the Cacophony Society, more of an underground arts group, but that too had eroded into vague remnants by the early 2000s.

"How about Chaos Order!" Lydia interjected.

She knocked a splash of Bloody Mary onto the bar in her excitement. I cringed. She always tried to please Leo, but I played along.

"Yeah. That's kinda funny! The words, they cancel each other out. Chaos—Order—," I said, geeking out on the creative wordplay rather than the implications. "Not bad."

I caught the barman's curious eye. He swabbed at Lydia's spilled tomato juice with a nubby grey rag.

"You guys, you're from the Freeschool, right?" he asked.

"Yeah," Lydia answered. "You been there before?"

"Sure. Just down the street, right? I took a class on making goo balls there. Had a big crop, didn't know what to do with it all. I've been to your show at The Box a couple of times, too. I thought I recognized y'all. I heard you talking about this Chaos Order idea —sounds interesting. What is it exactly?"

"That's what we're figuring out. No spectators. That's for sure. If you wanna watch, go home and follow us on Instagram. We question everything. We're anarchists, but we don't take ourselves too seriously—no pipe bombs or inciting riots or that kind of shit. Our attacks are on conformity, not directly on political or corporate powers, more like disruption of the norm; defiance, art. And it's definitely about overcoming fear. That's the main focus, I think. You become invincible if you overcome your fear of death. Of course, it takes massive balls to join," Lydia came up with on the fly.

I glanced at Leo to see if he was impressed with how thoroughly Lydia understood his vision. If he was, I couldn't tell.

"Check it out," Leo said. He tapped his SmartCuff to pull up Weather Girl's video. The four of us huddled around the replay once again.

"Is that for real?" the barman asked.

"Hell, yeah," Leo said. He gave Lydia a pinch under the bar. She squirmed. "The three of us get into places we're not supposed to. We scaled the Golden Gate Bridge plenty of times. A fair amount of breaking and entering, but not to steal stuff. Just to check out abandoned buildings and restricted places. Did you know there's a whole damn network of tunnels under this city? There's a fuckin city under the city. We post what we get up to, but that old stuff is as boring as security camera footage compared to last night. Fort Point was a spectacular breakthrough," Leo said.

"Fuck, you guys are hardcore."

He dropped his rag into the ice well and topped off our drinks.

"What's your name, by the way?" Leo asked.

"I'm Herb."

"Well, I'm Leo, that's Evan, and this is Lydia. We've been a threesome for a while, but, today, we've decided to invite more freaks to the show."

"Well, you got me! I want in! How do I join?" Herb said.

"You know, Herb, I think you may already be a member."

§

Back on the street, and armored against the cold by a snug blanket of booze, we stumbled down Mission Street on the prowl to our favorite burrito joint. La Cumbre was the only place left in town where you could get a football-sized burrito for a reasonable price. All the alcohol sloshing in my gut needed some serious sponging. I lost count of how many cocktails Herb fed us on the house. The infamy of Leo's show at The Box and the Freeschool's clout meant we rarely paid for more than a drink or two in local dive bars.

Red plastic trays slid down the buffet rails inside the mural-covered taqueria. Behind the plexiglass, steel pans of meat steamed over water baths—pastor, carnitas, pollo, carne asada, tongue, and tripe. Today, I wasn't up for an exotic wrap. Instead, my mouth watered for plain old shredded chicken.

A brown girl with curlicue letters tattooed down the line of her jaw piled the filling high on top of a tortilla the size of a manhole cover. She passed my lunch to the next set of hairnet-covered attendants. Cold toppings fanned out. I pointed at white cheese, avocado, lettuce, sour cream, and little cups of extra Verde sauce. The masterpiece was rolled in a blur of dexterity, wrapped in paper, and nestled among house-fried corn chips in a brown bag growing translucent on the bottom from the peanut oil soaking through.

On the way back to Rain Dogs with our to-go bags, we passed the permanent tent city clustered around the 16th

Street BART station. Tents, tarps, and cardboard shelters were misshapen from the bad weather, but the tenants had not vacated. Where else did they have to go? Both colorful and sad, the culture of the homeless had its own rhythm and clock.

"They're so ugly," Leo said.

"Who are ugly?" Lydia asked.

"Look up."

I thought Leo meant the people too, but instead, he pointed to a billboard mounted on top of a four-story building half a block away. Old-fashioned sash windows set into grimy masonry glinted as I studied the looming ad. Hazy and inebriated, my thoughts wandered to what it would be like to work in one of those tiny offices, walls runny with tobacco stains. The ghost of a noir dick peered down, whisky in his coffee cup, the gravity of the girl who got away tethering his spirit to Mission Street forever.

"A pretty face is not safe in this city. Fight back with HERE Urban Playground, the latest in immersive 3D gaming. Kickass!" Leo read aloud, snapping me out of my black-and-white daydream.

Perched over the traffic was a glowering ice-queen in a waterfall gown of silver, slit to the thigh—her skin, radiant photoshopped perfection, diamonds aglitter, and heels like knives. Movie-set bums and orphans—straight out of a sooty, futuristic Dickens tale—admired the dark media goddess from their repose in the gutters as she gleefully gunned down indigents with an assault rifle. Ethically repulsive, but I had to admit, the image gave me a perverse thrill. Whoever selected the ad's location hovering above Skid Row has a real sick sense of humor.

"We should do something about it," Leo said.

"You mean because it's disgusting?" I asked.

"We could protest! There's an initiative to ban billboards in the city. Giant ads everywhere are–" Lydia chatted loosely.

Leo cut her short with a switchblade glance.

"You think I give a rat's ass about initiatives. Picket signs? Pffft. Anyway, think about it, protesting billboards with picket signs, ironic. No, it's stupid. And ineffective. No, let's do something *to* it!"

"Right, right? Okay... How 'bout we spray paint her a new, shiny latex catsuit and a riding crop," Lydia offered.

"Good concept, but too low rent—we need more of a high-end statement—graffiti that you can't tell is graffiti. The print shop on 24th does large-scale posters. We're gonna reshoot the whole scene. We need a lot of glue!" Leo said; his 5-star general of chaos surfaced, hands waving like semaphore flags calling in the troops.

§

When I first heard about Leo, he sounded like an overrated buffoon. My comic book store regulars kept urging me to check out his act. He hosted some sort of live game show down the street at a place called The Box. "It's like terrible reality TV, except for on acid. You gotta see it," I was told.

Boredom and loneliness pushed me out the door one

Wednesday night. The doorman scanned my Cuff for payment and admitted me into a sea of hipsters covered in a vomit of cosplay accessories and vintage mishmash. In the Lysol haze, red and white spots streamed columns of dusty light to pick out an oriental carpet, three messy desks, and a giant gong on stage. Classic EDM Trap and the crowd's chatter echoed around the acoustically imperfect venue—little more than a bar and a little less than a nightclub.

I ordered whisky rocks and sat in an empty foldout chair toward the back. The pre-show music transitioned into a bizarre theme song—it sounded like *Let's Make a Deal* played through the tinny speakers of a derelict merry-go-round. Leo climbed the stairs to the stage and chatted animatedly with the cast while they took their marks on the set. Finally, he walked to an old fashion mic on a stand.

"Hello, Freak Show!"

Not much to the eye. Leo was short and wore horn-rim glasses, a t-shirt from the BBQ joint down the street, Carhartts, and chunky work boots. He looked like a regular neighborhood guy, but his presence propelled the crowd into fits.

Hoochie girls from a black and white era drifted across the stage like spectral window dressing, holding title cards, or striking pouty pinup poses. While the audience watched the mayhem on stage, one of the showgirls climbed to perch on a trapeze moon over the spectacle. A wistful goddess in satin slippers hanging just out of reach. I could smell her perfume.

Leo turned out to be more of a straight man surrounded by a hilarious cast of characters. Somehow, he channeled the talent of others like a conduit. Leo brought out boldness in the shy and humor in the serious. He was funny in a dangerous way—caustic, full of himself, and deprecating. There was something egalitarian in the way he drew everyone in. If it weren't for Leo, the quick wit of the bartender or the clear, strong singing voice of the sound engineer would have remained hidden.

At its heart, the show was a procession of truly awful amateur acts. A drunken *talent show/open mic* gimmick featuring ear-splittingly bad singers or silly dance numbers with bulging spandex.

The fifth act was special. The contestant was a drab-looking girl, with shoulder-length blond hair and an athletic build—fit except for her disproportionately large boobs. I noticed her chest because when Leo called her up on stage, she took off her jacket with a flourish to reveal a t-shirt cut from the neck to the navel. She had safety-pinned the two fabric flaps open to showcase ample cleavage in a pushup bra.

Directing the room from Leo's mic, the girl ordered a longneck Budweiser and the bartender ran up to deliver the beer in seconds. The contestant twisted the top off the beer with her teeth, spit the cap at the audience, and wedged the base of the bottle firmly between her breasts. She called for a drumroll from the sound girl, opened her arms wide to the audience, and turned profile.

Contortion began as she curled down to lock her lips in a tight seal around the Bud. With the beer still nestled between her mouth and boobs, she bent deep at the knees until the top of her head touched the stage.

Then an amazing thing happened; she turned a somersault, then another, and another. Placing her palms flat on the stage, she stretched her legs up toward the roof in a perfect handstand, following through with a cartwheel, popped the bottle out of her mouth, and took a bow. Fizzy beer sprayed the first row. The crowd leaped to their feet like they were spring-loaded—they screamed—I cheered. It blew my mind. Now fully immersed in so-bad-it's-good entertainment, the raucous effect satisfied as nothing had before.

After the show, the Rain Dogs regular who urged me to The Box in the first place offered me—or rather, my building—to Leo. Behind cold eyes, I could see Leo's assessment. Space—San Francisco's most precious commodity. The girl from the trapeze sidled up. Floating above the stage, she had been ethereal, but up close, she was gorgeous. Flushed and primal, she wore frilly bloomers and a white satin corset. Her breasts were pushed up to her chin and her cheeks were painted with red circles. She looked part Edwardian prostitute, part doll. Leo introduced her as Lydia.

"I'm Evan."

"I know who you are," Leo said.

"You do?"

Leo slid his hand to the center of my back to steer me away from the cast and groupies that trickled in through the backstage door. A warm tingle crept up my neck and to my face. I didn't know how or why Leo knew me. But whatever the reason, it was flattering to be known by the star, especially after witnessing his sold-out show and rabid fans. He clearly had an intense following. Like the Rocky Horror Picture Show, the audience had responded to Leo's cues in call and response—a script only the insiders knew.

"Lydia, give us a moment," Leo said. "I have some business to discuss with Evan." She drifted to a cluster of performers joking and laughing on the other side of the room.

"Listen, Evan. Lydia's one of my lieutenants. My favorite, in fact. She asked me for a favor, and I'm inclined to make it happen for her. Lydia has this idiot idea that school should be free. She's obsessed, and I'm tired of hearing her prattle on about education reform. Not much of a business model, in my opinion. Regardless. From what I've heard, you might be up for hosting her Freeschool at your shop. Could be a win-win. Am I right? More customers and cred for you, and a school for Lydia. I'd owe you a favor in return. Think about it."

Leo didn't try to close the deal. Instead, he disappeared into the club, leaving me in a dark corner of the greenroom to witness the flurry of activity that sprung up in his footsteps. He was maneuvering, but despite the transactional feel of our chat, I wanted to be an insider too.

§

NEARLY TWO YEARS LATER, Rain Dogs had become Lydia's and Leo's home away from home. Lydia's loft was spacious, but it was across town on Spear Street, by Pier 24. Leo berated her for living in a bourgeois sham of an artist's warehouse. I really didn't understand what he meant. Lydia's place was comfortable and clean. I like spending time there.

On the other hand, Leo's studio was an honest-to-goodness shithole. One of those long railroad apartments, little more than a hotplate and a futon crammed into a tunnel with a tiny window at the far end. I could spread my arms across the space and almost touch both walls. There wasn't even a private bathroom, instead, he shared a toilet and shower with an entire floor. You couldn't pay me to hang out in his claustrophobic, roach-filled sublet.

Back in the break room at Rain Dogs, we unwrapped our burritos. The huge floury lumps didn't look like much, but the aroma was intoxicating. I popped off the top of a plastic cup and drizzled the green salsa into the nooks between shredded chicken, whole frijoles, avocado, and shredded cheese. Nutrients seeped into my blood. I hadn't eaten since the day before.

Leo shared his plan to free the billboard from its own bad taste by transforming it into something in much poorer taste. One thing I knew for sure: he didn't care a dime about the homeless problem. In fact, he once paid vagrants fifty dollars each to fight on stage at The Box like pit bulls in a dogfight. If anything, Leo was the real-life embodiment of the exploitative figure glamorized on the game company's billboard, minus the evening gown. He only pretended to be charitable when it served him. Leo's protest was just another performance on his list of endless sideshows. Something to follow on the heels of the success of our Fort Point adventure and keep his new admirers interested. He was after more visibility.

"I want to recruit as many people as possible for the billboard event, but they have to be fearless, irreverent. A black sense of humor is at the top of the list, too," Leo said.

"They will need to pass some kind of badassery test for us to know all that," Lydia said.

"Right you are! I've already figured out how. We'll run a Freeschool workshop this weekend. Call it *Enter the Unknown: A Class in Chaos. Hijinx and high times for all.* Whoever gets through *my* barrage will be up for anything," Leo said.

"Okay, so, say they make it through the workshop. Then what?" Lydia asked.

"Then we need to test their real mettle. Put them in a dangerous situation." Leo said.

I considered the repercussions of expanding our illegal capers to a larger group. For a long moment, we ate without speaking. Lydia's cigarette burned in the ashtray beside her, stamped with the Japanese Hanko of her ruby lipstick.

"Okay, let's do it then. What do we need?" I asked, breaking the heavy silence.

Leo dictated, and I scribbled a list of tasks and purchases on my tablet as we talked:

- Large scale printing
- Photography
- Costumes, hair, and makeup
- Poster paste
- Climbing gear
- Cement drill
- Street team
- Copywriting, web updates, social media, flyers

SOME SIMPLE ADDITION and I knew I was in it for a lot of money and time. It was useless to complain. If I did, Leo would just storm out. I'd be lampooned as a weenie rich boy at The Box for as long as it took to apologize and rejoin the fold. The public shaming of enemies by ruthless roasting was part of Leo's act and personality. His game had been directed at me once before. It was an ordeal I didn't want to repeat.

At *Enter The Unknown* on Saturday, we ran out of folding chairs. Lydia made an emergency trip to the neighboring junk store to pick up a bunch of pillows for the floor. The curious filtered into Rain Dogs in a steady stream drawn in by the bizarro flyers I had plastered across town. The P.T. Barnum copywriting and clip-and-paste punk zine style my aunt Cloe had taught me drew a crowd far larger than I expected.

Leo and I watched the arrivals from the break room. I recognized Herb from Wormwoods as he ducked under the low frame of Rain Dogs' doorway. "Muscle. Exactly what we need," Leo said. In the main lounge, the mountain of a man was contemplating the pillows with an expression of anticipated discomfort. Leo sent Lydia to extract Herb from the audience. When they returned, Leo shut the door. Herb grinned like a fanboy, happy to be included.

"Let them wait. We'll see what they do with no instructions for a while." Leo said. Hiding out in what passed for backstage, the four of us listened to the plan.

"Okay. Here's what we do... Fill these up," Leo said, handing me a stack of pie tins. I had wondered what the hell was in the garbage bag he had hauled into the shop. Now I knew. Foil plates and three restaurant-sized tubs of Cool Whip.

"Okay, before I get started, Lydia, Evan, Herb, lay the pies out on the card table next to my mic. When that's done, I'll make my entrance and explain the Chaos Order's principles to the group. Herb, your job is to run interference. If anyone has a shit-fit, just escort them outside," Leo said.

It dawned on me what was about to happen.

"Jesus Christ, Leo, this is my store! It's going to get fucking trashed!"

"Worth it." Leo winked. "So what if your shitty couches and carpet get messed up? You can deal with that. The comic books are far enough away from the performance," Leo asserted matter-of-factly.

I whistled a long breath, but I knew there was no turning back. We had a full house. Unfurling my clenched fists, I reached up to massage the hinge of my jaw. It ached a lot these days.

"Showtime. Boop." Lydia said, dabbing a bit of Cool

Whip on my nose. She gave me a playful smile and a kiss on the cheek. Her cherry-print dress, ankle socks, and platform Mary Janes deflated my annoyance. She even smelled like SweeTARTs. Lydia used sex appeal like a hammer. Defeated, I followed her to the lounge with a pie in each hand.

Lydia whispered, "Make it look like we are laying out a buffet. Be nonchalant."

We finished arranging the arsenal in the nick of time. Leo was in motion, prompted by some internal stage cue, he burst from the break room door, arms stretched wide.

"Hello, Freak Show! Chaos Order principle number one: expect the unexpected."

Leo gave Lydia the signal and it was on! A girl in a cloche hat in the first row got the first cream pie square in the face.

Splat!

"Control is an illusion!" Leo boomed.

Startled by the sudden amplification of his voice, I looked away from the whipped cream-covered girl. Apparently, Leo had also brought in a battery-powered mini-megaphone in his magic Hefty bag. He shouted in a hypnotic cadence as he leaped up to the spine of the sofa filled with people and walked it like a balance beam.

"To care what others think is to lose the game," crackled through the speaker.

"Comedy is a very serious matter!"

Anarchy took over the room. Half of the audience rushed to the pie table to grab their own ammunition.

The other half didn't know what the fuck to do. Several dashed for the door.

"Extreme acts elicit extreme responses. Be prepared!"

Shrieks and laughter erupted as chairs crashed to the floor. A group of well-dressed girls cowered behind the register, clutching their handbags—their expensive outfits and perfectly made-up faces, like bullseyes.

Leo pied Lydia in the kisser. She gave chase, but he evaded her as he wound through the crowd cackling at her through the megaphone.

"If you are caught, claim that you acted alone! We come here to overcome our fear!" Leo roared. He stopped abruptly. A calm descended. Monk-like and still, Leo let Lydia catch him. It seemed like slow motion as Cool Whip squirted in all directions. She backed away, suddenly sorry for what she had done, pie foil still clinging to Leo's face. He peeled it away.

"Chaos Order principle number seven: finish the game," he said, in his normal voice, megaphone at his side.

A quarter of the crowd, furious over their ruined outfits, left before the pie fight was over. Herb mitigated and explained the no-refund policy. I, for one, was pleased to have him on our side. At least the angry people had paid the entry charge. That would cover the carpet and upholstery cleaning. Nearly another hundred prospects petered out as Leo mocked everyone and everything. By the time he had revealed his true intention of vandalizing the billboard on 16th, the remaining thirty had been converted to hardened anarchists and unabashed fans of Leo. Herb was among the most ardent.

§

Homelessness and street life were the theme of Weather Girl's photoshoot for the billboard replacement posters. Lydia was cast as our BDSM queen. Other models were dressed in ratty trench coats, knit caps, alien skins, and clown makeup. Lydia, always a showbiz pro, arrived in wardrobe with her hair and face already done. Rain Dogs buzzed with activity.

At the site for the shoot we pried open a rusted padlock to reach the abandoned barracks I had scouted. Our Uber wouldn't cross into the shipyards. The restricted area glowed red on the dashboard map.

"This place gives me the creeps. It's radioactive. Seriously, it glows at night," Lydia said. Her breath, an icy haze in the air.

"A few rads won't hurt you. Anyway, that's the point. This is the most apocalyptic setting I could find. Plus, no one will bug us here," I told Lydia.

Bleak and crumbling, the abandoned neighborhood exhaled the failure and futility of modern American wars. Not a soul on the streets. It was perfect. Lydia and the models spread out to explore the empty bungalows while Weather Girl marked Xs with orange spray paint and set up her tripods and lights. The call of gulls and the smell of sea air put me in a vacation frame of mind. But out here, it was an eerie, dystopian holiday. Only the most tenacious plants, cheatgrass and foxtails, clung to the soil and pushed up through cracks.

"Zoning out, as usual, Evan," Lydia said. I ignored her pointedly, not wanting to share my meanderings.

"Are we ready?" I barked, a little too sharply.

"Ready for my close-up, Mr. DeMille," Lydia replied. She snapped me with her riding crop.

"Take your mark. Let's do this," Weather Girl said.

Lydia clipped a leash and collar on Herb. She reached back to pluck a Martini from a silver tray carried by another faux street person. Very, very tacky. Just what we were going for.

3

VANDALS OF CHAOS

Twenty-six people sneaking down Mission Street at 2 a.m. was an exercise in folly. Fortunately, in San Francisco, nobody paid much attention to odd people doing odd things at odd hours.

"Cross the goddamn street! Get your asses out of sight!" Leo shouted.

The rope ladder on my back pitched to the side and almost toppled me over as I turned to see what the holdup was. I stepped wide to steady the weight. Some fuckups had started an impromptu game of hot lava—the rogue faction skirted the circles of light cast by the street lamps, trying to push others into the no go zone. Some wore black body stockings or urban camouflage, an appropriate choice. But most wore outrageous costumes—red noses, Groucho glasses, boas, or clown onesies.

In the Order's first top-secret email, I suggested disguises for tonight's event. I had meant to dress on the down-low—dark colors, blend in, but cosplay was how it was interpreted by our confederacy of dunces. I shook my head as I watched them run and laugh.

"This is serious!" Leo called again, even more pissed off this time.

Except, how could anyone take him seriously—his own yeti costume stuffed into a knapsack, bits of fur poking through the flap on the top? Joke or not, trespassing and vandalizing could mean jail time. If he couldn't control the group, this would end before it started. I'd take a bullet for the cause, but not unnecessarily.

Even at this late hour, the hum and honk of traffic echoed through the alley. The smell of garbage filled the narrow space despite the cold. Chain link barricaded the far end and a stripe of stars rolled out over our heads. Leo crossed his arms. Impatience narrowed his eyes and curled his lip.

"Okay. Listen up, Freaks. First, until you prove your name is worth remembering, you are all anonymous to me. I don't care what your mama called you. Lydia here, who has earned her name, will climb the building and throw a ladder down for the rest of us. In case you don't know, she is a professional aerialist and an urban free-soloist, so don't worry about her. She knows what she's doing. And for fuck's sake, keep quiet and stay out of sight. I'll climb up next to install the pulley to lift all this stuff. Evan will be your man on the ground. Climb up one at a time. And when Fatty over there climbs, everyone, stand back." Leo chuckled deep and low and to himself.

Maureen must have weighed close to 300 pounds. I wasn't sure if Leo was body-shaming her or he had actual concern for the group's safety. Probably both. Hard to tell with Leo.

A coil of paracord glowed neon pink on Lydia's back as she ascended the wall. Quarter-inch toeholds in the brick facade made her awe-inspiring climb possible. As soon as she disappeared over the corner of the roof, the brightly colored line snaked down through the dark. I fastened my rolled-rope ladder to the end. It spun and bumped off the bricks as Lydia hoisted it up. I could just make her out as a silhouette while she tightened the steel safety hooks and dropped the ladder's length down with an ass-puckering clatter. The noise triggered my flight to the end of the alley to make sure no one heard the loud sound. The coast was clear.

When I got back, Leo was already climbing. Once on the roof, he had moved a few yards away from where Lydia stood. The low whir of his cement drill started as he affixed bolts to the parapet to haul up the rest of the gear. When I finally climbed to the rooftop over an hour later, the mirth had been sucked out of the Freaks who huddled against the cold on the grungy rooftop. Lydia hung back from the crowd as Leo recited the plan. She knew his spiel as if it were her own. We had heard it many times. The pulls of her cigarette bloomed and faded against her barely visible shape tucked in shadows across the rooftop expanse.

"Now that we're all up here, no one can leave. Period. That's the most important rule. It's for your own protection and the protection of the group. If we scatter, we increase the risk of being seen and caught. Leave, and you're out of the Order before you get in," Leo said.

"Hey, Herb." Lydia called across the space. "Come over and grab these bags."

Herb stood taller, pleased to be singled out. Underneath his bulk and height was an affable and big-hearted goof who already adored Lydia.

As he went to do the heavy lifting, Leo continued, "Right. I need four volunteers to work up on the catwalk." He scanned the faces of the recruits.

"Why aren't you, Lydia, and Evan going up there? The others don't know how to do this stuff," Herb said to Leo as he dropped a bag of ropes at his feet.

Leo's look was withering. Questioning Leo's plan was not allowed. Although he didn't know it yet, Herb was on the verge of becoming an insider. This breach had cost him.

"That's the point. I'm not the one being tested here. All of you are. There are members, and there are *Members*. Put yourself in real danger, face your fear, and you level up," Leo said with an unwavering menace directed at Herb, who slumped down an inch or two.

When no one stepped forward, Leo snaked through the group. If a recruit didn't squirm and try to back away when Leo got in their face, he put them into the suitable climbing group. Despite what he said to Herb, or maybe because of it, Leo led the chosen Freaks up the scaffolding to the billboard base. It didn't matter to Leo if his words matched his actions. Uplighting illuminated the towering advertisement and shone on the aircrew, picking them out like a lineup of criminals. Leo unscrewed the bulbs to hide their illicit work.

Smart, I thought.

Lydia's Cuff rang.

"Yep. Okay. I'll get it ready," she said and hung up.

"Okay, Freaks. Leo says to move the paste, rollers, and posters to the base of the billboard. The crew will lower down gear bags for you to load."

Herb jumped to his feet to help. Most of the recruits followed his lead. They bumbled and bumped into each other. Too many hands, not enough tasks. I knew Leo had a special admiration for the ones who remained planted firmly on their asses. He liked leaders, skeptics, and rebels. Followers were fodder to him. Sometimes I wondered where that put me. Hiding in the shadows, I eavesdropped. Predominantly, the Freaks made small talk or exchanged nervous jokes, but everyone had an opinion about Leo and his dynamic with Lydia and me.

After another long stretch of waiting, the last of the four panels was pasted into place. Leo screwed the lights back in, and the results burst into the world. Brilliant. A billboard born anew. My chest rose as I surveyed the finished art. I organized the photoshoot with Weather Girl, purchased the costumes, edited the images to hyper-real perfection, and picked up the posters from the printer. Lydia looked stunning... and scary, fifteen feet tall in her thigh-high, stiletto boots. The barracks at Hunter's Point made the perfect backdrop for our latex-covered dominatrix surrounded by insane hobos, yetis, ninjas, and space aliens. Lydia held the end of a leash, a diamond collar secured around the neck of Herb, our gentle giant clad in shabby rags with blacked-out teeth and holding a bottle of Night Train in his colossal fist. Lydia planted a fetish footwear-covered heel in the middle of his chest. Emblazoned over the scene were the words Leo had carefully chosen:

FIGHT MEDIA CONTROL *with Transgressive Art*

I HARDLY HAD a moment to bask in the pride of success before Leo's shout came booming down from the catwalk.

"Fuck! The cops are here!"

My skin electrified. My mouth went dry. The others swarmed like bees from a fallen hive. Leo slid down the ladder, impressive to watch, but the circumstances were bad.

"Okay, we knew this could happen. The cops are here," Leo hissed as he rushed at the panicking crowd. He corralled stray Freaks to the skylight where Lydia had been assigning tasks.

"What do we do? Can we escape through the alley?" Maureen asked, as spooked as a horse in a burning barn. She bounced from one foot to the other.

"No. We're surrounded. I saw at least ten cars coming. If we climb down, there's no way out. It's a dead end. We'll be cornered," I said.

"So, we're just caught, then?" Maureen asked, her words rising to a pleading squeak.

A burst of a bullhorn interrupted before Leo or I could respond.

"This is the San Francisco P.D. The building is surrounded."

Leo went straight to plan B. He zipped open his backpack and yanked out the yeti suit. He pulled one furry leg, then the other over his boots and Carhartts. Nervous giggles from the Freaks burst the tension like a rotten peach.

"Hey, Fatso, you come with me. A fat lady and a yeti will double our comic effect. Evan. Lydia. Stay back here and keep everyone calm," Leo ordered.

If Maureen minded the insult, she didn't show it. Clearly funny looking in her own way, she played up her look—wild curly red hair worn loose, a spray of freckles across her nose, and a low cut, muumuu-ish shirt covering her enormous breasts. Not that the police could see the freckles. But the boobs, the boobs they would see.

"I'll do the talking," Leo said to Maureen as he walked her to the edge of the roof.

"Shit! Evan, come over. You gotta see this," Leo called to me. I joined them. "It's the press. Look at this shitshow," he said.

Five news vans blocked the street. Drunks and bums gathered in pockets to gawk. The idea was to get the police laughing if we got caught. Leo knew that cops had the discretion to either arrest us, ticket us, or let us go. He said that he could convince them to release us with a warning. I wasn't so sure.

"Shit, Leo, there's no way we can fast-talk our way out of this now. They'll never let us go with the press swarming everywhere. We can't play the joker card anymore," I said. My voice rose with alarm.

"You don't know that, Evan. Stop pretending you can predict how people will react. I hate that about you. You don't really believe in chaos, do you? I'm doing the King Kong bit and we'll see what happens. If we can't laugh our way out of this, at least we can shoot for national coverage and some more viral clips," Leo said.

On the street, the commanding officer refused to acknowledge the odd sight of a fur-covered Leo on the parapet, but the brightening array of lights from the news vans made it clear the press watched every move. Leo aped and turned cartwheels. I nearly shit my pants over his gymnastics on the edge of a fifty-foot fall.

"Back away from the edge. Do not exit the building. We have fire trucks on the way. We will escort you off the roof," the police chief called through the bullhorn, no longer able to ignore Leo's act. He was a salty old cop. A bit o' the Krispy Kreme on that one. I could see the rookies standing in the lights of their squad cars. Even if Commander Donut didn't want to acknowledge the yeti on the roof, the younger cops pointed in awe.

The first of the fire trucks swung around the corner. Sirens blazed. The whir of an air pump started. Flat white bags puffed up into giant marshmallows. A young cop stepped from the frontline to mount the rescue ladder. He was followed by an athletic blonde, her hair pulled back in a ponytail. Commander Donut must have singled out these two for their physical fitness. The majority of the police on the street were older, chubbier, and tasked with keeping the after-hours bar crowd out of the cordoned-off zone.

"Stand back! Hands up!" The lead cop shouted to Leo, Maureen, and me as he readied to step onto the rooftop. His partner followed him over the roof wall.

"Jesus!" he exclaimed when he realized nearly thirty people were lurking in the shadows. He turned to his partner and spoke low, but loud enough to overhear. "We're not going to get them all down the ladder safely. We need to get the keys to the building. Taking the stairs is the safest way," he said.

"You," he turned back to us, pointing at Maureen first. "Stand with him," he said with loud, cardboard authority.

I snickered to myself when the cop started to frisk Leo. I sincerely doubted he could feel a weapon—even though I knew there wasn't one—under all Leo's faux fur. He whipped off Leo's yeti mask and threw it on the ground.

"On your stomach, hands behind your back!"

Once Leo's hairy wrists were zip-tied, the lead cop spoke into the radio clipped to his lapel.

"Requesting back up. There are a couple of dozen people on site. We need the keys to the building. Call the building owner or the superintendent."

"What's your name?" I asked him gently, drawing his attention from the squawk box in his hand.

Indecision flashed across his face.

I soothed. "We're cool here. This is just a prank. See, look at the billboard. It's art. Just art."

He released a long breath. "I'm officer Cole. This is officer Bantam. Who's the leader here?" he asked.

I had calculated his need for an ally correctly.

"That would be the yeti. But this is just a joke. We won't hurt you. We were just messing around. The billboard looks much better, right? Stay cool," I said.

"We don't want any trouble," Cole said. "Cooperate, and this will go far easier on everyone. We are going to sit tight and wait for reinforcements, then figure out how to get you down."

4

THE SLAMMER

The police station receptionist was a gum-snapping scowl topped by a bad dye job. Her desk faced the rows of hard-molded plastic chairs where we waited. Runny-faced clowns, a fur-covered Leo, and the assorted Chaos Order riff-raff in Halloween Headquarters cast-offs ceased to be a novelty to her and the passing patrolmen and civil servants as our time in holding stretched into hours. Booking twenty-six jackasses for trespassing and destruction of private property was a long ordeal, one made longer by the solitary desk cop assigned to photograph and digitally fingerprint us.

"Next," he called in a flat monotone voice.

By the time we moved into the side-by-side men's and women's cells, the pale light of dawn showed through the bullet-proof windows. Maureen sat on her cot like Boudicca crowned in a riot of red hair. Lydia was a statue, watching Leo through the barred wall. He paced like an animal. Some of the other girls cried and clung together. Glitter, mascara, and clown white mingled and streaked their faces. I lowered my gaze to my hands. Did they blame me? A cold stone of guilt settled in my stomach.

Unlike the women's cell that shared an exterior wall with the station, the men's cell was barred on all four sides and had no natural light, only buzzing fluorescent tubes behind a protective metal mesh. There was one filthy shitter in the corner, four cots, and the Freaks packed in like sardines. Lungers and gum and god knows what else clung to the ceiling in disgusting stalactites. The place smelled of piss.

Lydia reached her hand through the bars to brush Leo's sleeve when he passed close enough to her in his whirlwind of mania. If he felt her touch, he didn't acknowledge it. Instead, he made a beeline for the female guard who sat sentry. She reminded me of Lydia—a pretty brunette with thick, dark brows and a broad, lipsticked mouth. A signal flare to Leo.

"Nice place you got here," Leo called to the guard. He leaned against the wall, resting a work boot on the lowest crossbar.

"You like it? I decorated it myself." She looked up and smiled.

Fish on! Leo got her attention. Now for the razzle-dazzle. I had heard Leo's pickup lines hundreds of times before, but his signature mix of absurdity and negging was all new to this mark. Superhuman confidence was his secret.

"You know, I thought it was just going to be the two of us tonight."

Leo was looking for a transaction from her, but his cringe-worthy flirtation was useless; worse, delusional. I knew our release was off the table. We were in the system. There was nothing the guard, god, or anyone could do other than let the wheels of justice spin.

When Leo realized the best he could achieve was some future hook-up, he grew bored and turned his attention back to the Freaks in the men's cell. Instead of apologizing, Leo spun the arrest and our night in jail into an honor.

"Chaos Order badges for you all! We'll sew them to our sashes next meeting," Leo joked. "Anyway, this is better than we imagined! We finished the billboard and got a ton of press. Man, this is the big time," he said, confidently patting the most enthusiastic of the Freaks on the back, and pointedly shunning the less sure.

I sat back, disgusted in Leo and our situation. To distract myself, I read the jailhouse scrawl on the water-stained walls. Everything from banal, *Here I sit, broken-hearted,* to clever; ★ ★ ★ ★ ★, *Great service, spacious rooms.* I must have fallen asleep because the next thing I knew, I was being shaken awake.

"Your bail came through. The women were released while you were sleeping. A clerk will return your belongings and let you call for rides in booking," the pretty guard said.

"Thanks. Maybe I'll see you at the next Chaos Order meeting," I said with a groggy creak in my voice.

"Maybe you will. Here, give Leo my number," she said and airdropped her contact info to my Cuff. "I woke you first since you paid the bail. He's still sleeping."

She pointed to a cot on the opposite side of the room. Leo's mouth hung wide open and omitted wet snores. The other Freaks slept in huddles against the walls. Some shared the remaining beds. On the floor, Herb's generous flank served as a pillow for four of the guys. They looked like piglets suckling a sow.

"Give me a minute to rouse the troops," I said to the guard. "Anyway, why don't you give Leo your number yourself?"

"Nah, my shift's over. Just go to the window at the end of the hall and get your personals and the paperwork for the hearing."

She wiggled her ass as she walked out of sight. Minimize exposure, maximize mystery—one of Leo's favorite games.

"Wake up," I shook Leo's shoulder. "Bail came through. The girls have been released."

"What time is it?" Leo stretched and looked around.

"Close to eight in the morning." I didn't say anything to him about the guard.

Why didn't Lydia wake us when she and the others were released, I wondered to myself. Maybe they were told to leave quietly and not disturb us. But how could I blame Lydia for being angry with Leo? His disregard for her had been blatant and public—his flirtation, painful to watch, even for me. Lydia and Leo weren't a couple, but it was obvious to everyone that Lydia had feelings for him.

The morning fog outside the station felt unreal. It rolled low along the street. Early morning delivery drone whizzed by. One passed so close it left the trailing scent of coffee and bacon in the air.

Exhaustion had finally gotten to even Leo. I dialed for an Uber and asked if he wanted to share with me. Rides pulled up, even a few moms, to peel the Freaks off from the group one by one. The thinning herd of Order members drew closer together for warmth. Leo got in the back of our Uber sedan.

"We need an attorney," Leo called from the warmth of the passenger compartment. Hurry up, get in, we'll talk on the way home.

"I know, I'll pay for our defense," I said. I was too worn out for anything other than simple agreement. The back of the car was a comfort after the cold, damp cell. I had opted for the Lexus upgrade. It had four dark leather seats in facing pairs and tinted windows. All I wanted was sleep.

"Nah. Let's get a lawyer to *join* the Order. We're going to need a regular one, anyway. Pro Bono is the ticket."

Not a bad strategy, I thought. Leo didn't typically consider the business side of things. Impressed, I pulled out my phone and scanned my contacts for a few choice candidates. Todd, maybe Paul. They were not good lawyers, but they did fit Leo's criteria. They would join the Order.

In an uncharacteristic show of compassion, Leo said, "Don't worry about it now. Get some rest first. You look beat. You know, I don't blame you for getting us caught."

Touching, even though no sane person would judge

what happened to be my fault. But for Leo, this topsy-turvy brand of forgiveness was a monumental gesture.

The car dropped me back at Rain Dogs. As I climbed the stairs to my apartment, intense fatigue hurt my skin, but my mind wouldn't relax. Gazing out through the sagging Victorian glass of my living room window, I tapped my fingers on the worn fabric arm of an upcycled wing chair. There were at least thirty charges to deal with. I knew a lot of attorneys, but one in particular would take the case for free. I scrolled my contacts on my Cuff.

"Connie Bouchard," she answered.

"Mom."

"Evan, is that you?"

"Hey, Mom, how are you doing?"

My mother was one of the best litigators in Orange County. I didn't want to let the Order down. These people had trusted me. They signed up for this debacle on my property. I'm the one that reassured them. A life-changing experience, I said. Now they were facing serious charges and fines. Maybe jail time.

"I'm fine, honey—what's going on? Are you in trouble?"

There it was. Trouble. Mom made an assumption, and she was right. I knew small talk wasn't her thing, but—*are you in trouble?* Maybe she saw some of what happened on the news. The arrest was all over the feeds. That must be it.

My spine collapsed further. To my credit, I didn't hang up and call my lawyer-buddy Paul "The Hammer" Campbell, at 1-800-CASH4U2. He would do this for us.

He'd even join the Order like Leo wanted. This case was right up his alley—a media spectacle. Leo would think The Hammer was the perfect fit.

I could have back-peddled, but the matter was much too serious to not take responsibility for. I couldn't trust Leo to do the right thing. The lives of twenty-six people were on the line. Paul was not the man for the job; mom was.

"I guess, I guess—Yes, Mom, I am in trouble."

When I was thirteen years old, my mother had to pick me up from the eMart Mall security office for shoplifting. That shame had been catastrophic. But this felt much worse. I heard myself explain what happened. My face burned with the ridiculousness of the situation. Good thing I wasn't on video chat, or my mom would have known precisely how I felt.

We scaled a building, pasted up a twenty-foot-tall, explicit and subversive image. Nearly thirty people were involved. Weeks of planning. Felony destruction of property.

I reconstructed the events for her. She listened and asked the right questions.

Who paid for it? What was the intention? Whose idea was it?

The answers didn't make me look good, but I took the full blame.

"My dear boy, why?"

I felt like I was back on that cold metal chair, staring into the buzzing blue light in the mall security office. That was fifteen years ago, but the shame felt exactly the same today. I didn't feel worthy of love—hers or anyone's.

My mom's voice buzzed in the air like an efficient insect. "I'll get the court date, file the papers, and book a flight. I think I can take care of this. But why are you associating with these criminals? None of this makes sense, Evan. You and Cloe, I'll never understand—"

How could I explain? It embarrassed me to consider the answer: my friends, Leo and Lydia, filled a vague hole, one empty of the kind of love missing from my life. The type of acceptance she never gave me. Love free from judgment, conditions, and the pressure to be someone I wasn't. My prodigious ability to code had only frightened my mother. She had ridiculed me, calling me a mushroom, and pushing me to go play outside, make friends, ride a bike, and be normal. I buried the queasy thoughts. God, I wanted a drink. Instead, tapped the Instagram icon on my Cuff while I finished making plans with mom.

I choked. Eleven million new followers!

"Okay, mom, love you, gotta go. Thank you so much for this. I'll see you in a few days," I hung up.

Holy shit! The photos and video of the arrest were off the charts. It had to be one of the biggest stories of the year, and it was being applauded by millions.

5

CONNIE

An hour-long commuter flight was all it took for Mom to enter back into my orbit. I was neatening up the window display when she pulled up in her rented Tesla SUV. It took a lot of convincing to get Leo to even meet with her. A courtroom circus was what Leo was after, even if he didn't admit his need for a big show to me. Jail time, fines, major disruptions, he could face all of that. Wanted it, even. More press. More attention. And he was willing to force the others to do the same—for the cause—for his cause.

My hope was that the HERE corporation, whose billboard we destroyed, and the building owner would simply drop the charges if we followed my mother's orders. She had moved mountains already. That all twenty-six of us would have to appear in court looked less likely.

What was harming us more than anything else were

the copycat vandals. I did my best to boost the word on the street that these acts derailed our attempts to get HERE to drop the charges. But Leo's ideas were spreading and we didn't control their manifestation. The more damage that dotted the city, the less likely the decision-makers would accept our bargain. But how to communicate that to an uncontrollable radical arts community? It didn't help that Leo was working against me. He was thrilled by the spreading chaos.

"Hi, Honey."

Mom kissed me on the cheek, then held me at arm's length for an inspection, her French-tip manicured hand resting on my shoulder.

"Have you been sleeping?" she asked.

"I'm okay. No, not sleeping much. But—actually—this whole thing has been pretty good for business. If there aren't any big fines, the shop, the school, the Order, they're all getting lots of publicity. So that's good."

It was a stab in the dark. Sales at the shop or media coverage for the Order would never impress her. She studied me like a lab specimen. I wriggled under her steady, burning gaze.

"I'm glad your store is doing well, Honey. But I'm not happy about this Chaos Order thing. It's childish, Evan. These are not good friends, and they are not good for your future," she said.

"Before you push your own agenda again, Mom, you should give Lydia and Leo a chance. You're representing them, after all," I said.

Deep down, I knew it was useless. Mom would

disapprove of Lydia. And despite the thrall Leo held over our peers, mom would see right through him. She already thought of Leo and Lydia as grifters, and maybe she was right. Her disappointment seeped into my bones.

"Evan, I love you very much. But you also know I'm not wild about your life choices. You're such a smart boy. A genius, really. I blame Cloe. She got you all turned around."

Cloe had been Connie's sister. Had been, until she died of cancer. Even after her death, that Cloe was my role model was unforgivable to my mother.

I sighed. I hadn't bothered to tell my mom I was working on my Master's at Berkeley. I had enough money to pay the tuition with the income from the building where we stood, with its six rental units and the shop. This place, my inheritance from Cloe, was a thorn in my mother's side because it was my freedom. That I was back in school would have made things worse, not better. More pressure. More expectations. The greatest pain was that she didn't respect or understand my life choices or my natural temperament. Without some external validation from the world, what I did was meaningless. Pursuing an advanced degree, yes, and that would have thrilled her. However, I wasn't planning on following the accompanying career, and that would have been baffling and infuriating to her. So, I kept quiet. Social media influence, underground fame, the arts—all this was detritus to my living family, especially my mom. Transgressive expression remained my domain. The memory of Cloe stabbed at my heart.

"They'll be here soon," I deflected, "We should meet in the garden. I'll bring out some snacks. Why don't you get settled?"

I led her out the back door of the shop. The February weather was crisp, but commercial heaters made the patio a comfortable and airy space. The mismatched aesthetic of Rain Dogs extended to the outside reading area. Mom smoothed her cream-colored skirt suit, pulled out her phone, and tucked her handbag under the wrought iron garden table as she sat down among the curlicues of the matching chair.

"Be right back with tea," I said, hating the pansy-boy way that sounded.

The shop bell rang while I sliced a baguette in the break room.

"Back here," I called to Lydia and Leo.

Mother Mary and Joseph of God, Lydia was in her full Jackie-O regalia—a cheap pale-pink bouclé Chanel knockoff, pillbox hat, and pink patent leather clutch. My guts churned. My mother would see the outfit as the mockery it was.

"Daaahrling," Lydia said, dropping her hand from a limp wrist. I wanted to die.

She plucked a round of bread from the cheese plate I was arranging and popped it into her mouth. Leo looked normal for Leo—long sleeve t-shirt, tuxedo slacks, and boots. I shook off the heebie-jeebies.

"My mom is doing us a huge favor. Please be cool. You don't realize how much this would cost us if she hadn't stepped up," I said.

"Zero is what it would have cost us if you had done what I told you to do," Leo said, his scowl burning into me.

"We can't talk about this now. She's out back. Come on, follow me."

Mom stood, gracious as usual, as Lydia, Leo, and I crossed the threshold to the patio.

"How do you do?" she said to Lydia, barely acknowledging the absurd outfit with more than a glance.

"Nice to meet you," Lydia said.

Lydia suddenly seemed less sure of herself. My mother had that effect on people. I think it's something she learned in law school, or maybe being impressive was natural for her. Connie was like a thin, blonde mountain.

"And you must be Leo," she said, extending a hand.

"No, I'm Ronald fuckin' Reagan; of course I'm Leo," he said, taking a seat without accepting the shake.

I put down the tray with a loud rattle and went back for the cheese and bread plate, trying to hide my burning cheeks. *God, Leo was such a douche.* Yet, deep down, I was thrilled that my mother didn't impress him.

Back inside, away from the unbearable first encounter, I laughed aloud and and willed myself to relax a little. Leo's irreverence *was* hilarious; it's what I liked about him. Mom easily won over every room she entered, but Leo played a different game. I picked up the hors d'oeuvres and headed back outside, curious to see how the meeting was progressing.

Everyone had settled. Leo spread out, with one arm draped over the back of an adjacent chair and his feet planted wide. Mom and Lydia sipped tea as Leo recited his Chaos Order manifesto. He poked the air with a finger to punctuate his points. To my surprise, my mother seemed entertained by his rant, interacting with him at appropriate moments.

I took the remaining chair but lost interest in Leo's speech—I had heard it before in all its forms. The radiant circle of the patio heater was soothing; the hiss of the propane kept the wintery garden at bay. A blue crested jay turned one onyx eye my way from his roost in the papery branches of a white birch. Patches of greens and even small flowers still grew in the overgrown garden, but the overcast sky and pale light cast the scene in pleasant melancholy.

"Evan, are you listening?" My mother asked pointedly.

"Sorry, Mom, I am," I turned my full attention to the conversation.

"Leo, don't get me wrong, I want to understand why you did what you did and why you did it in such an extravagant way. Your politics and philosophy are fascinating. But what is important now is your power to stop the actions you inspired in others," my mother, the great Connie Bouchard, said.

"I don't want—" but my mom didn't let Leo finish.

"Clearly, you're charismatic, and I see why people follow you, including my son. However, the problem is this. The company involved wants a stop to the destruction of their property, but more than vandalism to the physical advertisements, the damage to their brand is their primary concern. Your grassroots accusations of ethical disregard and lack of compassion for the homeless on the part of the HERE corporation is what the prosecuting attorney is suggesting we repair. They don't really care about monetary recompense for a billboard. It is a pittance to them. What they have requested is a public apology campaign to control the damage to their image and property. They want you, Leo, or a spokesperson for the Chaos Order to film an announcement where you declare your actions were misdirected and that you condemn the actions of others who are following suit and vandalizing billboards and advertising around the city.

Furthermore, they would like you to endorse their game platform. Play the game. Give it your endorsement. If you do this, they will drop all charges. You three and the twenty-three others will have nothing on your records, no fines, and no further action will be taken against you," She finished. She folded her hands on the table in front of her and waited for a response.

Her patience was not rewarded. Leo told her he needed time to think about the offer. She left to check into her room at the W Hotel without receiving a direct answer, amazed that the deal she had secured was not welcomed with open arms.

"This is exactly what I told you would happen," Leo blasted his frustration at me as soon as the distant jingle of the door marked Connie's exit, "She's part of the system. There's no way I am going to publicly apologize. You don't get it, Evan. I don't care if I spend the rest of my life paying off the fucking fine. Money is just paper; a symbol, it has no real value. What matters is that people see, clear as day, that they are not at liberty and that they must fight for that freedom."

"First, it's not your money or your freedom we're talking about, Leo. If it were, I'd let you do whatever you want. It is the others' money. Twenty-three people, most of them we barely know. They didn't know what they were signing up for. These people are scared and confused. You're messing with Lydia's family. My family. It's Herb's freedom we're talking about. You wouldn't understand because you don't even have a family, Leo. Your mom's insane, and your dad's dead!" I said.

"Don't bring Leo's parents into it, Evan!" Lydia defended, shocked by my use of personal details Leo had once uncharacteristically shared during an Ecstacy bender.

Too far, I went too far. I wanted to suck back those last words.

"Oh, shit, guys. I'm sorry, I didn't mean that," I said, back-peddling, but the apology made my breach of trust worse.

God damn it, I should have followed Leo's instructions and asked some ambulance chaser to join the Order. I should have followed the code. Fear of fines, jail, and a media circus was normal. But normal was not acceptable to Leo. Normal is what Leo fought. What was I thinking, bringing my mother into our world? It was a world in which she didn't belong and one she would never understand.

"Leo, I'll do the videos myself. Please. They won't

know the difference," I said, "Come on. I'm sorry. I'll take responsibility for everything."

His calm was horrifying.

"First of all, you don't *let* me do anything. That's not how the Order works. You went against my express orders. Lydia and I discussed what we'd do if you went conformist on us. I expected this from a trustafarian like you. Do the video or don't do the video, I don't give a shit. We're moving the Freeschool and the Order to a new location." Leo put his hand on Lydia's shoulder and looked me straight in the eyes. The look said: *The Order doesn't include* you *anymore.*

"I'm done with you. You're broadcasting the wrong message, Evan. You can't run back to mommy when it serves you. Not if you're a thought leader in the Chaos Order. Yeah, maybe we will get off easy because your mother is a fancy lawyer, but what does that say about us? What does that say about our integrity? It says we are weak. Most people think transgression means freedom to make macrame underwear for a living or have sex in public. That's the type of meaningless bullshit wage earners dabble in to feel something other than numb. I'm showing the world that transgression includes murder, suicide, theft, domination, hatred, and war. Our human nature that most people can't even look at. Pain, pleasure, good, bad, it's all meaningless and ultimately the same. Our boundaries extend to the very limits of human capability. I'm not planning on eating babies any time soon, but what you did is against everything I represent."

Tears welled in my eyes as Leo escorted Lydia to the

door and out of my life. Rain Dogs was not going to be the headquarters any longer. Not for the Order. Not for the Freeschool. They still needed me. I was too integral to their operations and I worked for free, but the new location that Leo talked about excluded me. He had made that perfectly clear. I was just an employee now.

6

EVAN BOUCHARD

Aunt Cloe's eyes were sunken; her cheeks hollow, but the smile that lit across her face when I knocked at her door unexpectedly three years ago is something I'll never forget. Her cancer had progressed, and insurance didn't cover in-home nursing. I knew things were taking a turn for the worse from our daily phone calls. Against my mother's wishes, I put off UCLA to take over her palliative care. I didn't want my favorite person in the world hidden away in a state run hospice where she would be just a room number and a chart to an overworked staff. I had no experience with death, but I loved my aunt. Since puberty, my bones had been picked clean by Mom's relentless expectations and judgments. The choice to nurse Cloe instead of starting pre-law was a triumph over the iron-fisted governance of home.

Cloe was the coolest. She had been in a punk band

that got a lucrative recording contract in the 90s. Her band, Tokyo Montana, was big in Asia, and she had kept a tiny apartment in Seoul before she got sick. Cloe owned the apartment building and retail space in San Francisco as an investment. Now that she had lost her mobility, she lived in a first floor apartment on the property full-time.

My mom feared her sister—a dark horse that was not to be trusted. Once a junkie, always a junkie, she said. Connie always reduced people with simplified and dismissive labels. It was her way of keeping the world safe and orderly. I loved my mother, but compassion and understanding were not among her virtues.

As soon as I moved in and had settled into cooking, cleaning, and taking care of Cloe's medication and doctors appointments, I suggested a road trip to Costa Mesa for a family reunion before I started my first year of undergrad at State. My assumption was that my mother could put aside her harsh judgments to say goodbye to her only sister. I wanted my aunt to resolve the family conflict that my mother had inflicted on her, which, in retrospect, was unfair of me to ask. Cloe's only offense was living an authentic life on her own terms, and I was made in the same mold. Mom's acceptance of her sister would have meant she accepted me too. My desire for reconciliation was a selfish one.

Cloe slept during most of the drive down south. Bald from chemo and tattooed with bees and bouquets tied with ribbons, her head rested on an inflatable neck pillow. The I-5 cut off to 55, and we headed toward the sea.

"Wake up. We're here." I shook Cloe's shoulder.

"Huh? Oh, shit. Was I snoring?" Cloe asked.

"Like a jet engine," I said, my comment earned me a punch in the arm.

Rows of gated mansions receded into purple shadows. The aroma of backyard barbecues on charcoal grills floated through my open car window. Garden lights blinked on, spilling ponds of gold over the rolling country club greens. Mom opened the front door as we drove up the long driveway. The force of her scowl turned the summer to ice. Cloe and I grimaced at each other, not wanting to get out of the car. Maybe this trip wasn't such a good idea.

"Cloe, you're going to crush my elbow. Ease up," I whispered.

"Oh, god, I didn't realize–Sorry." She let go, and we got out of the car.

"You want to turn around?" I asked. But we both knew that would be ridiculous. We'd come all this way.

"Hi, Mom," I called up the walk. I could feel Cloe close on my heels.

"Good to see you, Connie," Cloe said from behind, but her voice rang strained and squeaky.

Stiff as an Old Glory waving flagpole, Mom wrapped her thin, tan arms around me, then turned to Cloe when she got close enough. Connie gave her sister a pat on the back. Gold bracelets clacked together.

"You should wear a wig. Those tattoos look ridiculous."

"Hi, Mom," I said again. "It's been a long trip. Traffic was awful."

"The prodigal son speaks," Connie said crisply.

Mom gave me a brisk up and down and moved aside to let us pass. Her harshness made me sick. I assumed Cloe felt the same, but she wore a brave face. Inside, Dad's football game echoed through the marble entry.

"Tom and Candy are in the game room with your dad," Mom said like a push.

An anonymous sportscaster shouted, "Touchdown!"

Cloe and I followed the sound of cheering to the television. My brother, sister, and father turned to us with cold, blank faces as we stepped into the room. Ass-deep in his favorite leather recliner, Dad pressed his thumb on the big screen remote. Tommy and Candy flicked their eyes back to the TV for the field goal.

"We're pariahs," Cloe mouthed to me with sad eyes.

"Come on, let's get drinks in the kitchen," I spoke up to be heard over the game. I knew that the family disapproved of my choice to live with Cloe. But what kind of assholes would treat a dying relative this way?

In the kitchen, Coco's welcome was as warm as the rest of my family's was cold. Soft hair was pulled back from foxed eyes. Plump, motherly arms crossed over her chest in a gesture of impatience, but her smile revealed that this was a joke. Clearly, she knew we'd seek refuge with her. She was ready with my favorite snacks— Coco's signature lumpia; onion dip with Lays potato chips, original flavor, of course; and Brie with pesto and sun-dried tomatoes.

"My baby, I miss you so much. It's so boring around here without you." Coco ruffled my hair. "And Miss Cloe, you're so skinny. Eat, eat. I have gin and tonic, Pimm's, beer, and lemonade. You take a seat in the garden, and I'll bring you whatever you want."

"I'll have a Pimm's. That sounds wonderful! Thank you," Cloe said.

I kissed Coco's cheek.

"I'll have a Fat Tire," I said.

Cloe and I took a seat under the pergola. Wisteria and honeysuckle were in bloom; the aroma was heady in the Southern California swelter. The tsst, tsst, tsst of the Rainbirds dotting the lawn brought back pleasant childhood memories of backyard birthday parties, pony rides, and bouncy houses. Mom wasn't all bad. She meant well. But the ideal childhood she crafted was crushed by expectation of perfect GPAs for transcripts that UCLA would see, my mother's alma mater. When I turned twelve, the hammer came down, and my dishrag of a Dad did whatever Connie wanted. But I wasn't interested in the slew of extracurricular activities that would look good on college applications. Moreover, I didn't want to study law. My interests were philosophy, the arts, coding, and gaming. Mom didn't understand. She wanted me to play sports and dominate the high school debate team. Basically, she wanted me to be her.

"Well, looks like we're in for a long night," I said to Cloe.

"It's okay, Evan. I forgave my sister a long time ago. I appreciate that you tried, though. That's what matters."

That night, Coco carved the roast on the sideboard in the dining room. Dad rattled his knife against his plate impatiently. The phone in my pocket vibrated. It was Tom from across the table. What a dick! Texting me when I was looking right at him.

What R U trying to Do? This is a HORROR SHOW. Cloe looks like a zombie. Braaains.

I wrote back.

You're 24 going on 9. Grow up.

That Tom and Candy thought Cloe was an object to be mocked and feared saddened me. Who were these people? How could Cloe and I be related to this pack of superficial jerks?

Mom presided over the table like a judge, her conversation, a strict agenda. "Abigail from church asks about you, Evan. She's at UCLA now. Maybe you can visit her in the dorms before you take Cloe home. You two were so sweet together in high school."

"Ahh, yeah, probably not, Mom," I replied.

My sister Cadence talked to Tom about the new sailboat he had bought like it was any other day. Tom bragged that he had used his connections to jump the waiting list for a coveted slip at Dana Point. Dad hovered over his plate, silent as the grave, letting Connie and Candy run the show as usual.

No one talked to Cloe. She had faded away, a ghost already, that's how they treated her. Her extraordinary life and art didn't merit a mention, even now, when a retrospective and remembrance was her due.

7

YOU ARE HERE

I stopped opening Rain Dogs altogether. Serious shoppers could use the website or reach me by phone. In reality, street traffic had never really amounted to more than a memorial to Cloe and some pocket change. In the weeks after Leo and Lydia moved the Freeschool out of the shop, I spent my time tucked safely in a virtual world, or working on my thesis, or looking for internship hours.

A crunch in the snow heralded the attack. I whirled as I drew my katana from its sheath. Icy mist hung in the air, exhalations like clouds. Cold numbed and weakened my grip, but my sword hand warmed with the thrill of engagement. The assassin's blade rang as the first blow deflected off my armor. I fell to one knee and rolled as I pushed off with the other leg. Gale winds poured down the snowy peaks above. My billowing cape filled with a gust. Whump! Coal-black fabric flew into the face of the attacker, momentarily blinding her. An unexpected diversion! The arc of my blade sliced through the padded jacket of the ninja. Cotton wool mixed with blood erupted, leaving a trail of rubies in the pristine snow.

"End game," I said.

The snowy scene evaporated into sleep mode. I sat, savoring the humming dark of the virtual in-between. Some days, I'd sit in the void for hours, studying the grid of light points stretching to infinity. Not today, though. My thesis was due soon, and anxiety from the deadline stabbed at my brain. I tipped my VR visor up, peeled off my gloves, and took a gulp of energy drink.

Back at my vMac, a cursor hovered in the air, tapping its impatient finger at me. I had written my final paper once before, but my perspective and the technology changed in a few short months. The target kept moving—

We mustn't lose sight of the heart of the game, which is **a never-ending story brought to life.** *The mantra of 'story' for those entering the field of situational design is of the utmost importance. Games are replacements for the rites of passage and meaningful initiations that have been driven to near extinction in the conditions of the modern world. Extended reality game (XRG) players do not know where the game begins and where it ends. As developers, designers, and socio-engineers, we wield great power. XRGs offer permission for people to design their own worlds. Users are the architects of their culture within a unique virtual realm. Transgressions do not come under scrutiny here. XR is a safe-zone for expression, be it biological, emotional, sexual, or political. Instead, experiences are compiled in data cohorts to adjust the environment to the user and to create community. We, as* *situational designers and alternative reality technologists, will re-engineer the way audiences interact with media, the space around them, and with each other.*

I had written and rewritten this intro so many times I lost count. After an hour, I gave up yet again and logged in to the HERE Urban Playground Project. HERE UP was an unreleased game available to CS grad students through the Berkeley student affairs office. Beta testing counted toward internship hours, so, technically, I wasn't wasting time. That HERE was the same company whose billboard the Chaos Order destroyed was an irony that hadn't escaped me. To the contrary, the secret betrayal made the time spent beta testing more satisfying. Plus, HERE UP had potential, a lot of potential, but it was missing something—playfulness, immersion, originality. The luxury branded violence and lack of humor were what made HERE's billboard a target in the first place.

The central concept of the game was real-world exploration—a virtual adventure that used the actual streets, businesses, and alleys of San Francisco as its world. Of course, the first place I explored was Rain Dogs. I don't know how they did it, but the virtual rendering of my shop was accurate down to the floor plan, shelves, and lounges. I could pick up a comic and read or buy it through a gateway, albeit an Amazon one. Margins on purchases made in my shop were automatically credited to my business account. I had the uncanny feeling that I could walk up to myself at the register and ask my own avatar for the meaning of life.

The augmented reality components of the XRG were

primitive at best. It worked through an interface between my SmartCuff and my mixed reality gaming headset. It wasn't true augmented reality yet since the environment was rendered with passthrough cameras on my visor. I looked weird walking around the city in my gaming gear tethered to my Cuff, but I didn't care. HERE UP had several quests and adventures to complete in the prototype, but the game was glitchy overall. However, I was impressed that the developers implemented fixes within days or even hours after I reported them. It was clear that HERE had an ace programming team working on the project 24/7. The improvements to the game since I first logged in were astounding.

A notification appeared in the upper right corner of my display. The icon looked different than the usual bell shape—it was the HERE logo in miniature. In the game's communication center, a message from HERE's director of game marketing awaited my attention.

DEAR MR. BOUCHARD,

Thank you for your interest in HERE. Your contribution to the Urban Playground Project has been noticed. In fact, we have found your suggestions to be revolutionary.

I have contacted your counselor at the University of California, Berkeley. We are impressed with your credentials and would like to meet you to discuss your future with our company.

Please contact my secretary to schedule an interview. Thank you in advance for your consideration.

$$\cdot\ \cdot\ \cdot$$

HAD Ms. Weele caught me at any other time in my life, I would have ghosted her, but I was desperate for intelligent human contact. I had never met Jol, but I knew her name from meetings with HERE's marketing department. After Lydia and Leo walked out of my life, I was the one who stepped up to endorse HERE's products. My mother pushed through the agreement for sponsorship and the legal settlement despite Leo's refusal to participate. That I was the Order's so called spokesperson was the final nail in my coffin with Leo and his growing cult. I had commodified the Chaos Order's name, an irredeemable sin, but I didn't know what else to do. The alternative allowed criminal charges to be filed against me and all of the people who had trusted me. I didn't realize until it was too late that the majority of them would have preferred to pay fines and even serve time.

Connie had stayed at The W for two weeks to finalize the contract with HERE. She had me sign off on the video scripts and advertisement campaigns and made sure I followed through. My mother's proximity and pressure opposed to Lydia's and Leo's complete absence made it feel like I had no other option. Under the bright studio lights, I claimed that the billboard caper had been a planned collaboration between HERE and the Chaos Order. An embarrassing and unforgivable lie.

§

THE BITTER SMELL of the coffee bar dominated the atrium of HERE's headquarters—a torus-shaped building that took up an entire city block along South Park. It didn't escape me that the location was an ironic nod to ground zero for the Bay Area tech explosion in the 1990s. Androgynous, sun-deprived workers swooped the breakfast bar like bats to snap up free mini-boxes of goji berry Muesli, green smoothies, and espresso shots.

Why the hell am I here, I thought, looking down at the digital tablet on my lap. *Evan Bouchard—3 pm interview—Jol Weele* scrolled across the top. Absentmindedly, I clicked checkboxes next to quiz questions. Puzzles were part of the application. I momentarily immersed myself in manipulating a hologram of a manhole cover.

"Mr. Bouchard, Ms. Weele will see you now," the receptionist announced.

Before I had time to turn and escape to the relative comfort of the street outside, Jol emerged from between two towering ferns. Like hiding prey, my breath stopped as she scanned the lounge. Her eyes were dark cabochons above wide, high cheekbones. In the sun streaming through the atrium glass, the suede of her hair glowed two shades lighter than her deep brown skin. Her slim, tailored suit was made far more exciting by enormous hoop earrings and the multi-color beaded collar she wore. She saw me cowering and I stood.

"Mr. Bouchard?" She asked.

"Please, call me Evan."

"And you can call me Jol," she replied in an accent that sounded like music.

Jol took the pad from my hand and led me to what looked like a paneled wall. A french-tipped press on the thumbprint scanner opened a discrete door into the interior hall. Inside, thick glass bricks like ice cubes flanked the private corridor. The walls were cool-white. I shivered, even though the cold was visual, not physical. Jol was the only warmth here. Her honey and amber scent and the glow of her skin kept me close.

Jol pressed her thumb onto another keypad and we stepped into her office. Thirty-foot-high floor-to-ceiling windows looked out onto the gardens inside the inner circle of the campus. The faux-leopard chair on which Jol motioned for me to take a seat was flanked by a profusion of plants—tall palms, philodendron, fig, and bamboo. She sat on the other side of the desk and tented her fingers.

"Welcome to HERE," Jol said, "I want to start by letting you know that this won't be your typical interview. We know a fair amount about you already. We are interested in your prodigious programming skill, but also in your association with the Chaos Order."

I shifted uneasily, feeling trapped in the belly of the building. Unless I wanted to leap through a window, I was dependent on Jol to let me out.

"Okay, that's unexpected. I worked with your marketing department under threat, but it wasn't sanctioned by the Order, and they have been clear about that in the press. I'm lucky they aren't a litigious group or they'd probably sue me. I don't think I'm your point of entry," I said.

"Yes, well, we will get to that. Your unique combination of skills is what makes you so very interesting to us. As you know, HERE's XR environments are photorealistic. The more the game is played, the more the AI renders a true version of the city through our extended reality interface. What you haven't experienced yet is our breakthrough XR hardware. It's next generation. Our hope is to introduce HERE's revolutionary near-eye hologram headsets using experiential gameplay in the real world. A cyberpunk aesthetic overlaid on the everyday world outside. A secret society moving among the crowd. Like the Chaos Order."

"I guess you don't want to see my resume then," I joked, but she said nothing in response.

"Yes. Well. I know about your actions. The billboard, of course. But also the various events and the internal politics of the Order. We know about Leo's personality— that he is a loose cannon."

"Then you know I've had a falling out with him. I'm not part of the Order anymore. Really, you probably know far more about the Order's current inner workings than I do," I said.

"I suppose we do. However, Leo is unmanageable without you, and of course, he can't code. I realize, Evan, you could have written HERE Urban Playground on your own. Your genius and your multiple talents aside, you have more influence over the Order than you know. Maybe not through Leo, but by other avenues."

"Jol, this is intense. And untrue. I feel cornered. Traitorous even," I said.

"I'm sorry, Evan. I've been told that I come across as direct. Please, let's take a walk in the courtyard and I promise, I'll lighten up. Let's get to know each other."

Jol pressed a button on her desk. A featureless door— all but invisible—opened to the gardens. She smiled the most beautiful smile and led me into the light. The landscaping outside felt weird and unnatural— formal like the gardens of Versailles. There were no sounds from insects or birds. Tight geometric squares of clipped lawn were crossed with a labyrinth of walking paths. Some of the checkerboard greens held topiary or a Zen-like boulder. Wild and free, this was not. An orange tree blossomed in the late February sun, its scent shockingly sumptuous and sweet.

"Let me start again," Jol said, "As you know, we are developing a full immersion experience. Pokémon Go, for adults, but far, far more sophisticated. The story arcs of HERE will lead players to clues in the real world. It will transform the civic realm of San Francisco into an XR playground."

"Yes, I know. But how do I fit in?" I asked.

"Independent from HERE, you and Leo have already gamified the urban environment, and in an organic way. It's nothing our developers could achieve. Believe me, we've tried. As you know, our current prerelease is unimaginative when it comes to the storyline and popular cultural references. At least, compared to where we want it to be. HERE's partners and shareholders want a true "down the rabbit hole" experience. Twists. Surreal. Multimedia. Relatable. Hip. No matter what we try, our attempts come off contrived and conventional. That's where you and the Order come in. We want to bring HERE into public spaces and we want you to head the situational design project. You will be the bridge, coding the portals that will lead us between the virtual and the physical environments."

"I don't know, Jol. That this game will be hosted by a corporation will not sit well with the Order. I'm not sure how I feel about it myself. Tell me, what are your expectations for Leo and me?" I asked.

"Yes. That. We want to reunite the two of you. We want the Order to be the first group to play and promote the game. HERE would be the Order's sponsor, and vice versa. I know Leo won't trust HERE without you, and we can't bring him in without your help. I want you to understand, you are far more important to us than Leo. If we lose him, we can still proceed with your knowledge and influence alone. But if you refuse, the real-world design division ends now. I can't do it without you."

8

HEADQUARTERS

I t was the third reference check that finally got my attention. Notifications from commercial property managers pinged my inbox and distracted me from my thesis. What's more, my Masters degree now seemed irrelevant, which didn't help my motivation. My paper was never going to get done. Lydia seemed right—the expensive university program had no bearing on my marketability as a programmer. My real-world experience had attracted HERE, not a new letter on my diploma.

Mr. Bouchard, can you verify Mr. Leo Gault's employment, job title, pay, and responsibilities?

Mr. Bouchard, Mr. Gault tells me he leased an office space from you from 2012 to 2017. Was he a good tenant?

I could barely suppress my laughter. I mean, first off, Leo would have been six years old in 2012. Regardless, I gave out glowing reviews of Leo's character—responsible, punctual, ethical to a fault. When giving references, I imagined the opposite of what Leo's temperament actually was. An anti-Leo.

When the calls kept coming, I started to pry into what the fuck Lydia and Leo were up to. On the fifth reference check, I asked what Leo was renting and why.

"It looks like this lease is for offices on the 42nd floor at our 399 California Street address. Let's see—the company is—a—called—um, order.com. Yes. The application says it's a retail fulfillment company. Some sort of startup."

"Okaaay," I said, "Yeah, sure, Leo was a good tenant and paid his rent on time. You're welcome."

Offices in the Financial District? Totally nuts! Lydia and Leo couldn't afford that, they couldn't afford an hour's worth of time at that location. They had no revenue to speak of. A guerrilla arts society had no business being on California Street. Consultancies or mega law firms, that's who held space downtown.

Lydia was still secretly asking me to work on the Freeschool website through covert texts and emails. She claimed she didn't know how to post classes or schedule social media. I knew she was more technically adept than she let on. But I did it anyway, and I did it for free. I needed to keep that thin connection with Lydia and Leo, a last hope of reconciliation. As a courtesy, I hadn't poked around their new organization much at first, but if they were going to pull me in by using me as a reference, I had the right to know why. At least, that's what I told myself.

The back issues of the Order's newsletter didn't have a lot of information. It was mostly recaps of Leo's shows at

The Box. I found footage of the Order tossing chicken livers off the balconies at Rincon Center; that was pretty damn hilarious. I had to dig deeper to find any hints on the plans for a downtown office, that meant hacking into personal emails between Lydia and Leo. Breaking into their private communications was well outside my normal boundaries of prying, but I convinced myself that those boundaries had to move.

Leo had convinced Lydia to use her decent credit and to get her parents to cosign to take out a gargantuan business loan. With that money, Leo and Lydia planned to move the Freeschool and the Order downtown. The rents in the Financial District were some of the highest in the world. It was a doomed venture. However, if Leo said he could pull a magic rabbit out of his butt, Lydia was going to believe him.

I clicked Jol's bookmarked LinkedIn and called.

"Jol, it's Evan. Hey, I have an idea. Leo and Lydia are planning on renting an office space they can't afford," I said on the phone.

"Evan! It's so nice to hear your voice. Yes. I know. I don't think they will be able to get that space on their own. Even if they do, I would highly recommend they not take it."

"Well, hear me out. I'm not going to get back into Leo's good graces without a monumental gesture. If HERE pays for the offices, they will be dependent on us. We can't make it look like a handout though. It has to seem like grassroots fundraising. Listen, I could tell Lydia I know about Leo's plans from the reference checks and that I'm organizing a benefit in cooperation with HERE to raise funds for the new location. He'd believe that," I explained.

"Interesting—" The line went mute for a long moment. Suddenly, Jol was back. Her tone changed from reticent to enthusiastic. "It's a great idea. I knew I could depend on you. By the way, does this mean you want the job?" Jol said.

9

THE BENEFIT

J ol looked like a toy in a dollhouse standing in the middle of the Edwardian parlor in her gown and pearls. The perfect host, she greeted guests, and directed them through a large passage to the drawing room, dining area, and the gardens beyond. The furnishings matched the period of the house and the theme of the party—dark wood panels, tasseled draperies, and fireplaces in every room.

Although it was a costume party, the distinction between the Freaks and Jol's colleagues was blatant. The HERE crowd's fashion screamed Ballet Opening Night Gala with their jewels, hats, velvets, and ruffles. In contrast, the broad interpretation of Edwardian Gothic by the Freaks ran the gamut from Edward Scissorhands to powdered wigs, grease paint, and lingerie. I felt most comfortable among the elegantly dressed—gowns and tails, real dinner ties hand-tied into bows. Sure, we were trying to raise money for the Order, but I felt more in my element with the posh. Leo had always said that I was too bougie, and maybe he was right.

Leo and his entourage arrived raucous and late. Maureen was a riot of diaphanous chiffons in fiery rainbow colors. She had teased her hair into an electric shock afro, the shape of it roughly round, but the texture baby fine. Herb, in an undertaker's long frock coat and top hat, lurched around with a measuring tape to fit partygoers for imaginary coffins.

I delayed approaching. My comfortable pocket of conversation with some HERE executives turned unbearably stifling. Nervous about what Leo would think, I excused myself and went to the bar to refill my glass before making my way over. Although his overalls and pitchfork brought the devil to mind, I knew what he was going for—American Gothic. It always baffled me how Leo could make baggy old-man clothes look good.

Let him get his footing, I thought. In reality, I was the one who needed to find my ground. Nonchalant and relaxed, that's how I wanted to come across, but my chest was so tight I could hardly suck in a breath. I went to the bar and slammed down a Maker's Mark, then another before I started across the room.

"A pitchfork, nice touch, it suits you. Gothic formal. I get it," I said to Leo as I joined the growing crowd around him. My words sounded acid sharp and my skin felt tight. Leo narrowed his eyes. He could read my biology like a book.

"Sure, American Gothic. We don't got none tuxedees

down on the farm," Leo said with a flat country twang. His smile was broad but his eyes were cold.

"My god, Leo, be nice," Jol said as she swung up behind me, her presence signaled by the sillage of her amber perfume.

Jol, opposite of Lydia, stood the same petite height, but the similarity between the two women stopped there—the elegant silk taffeta, pearls, and diamonds against Jol's dark skin was a stark contrast to Lydia's blue gingham pinafore dress, red platform shoes, and yellow yarn wig. I couldn't figure out if Lydia was going for Alice in Wonderland, Dorothy of Oz, or the country wife counterpart to Leo's depression-era farmer. Whichever, she looked adorable.

"All this is for you and the Order, Leo. Show some appreciation," Jol said.

"I don't *do* appreciation. And who are you, by the way?" Leo asked.

"Leo, this is Jol. She is a director of marketing at HERE. And she's hosting this party for you," I interjected.

"So you're the one. You and your company are commodifying what I do. What about commandeering your billboard made you think I wanted HERE as a sponsor?" Leo said.

"You're here, for one. And, in a way, the billboard was a collaboration," Jol said, cleverly.

Despite his posturing, I knew Leo understood that the interactions between the Order and HERE created a history. He needed money, so he was testing the waters. I could also tell he didn't like Jol speaking to him in the knowing, scolding tone of a mother.

"Hypocrite!" I interrupted the tense exchange. Otherwise, Leo was going to explode at Jol. His muscles had tensed and he was building up steam. I could read him too. "You've been charging for your events since the beginning. *You* commodify what you do. You can't rent property in the Financial District with ideas and charisma," I said.

That I knew he was charging for membership threw him off his rant before it began. I had hacked into private emails and what passed for the Order's accounting books. Leo had raised the cover at The Box and started charging for his parties, urban explorations, and classes, at least to outsiders. Despite monetization, the Order's books were deep in the red.

"Let's get some air; it's a lovely night," Jol said, glossing over my outburst. She smoothed her skirt with one hand and gestured to the yard with the other. The three-carat boulder on her finger caught the chandelier light like an exploding star. "Come, Leo," she said, claiming the last word for the moment.

I took Jol's arm and walked through the open French doors to the jasmine-scented garden. Feathery waltzes filter through outdoor speakers. Leo and his motley crew followed behind on a path that led around the pool and to a huge jacaranda, now black and bare, its branches, like arteries against the night sky. Jol sat on the stone bench beneath the tree. Lydia, Leo, and I stood around her in a jagged semi-circle.

"Listen, Leo. If we work together, we can go the distance. I get that the Order is more than entertainment.

I understand that we are trying to wake people up, break the Matrix, but you're not going to get the attention you want if you don't widen your net. People with money and influence want to be part of the Order too. They can help. She swept her hand, indicating the partygoers. Look around you. Just because these people are wealthy doesn't mean they can't reject the conformity and banality of our culture. You preach radical inclusion, but you don't practice it," Jol said.

Leo seemed not to be listening. He shifted his pitchfork from one hand to the other and glanced at his Cuff like he expected a message. *He's definitely distracted. What is he up to*, I thought.

"Leo, what's on your mind? Aren't you listening? Do you understand what HERE and Jol are offering you?" I asked.

"You win, Evan," he said, rocking from one foot to the other. He looked at his wrist again and flashed me a cryptic grin.

I glanced at Jol. She looked concerned too. The menace was palpable.

"I need a drink. Come on, I want to make a toast," Leo said.

"Sure, Leo, but we need to talk," I said to thin air. He was already three strides down the path back to the patio. Despite what I fantasized, I didn't have the upper hand at all. Leo led us back to the crowd and rang his glass with the tines of his pitchfork.

"Join us," Leo called out over the crowd of partygoers in a showman's voice that resonated through the night air.

Jol cooperated by asking the bartenders to pour trays of Champagne for Leo's pronouncement. As we gathered to retrieve our flutes, a strange sound began—a gurgling roar. Startled, Jol and I turned in unison to witness a column of water erupt from the center of the swimming pool.

A cascade from the explosion flowed both over the edge of the pool and up. Low waves of water swept over shoes, indiscriminate of whether they were Converse or Christian Louboutins. The downpour came quickly as the pool emptied itself into the sky like a geyser. Chlorine-smelling rain drenched everyone standing in the yard. Leo hooted like a drunken redneck.

"Leo! Holy fuck! What did you put in the pool!" I demanded.

My hands balled into fists. I felt whiplashed. My concern for Jol and her home triggered a reaction that overrode all the control I'd developed for Leo's stunts.

"Aaah. Let me see if I can remember. I think the recipe called for ten pounds of potassium, ten pounds of sodium, and some other stuff. You know, Anarchist's Cookbook. Honestly, I didn't expect such a spectacular effect, though. I'm impressed if I do say so myself," he said, wiping his hands on the bib of his overalls.

"Okay, okay. Quiet down and listen up, everyone," Leo called. Feathered hats drooped like birds in an oil spill. Mascara trailed down faces. Yards of wet wool and silk gave off the distinct smell of dirty dog and bleach. The dry group, those who hadn't quite made it out to the patio for the Champagne toast, laughed and pointed at their drenched counterparts. Leo rang his glass again to calm the rowdy crowd.

"Freaks and the followers of HERE, you have been officially christened and united under the Order of Chaos. The game is afoot! Together we wake the typicals from their sleep of conformity. Another door opens tonight, for those brave enough to choose it. The door of infinite possibility!"

Jol took a somber sip of champagne as others clapped politely. She walked to the edge of the half-full pool.

"Cracked, right down the center," she said over her shoulder, "God, you're such an asshole, Leo—right—well —who swims in San Francisco anyway? I'll get some towels," Jol said, with mild disgust. She disappeared through the French doors.

"Jesus, Leo. You destroyed Jol's property. That's going to cost twenty, maybe thirty thousand dollars to fix. What were you thinking? Jol is just trying to pay your ridiculous rent and this is how you thank her?" I said.

"Chill out, Evan. You may have drunk the Flavor-Aid, but I'm still free to do whatever I want. You're the man now, Evan, but I want nothing to do with this sponsorship garbage. Jol, now she's a wildcat, I'll give you that," Leo said and winked.

He took Lydia's arm and walked inside. I was furious, but I followed them. Too angry to speak, I took a seat in an out of the way chair and sulked. What else was there to do? My appetite for the party had been killed by Leo's antics. Jol returned from upstairs in a loose-fitting but stylish shirt dress and bare feet. She handed out towels to the wet partygoers.

"Come, sit with me Leo, Lydia, Evan." Jol rounded us up on her way to warm herself by the fire. To my surprise, all three of us joined her. Ornate bronze andirons glittered in the shifting light. Lydia moved nearer to the blaze to dry her dress. Leo didn't bother with a towel or the fire, he simply claimed the last empty chair.

"We need to understand each other before we can reach an agreement," Jol said from her seat opposite Leo's, as if the pool incident had never happened.

"Agreement? I told you, I work—" Leo started, but Jol interrupted.

"To get anywhere with this tonight, we need some special leverage."

Jol retrieved a tiny vial with a dropper from a carved green jade box on the side table next to her and held it up to the light of a Tiffany lamp. The amber glass glistened. "At HERE, we microdose for creative brainstorming sessions. Tonight, we go full strength. It's been engineered to amplify insights. It's like LSD, but with the empathy enhancement of Ecstacy. It's called Alter."

"Drugs? Fuck yeah! Now you're talkin' my language," Leo said.

Jol had Leo's number. I knew nothing about this secret plan B. Did she have drugs hidden in boxes across the house? Pissed, I sat on the warm bricks by Lydia. Jol walked our small circle, communicating silently by sticking out her tongue, inviting us to mimic her. I sighed but accepted the dropper.

What else could I do? She dosed us discreetly, presumably, so no one around us would invite themselves along. I took off my damp jacket, shoes, and socks to prepare for my trip.

"I miss you," I whispered to Lydia after Jol was out of earshot.

"I miss you too. But listen, be careful, Evan. I'm not as helpless on the computer as you think." She held her hand up to her face. "I know you've been poking around, and not just in the calendar files. I haven't said anything to Leo, but you are putting me in an awkward position. I want the three of us back together. But all this HERE stuff? It's not what Leo wants, and you know it. He will take you back if you apologize, but you're pushing this way past the point of no return." I tensed, hoping her words were covered by the hiss and crackle of the roaring flames. Leo was engaged with Jol, or so he seemed. Knowing Leo, he could appear totally absorbed in conversation, but be eavesdropping all the same. But no, I could tell he couldn't hear us.

These drugs were quick. Onset seemed to take ten minutes, give or take. My irritation evaporated like drops of water on a hot skillet. Gravity seemed to warp the floor below me. Before vertigo set in, the world changed in an instant. The surroundings became light. I took in the whole room at once. It shimmered, each element so purely district. The subtle baroque music popped out of the background and became marvelous—almost visible in the air. Thoughts came lightning-fast. I made connections that were unimaginable moments before, my synapses offering up intricate patterns overlaid on the surfaces of things.

I fell into Lydia's belladonna eyes. She, no longer separate, had no ending and I had no beginning. The heat, the rumble and tinkle of the party noise in the air, smoke rising from the fire, everything blended into one consciousness, or rather, a consciousness now witnessing itself. Leo, however, stood out like a black hole in the sudden unity of my awareness. He looked at me darkly and saw into my soul.

PART II

10

PALACE OF FINE ARTS

Lydia

I had second thoughts about my plan looking up at the towering columns of The Palace of Fine Arts. At the party, a midnight climb seemed inspired, the opposite of the stuffy gathering that had been getting on my nerves. Climbing up the vertical wall of a Mission Street office building to hijack HERE's billboard was a cakewalk compared to this. My stomach lurched. I was tripping hard. Free-soloing the Place on designer acid, well, that might be tougher than I first imagined.

"I'm going to have to take these off," I said. I was absorbed in my glossy, red Mary Jane platforms smoldering in the light of the full moon. Lacy ankle socks overflowed the sides like frothy milk.

The sight of my growing muffin-top was another issue. I moved to San Francisco from Santa Cruz in peak condition. Cirque du Soleil, here I come! Or so I thought. Turns out the actual paying gigs, at least in the city, were in nightclubs and bars. That's how I met Leo. He picked me up with a few other circus rats outside the Circus Center. Leo needed showgirls. And Leo, in his usual direct fashion, went out and got them by the truckload.

At first, I had to use a fake ID to perform. This was no high art cirque, more like barroom burlesque. With burlesque and bars came booze and butts. Cigarette butts, yes, but also my big size-eight ass. The same one that had fit into a size three just last year, and a size zero when I left home to seek my fame and fortune.

"Dorothy can't get back to Kansas without her ruby slippers. Help me find a safe place to stash these bad boys and I'll grab 'em on our way out." I said.

"Sure," Evan said, "Look around the base of the rotunda. There are recesses in the walls. Stick your shoes in there. I'll make sure we don't forget them."

Sure enough, there were several small, altar-like niches tucked into the base of the dome. I peered into one dark hole covered by the broad leaf of a philodendron. There was enough room beside the melted candle wax and quartz crystals. I artfully arranged the shoes among the items some wayward Wiccan had left behind and beamed up at Leo, Evan, and Jol.

"The sacred slippers of Antioch," I said, rising from a squat, while brushing the dirt off my hands. I pulled aside the leaf curtain to show them the spooky-looking nook with my red heels at the center.

"He who is valiant and pure of spirit may find the holy shoes in the Castle of Aaaaargh," Evan bantered back in a god-awful English accent. Laughter granted a few moments of mirth to the silent stone angels perched on their plinths 150 feet above.

"Wait, isn't the Castle of Aaargh in Arimathea," Leo said in his low, deadpan voice, but his face burst into an unusual boyish grin.

"I don't know what you're talking about," Jol said in consternation.

Bawhahaha!

That Jol was not familiar with the Monty Python skit made the whole thing a hundred times funnier. She looked so childlike and awkward that I couldn't help but hug her. My lunge of spontaneous affection may have been more aggressive than I intended. She pulled back in a micro-moment of embarrassment but corrected herself by returning the embrace fully.

She had been an ice princess ruling over her kingdom just an hour before, inching toward the goal of making the Chaos Order hers. Now she was as lovely and as warm as a lap cat. Her confectionery scent enveloped me. We burned in this garden place. The Alter had done its work.

Evan and Leo split off from us girls. They were back at their fraternal horseplay like no time had passed. It lifted my heart to see them the way they had been before Leo's schemes had pried them apart. When they weren't trying to shove each other into the lagoon, I overheard them talking about Jol's offer in low whispers. Leo seemed a little more receptive now that he was high as a kite, but I had my doubts that his openness would last.

I missed the three of us. Leo did too, I could tell, although he would never admit it to me or anyone else. Evan and Leo laughed and chatted on a different plane— they were on a social kind of high. Me? I had dissolved into the surrounding melancholic Maxfield Parrish world, knowing things could never go back to how they were before.

"I like Evan," Jol whispered. Her breath tickled my ear.

Charmed by her and sad at the same time, I had imagined both Leo and Evan would always be my men. A group marriage, of sorts. But I liked Jol too. She was smart, powerful, and very original. The Freaks, they were strange, yes, but all in the same general way. I mean, we were outliers. Radical, sure, but I guess all subcultures end up as homogenous and as tribal as the societies they are rebelling against. Jol's true originality stood out by comparison.

A strong gust of wind off the lake caught my wig. The tangled pigtails of yellow yarn landed in a bush. Goosebumps raised the baby hairs on my arms. *I must be cold*, I thought, although I didn't feel a chill. Luckily, my light cotton dress had dried from the exploding pool gag. Evan's black suit was probably still damp with its folds of thick fabric, velvet lapels, and layers. I worried about him sometimes. To me, he seemed to need caretaking. I interrupted my own reverie with a plan of action.

"Okay," I called down to the water's edge. "Gather 'round. I'm going up."

The idea was to free-climb the colonnades. At the hot and crowded party, Jol had suggested we get outside somewhere to talk. The Palace was my solution.

These frilly panties are going to get their share of the limelight tonight, I thought as I mapped the ascent in my head. The distance between the columns was perfect, about two and a half feet. With my back against one, I would be able to wedge myself in and walk my feet against the surface of the adjacent column. I'd step, then slide until my legs were horizontal again. That way, I could inchworm all the way to the top.

Foot by foot, I rose by alternately sliding my back up one column and walking up the other. Cement sucked the moisture out of the body, especially from the soles of my bare feet. At the top, Doric ridges bloomed into pedestals of stone acanthus leaves. I swung one knee over the top and pulled up my weight. Now able to rest, I calculated the final climb up the cement skirt of one of the weeping maidens. I could use the folds of her robe and the keystone relief as footholds. The figures with their backs turned to the world filled me with a sense of sadness and ruin. Their expressions could not be seen from the ground. That facelessness had always seemed eerie and mysterious to me.

I'm sure it took far less than an hour to reach the top, but Jol's Alter made it hard to tell how much time had passed. On the ledge, my feet dangling, I waved to Jol, Evan, and Leo. They were hugging. Sharp whistles and cheers reached me through the whoosh of the night sky. A triumph. *Not too fat after all*, I thought to myself.

The entire city unfolded up here. Inland, blinking red lights of the skyscrapers looked like the eyes of dead dinosaurs invading the shoreline. When I looked out over the bay, rolling fog became great grey serpents looping up from the waters to encircle the Golden Gate Bridge. Their eyes shone and their streaming whiskers reached to the clouds. Container ships crept, like vast cities across the night.

I didn't linger long among the soot-filled crevasses, tomblike urns, and the wheeling bats that were barely visible against the dark sky. Gusts of wind off the angry bay filled me with foreboding. The feeling wasn't entirely unpleasant, but I longed for the company and warmth below. I was a wraith up here. Alien and alone.

"The weeping women, they have faces!" I said as I made a perfect dismount onto the spring and give of the dewy lawn. My body felt strong and energized. I knew I'd pay for my stunt tomorrow. But tonight, I was filled with triumph.

"You were amazing."

"Oh my god, I was so scared for you," Jol said.

"You are my goddess of Chaos," Leo said.

His praise and admiration shut everything else out. Leo took my hand and led me into the gardens. Awash in bright stripes of moonlight, the air glowed blue. Swans, spectral, drifted on the shining waters. I had never seen anything more magnificent. A wonderland to explore.

We left Evan and Jol under the rotunda. In a maze of

rhododendron, Leo started a game of hide and seek. We jumped out at each other and broke into raucous laughter again and again. Under normal circumstances, this game would have gotten old after the third boo, but we were high on drugs and my accomplishment. Endorphins from the climb made me invincible. I ran and Leo caught me. I let him catch me. In his arms, he turned to kiss me. A first kiss. A tentative kiss. He pulled back and looked into my eyes, searching for my response. I kissed him back with deep exploration that held the desire of years.

"Oops," Evan said in a loud voice. That this moment could be so easily derailed ignited a flash of rage in me. I would protect this moment with my life. Evan saw the threat in my eyes. "Jol, you know what, I think we need to see that sculpture over there again. That one was particularly—um— Greek, right, let's go."

Evan tickled Jol in the ribs. Their laughter faded and they were gone. Leo reached into his pocket and pulled out a bullet vial of brown glass. He clicked it one turn.

"Just a little. This isn't blow."

"What is it?"

"Lydia, meet my White Lady. No synth for me. This is pure, organic, top-shelf H. My little secret, but I want to share it with you tonight. You were amazing," Leo said.

I snorted the blast and felt the drug spread to my toe tips—numb, floating, blissful.

"Wow, that's good. Really good!"

Another rush rippled down my body and enveloped my being. Two more turns, click, click. Leo took a double-stiff hit. We slid down a wall in a cloud of pleasure and fondling. His tongue felt incredible in my mouth, when he moved to nibble my ear, he whispered, "I've wanted this for so long." *Did he? He knew he could have taken me at any point. Why now?*

Leo peeled down the top of my dress and unclipped my bra. His coarse hands crushed my breasts and he bit the tips of my nipples. I writhed, my back arching away from the cold, dirty cement. Pain and pleasure, warmth and cold—an ambrosia of sensations bathed in the phosphorescent moonlight. He pulled my lace panties off and slid two fingers inside my pussy. I felt a slick of wet warmth slide down my inner thighs. He unzipped his fly.

As Leo entered me, I knew this was as good as it would get—the Alter and heroin, the victory climb, the longing for Leo finally sated. I would never experience more than this, and that made me a little sad. The knowledge of a never again moment passed quickly as I drowned in the thrusts of Leo's cock inside me. I felt like a complete circuit.

Our love-making seemed both short and long. Spinning mandalas painted the inside of my closed eyes. When I opened them, the sky was a patchwork of interlinking shapes, like an Escher drawing come to life. Leo's motion was expansive and full. He grunted and his eyes rolled back as he pulled out. Cum shot across my belly. I had been too high to orgasm, but I didn't care. Leo wanted me, and I wanted him. This proved it. I knew we belonged together.

We clung in an embrace for a long moment but the patch we claimed from the ground lost its glamor. It was cold, dirty, and covered in bird shit again. After a long silent moment, I looked at my Cuff.

"4:30 am, we should clear out. Morning joggers will be around soon," I said to Leo.

I stood, clasped my bra, and put my dress back on. I snapped a quick photo of Leo with my Cuff. He said no, but I assured him I wouldn't share this adventure online. It was my special treasure. A trophy.

"Leo," I said quietly.

He heard me, but before he could answer, Evan popped his head around a column.

"Everything come out alright?" he asked with a smirk.

"You look a little rumpled too, my friend," I said.

Jol and Evan looked as guilty and happy as I felt.

"Okay, leave no trace, guys. Are we good on that front? Pick up your wig and socks, Lydia. And don't forget your shoes in the rotunda," Leo said. He looked blank. It was as if nothing had happened, back to business as usual.

11

MORNING AFTER

By the time we got back to Jol's, I was crashing hard. Jol had given us a quick tour of the guest rooms before taking Evan to her own bed. I was under the covers and half asleep before I realized Leo must be downstairs grabbing a nightcap or a smoke. Wrapped in a white terrycloth robe I borrowed from a hook in the ensuite, I crept into the hall. A shimmer of Alter in my peripheral vision trailed into infinity when I turned my head and the ticking from a grandfather clock whispered around me. I slid my hand down the balustrade on the dark stairs. On the ground floor, the kitchen counters were cluttered with piles of bottles, glasses, and half-eaten appetizer trays. No one was around. The only light came from the glow of a few remaining embers in the fireplace and the moon through the windows. I even opened the doors to the patio to see if Leo was out back. Nothing but crickets.

The room where I had settled was still empty when I returned—*had he gone home?* I pushed the door of what I thought was an empty room open a crack. It creaked softly. In the dark, I could hear Leo's heavy snores. A sob hitched in my chest. I wanted to curl up next to him and ask for an explanation—to hear that he just passed out on the first flat surface he came across—but I knew that I wouldn't be welcome in his bed tonight. I had witnessed his behavior with many other women at The Box and elsewhere. I knew he never spent the night and he never invited anyone home. His fear of commitment made him a perpetual one night stand. Less than a one-night stand. He'd kick the majority of his conquests to the curb before the condom hit the trash. That he hadn't left Jol's entirely might have had meaning, but at the Palace of Fine Arts, I felt different. Special. The first one to break through his mile-thick wall. Clearly, I was wrong. I crept back to my bed and pulled the comforter tight around my body. Exhaustion took me before I could unleash the full force of my embarrassment and disappointment.

I woke to the smell of bacon and coffee. My stomach revolted at the idea of food. Patchy memories of last night circled in my mind, and tendrils of shame curled around my neck and shoulders. When I opened my door, I could hear voices under the sound of clinking dishes and running water.

I needed to clean myself up before Leo saw me. Everything hurt. My knees were scraped and bruised. I had blood under my fingernails. Every muscle screamed from last night's 60-foot climb. Lucky to be alive, I thought.

Get it together. Chin up. I tried to soothe myself, but it was useless. In the mirror, I looked beaten and doughy. I had leaves and sticks in my matted hair. If I wanted to play the *it was just sex* card, I needed to look a damn sight better while doing it. Steadying my voice, I called down to Jol.

"Hey, it's Lydia. She's awake," I heard Jol relay to the boys.

A moment later, footsteps drummed up the stairs and she knocked on the door.

"Hi, Sleepyhead," she said as she peeked in. "Where are you? In the bathroom?" She spoke a little louder when she didn't see me in bed.

"Come in, Jol. I need a change of clothes," I said through the bathroom door.

The Ritz didn't have bathrooms half as nice as this— huge, plush apricot towels; a shower filled with high-end shampoos, conditioners, moisturizers, and salts; a built-in sauna.

My heart sank when I saw Jol. She looked gorgeous. And me, I was an extra from The Walking Dead compared to her.

"Jol, oh my god, what am I going to do? I'm a fucking disaster! I need something to wear and some makeup— concealer, eyeliner, lipstick, a surgeon." I took Jol's hands in mine and pleaded.

"Shit. Okay. Okay. We got this. Here's the plan. Shower. Deep condition. While you do that, I'll grab some clothes.

I'm glad you're small like me, I think we're the same size. You can't use my foundation, clearly, but I have a sheer glow cream that will diffuse what's going on here." She gestured to my blotchy skin. "You're going to be fine. Now, quick, jump in the shower."

I held back tears of gratitude. Some women crow and gloat when you're down. Not Jol. She was an ally when I really needed one.

The hot water and steam helped calm my nerves. I ached everywhere, but my spirits rose. By the time I had the hair treatment in, I began to feel like a fool for caring what Leo thought of me at all. Like him, I had countless one night stands. Anonymous sex wasn't my thing, but when in Rome, or San Francisco, no-strings fucks were a way of life. So why was I a train wreck over Leo simply sleeping in another room? *Seriously, girl, check yourself.*

Jol knocked.

"Don't worry, just come in. I'm combing out these knots," I called from the shower.

"Breakfast is almost on the table. I laid out a couple of outfits on the bed. Come down when you're ready." Jol said.

The plastic case she left popped up a pyramid of products when I opened it. I plucked a jar of LaMer and a tube of Chanel Sheer Glow out of her kit. No wonder her skin looked so pristine. Magical indeed. I looked more than restored.

Jol was right—we were exactly the same size. The outfits she laid out were all in pale pastel colors—a coral and a sky blue. The coral was the most flattering—an off-the-shoulder number that covered my paunch, matching leggings, and ballerina flats. I resembled a creamsicle, but it was a vast improvement over the ripped and filthy Wonderland dress that smelled like rat piss and swan shit. Although, considering Leo's punk proclivities, he might prefer a dumpster dress. After a moment's deliberation, I went with clean.

I peeked around the stairs and into the kitchen. Damp hair swung heavy.

"Good afternoon, Little Mary Sunshine," Leo said.

"Is it afternoon already?" I asked.

"Almost."

Leo kissed me on the cheek and slid his hand from my shoulder to my hip, taking me in.

"The natural look," he looked me up and down, "Hmm."

This was not going at all how I thought it would. Leo was warm and sexy. The ice queen game I had planned to play wasn't going to work unless I wanted to look like a total psycho-bitch.

"Yeah, I'm chucking everything over to pursue my true passion to become the world's best Zumba instructor. No offense, Jol." I stuttered a little, feeling unkind for poking fun at her expense after she saved my ass.

"None taken," Jol said, "I wear that outfit to Zumba all the time."

Riffing with Leo was our usual routine, but I hadn't expected business as usual. It was like every other day, but with a little more body contact. That, and Leo was cheery, which was uncharacteristic for him. I needed to get my footing.

Jol handed me a cup of coffee with a wink. The kitchen was sun-filled and smelled wonderful.

"Half-and-Half is in the fridge, sugar's on the table," Jol said.

"You're lucky, you missed the party clean-up," Evan said.

"I would have hired a service, but we had enough hands," Jol added.

"You would have slept in too if you climbed the Palace of Fine Arts," Leo came to my defense.

Creepy. A nice Leo was totally weird. Suspicious, really. Anyway, at least he wasn't ignoring me, or worse, leaving me alone to negotiate with Jol and Evan. Me in peach-colored workout clothes and Leo being civilized was wrong. A queasy feeling sat in the pit of my stomach. Opposites day from hell.

Jol finished laying the plates for breakfast. The coffee in my hand was Philz, my favorite, and the cream was heavy and good. Bacon, eggs, and orange buns were laid on the mahogany table. God, I was starving. Nauseous or not, I needed nourishment. I heaped my plate, sat at the table with the others, and ate in silence until the hollow in my belly was gone.

"How do you afford this place, Jol?" I asked.

"I don't, it's corporate housing. I'm told it was a decaying mess when HERE bought the property. The Edwardian accents and design are original to the house, but they spent a mint on restoration. I've lived here since I relocated to the city from Singapore. I'm sort of the caretaker. Mostly it's just me here, but when guests of the company are in town, I have to offer up the rooms and play hostess. This is where HERE holds events and parties. A small inconvenience in trade for the perk of living in this beautiful home."

"Yeah, Peachy," Leo said. "But why are *we* here? Are we guests of the company?"

"In a way, yes. As you know, HERE's new game is a simulation of San Francisco overlaid on the real city. We need your help finishing the live component. Over the next six months, we want you three to take HERE to the streets, the real streets. Our people can't do what you do. We need artists like you to design the IRL experience. We believe your talent as a showman and promoter will turn the tables for HERE."

"Hm. Flattery. I'm no artist. At least, no one calls me that to my face. The point is, I'm not a corporate guy, and you won't catch me dead in an office," Leo said.

"Well, actually, aren't you renting offices on California Street?" Jol asked.

"Yeah, see, what you said right there shows you don't understand anything. That's a stunt; just a laugh at the expense of the downtown Pinks. Free clown classes and experimental art smack in the middle of all the law firms. It's funny. A gag. That's all."

That was a punch to my gut. To me, the Freeschool was not a joke. Not at all. It was my life's work. Rain Dogs had been the perfect space, and it had cost us nothing.

Leo had convinced me the office was the legitimacy we needed to level up.

Had Leo chucked my dreams overboard for a grudge and a joke? Was this all a very expensive pissing match? Going into debt was against everything I stood for and it made zero sense, but he talked me into borrowing from my parents and taking out astronomical loans. I signed the lease a few days ago. There was no going back. That it was for a laugh had not been a part of our conversation.

"It's a rather expensive joke," Jol spoke my thoughts aloud. "And it's not on your dime, is it, Leo? It's Lydia's credit and money you're using. Or really, her parents' money."

Even though she was defending me, my finances were none of her business. Jol had shockingly personal information and that was the biggest mistake she could make with Leo. That she knew my parents were involved was stalker-level creepy. Trouble was, I didn't know who I was more furious with—Leo for calling my Freeschool a joke, Evan for going corporate and spying on us, or Jol for playing dirty.

"How do you know all of that, Jol?" I asked, my voice shaking with fury.

Suddenly, I wanted to get rid of the responsibility for the California Street location and the money that I owed. I wanted out. This was going all wrong. Jol made me doubt everything. Last night, she promised my dreams would come true. Travel. Fame. The rent covered for the new offices. A broad reach for Leo's ideas, our ideas. It had sounded ideal under the influence of Alter. Today, when I was desperate and hungover, she acted like a friend, but it all appeared to be part of her strategy.

"Fuck this," Leo said and started to get up. He was going to lose his shit. All the signs were there.

"Wait, wait, you're taking this all wrong. What I'm saying is, HERE will pay your lease for five years to start and all your expenses. That's what I'm laying down. That, and you don't have to work at HERE headquarters at all, or even for HERE. You will be a consultant. Completely independent. Lydia too. We will pay you for the work you do for us, and we will pay you very, very well. Think about it. Think of what you can do with your offices free and clear, and with plenty of money for shows, events, whatever you want to do."

Leo sat down, his palms planted flat. If he had the ears of a wolf, they would be plastered flat back and his teeth would be bared.

"I'll be straight with you," Jol continued with a quaver in her voice. "I know you can't pay your expenses and you haven't even moved into your new space yet. I wish I had more time to develop our friendship, but I have a tight deadline. I had to put this on the table today." She realized she had overstepped the play.

"How do you know so much about our finances? Did Evan tell you?" Leo demanded.

"Evan had nothing to do with it. I hired an investigator."

A private investigator! The audacity of it! I thought.

"If I agree, which isn't going to happen, I won't sign any contracts with HERE. None," Leo said, still teasing Jol with the tiniest possibility of a deal.

That he signed nothing, I knew. Leo's apartment was a sublet, no contract. All of the papers for the downtown office were finalized by me. I also knew that HERE could never use Leo's services, contractor or not, if he didn't sign something. I hadn't considered any of this when I was high last night. Jol had painted a pretty picture of unlimited resources and artistic freedom.

"I don't think that's possible, Leo. You have to sign something," Jol said.

"What about you, Evan, have you signed a contract with these jizz nozzles? If you have, break it. You can leave with us. This is bullshit," Leo offered.

Jol interrupted, "Wait, wait, Leo, don't be rash. There is a lot more to negotiate. We've just started."

"No, we've just finished. Thanks for the nerd-drugs and the party," Leo said.

I actually felt bad for her. I really did. She had pushed too hard, too fast. Despite the fun we had last night, Jol had not gotten through to Leo like she believed. A common mistake. Everyone thinks Leo's on their side when he's not.

"Evan, I asked you a question," Leo demanded. "Are you coming with us, or not?"

Evan had been quiet since the negotiation started. Jol put her hand on his shoulder to stop him from standing, but he shook her off. His breakfast plate rattled with a pound of his palm.

"You've snubbed me for months, Leo. Moved out of Rain Dogs. Told half of San Francisco that I'm a traitor and a trust fund twat. Now you want to know if I'm with you! With you? Fuck you! I believed in you and your ideas. I gave you everything, my time, my money, everything, but this is too much. How about you stand with me for once?"

Leo stood violently and kicked over his chair.

"Lydia, get my stuff and meet me on the curb," he ordered.

He stomped through the salon and slammed the door on his way out. Jol's mouth hung open in shock and regret. When she noticed me looking at her, she quickly rearranged her face into a tight-lipped grimace of frustration and irritation. Jol had worked hard to plan the party, the private Alter trip included. She orchestrated the whole thing to win Leo's trust. She even sacrificed her swimming pool. Well, HERE's swimming pool, at least.

There was nothing to say. Or at least, there was nothing I had time to say. Leo was waiting for me. I rushed upstairs to pack up the things I had brought to the party and to grab Leo's backpack.

12

THE RIFT

When the Uber pulled up, I tapped *home* on my Cuff. Leo was out of control. A public place would not be good right now. Jol had triggered a violent frenzy in him. His jaw and fists were clenched. Hiring a private investigator was an irredeemable sin. Leo had his followers watch people all the time, but someone spying on him, well, that fed his deep-seated paranoia and general lack of trust. What had Jol been thinking? How was Evan even involved?

"I'll destroy them," Leo raged, "Fucking Evan and his fucking corporate bitch."

"I don't think Evan knew about the investigator, Leo," I soothed.

"Whether he did or not, I'm taking that whole damn company down if it kills me. Don't try to make excuses for Evan, or have you been fucking him too? You're a goddamn slut, Lydia. That's what you're good for."

Instinctually, I put my head on Leo's shoulder, resting it there, submissive and vulnerable. I didn't say a word, but the fight drained from his body. He took a deep breath and stroked my hair. Leo, at war with the world.

The Uber pulled up to my loft. I clicked the autopay. Pensive, Leo followed me to the door. The look of distaste on his face made my heart sink. My parents had given me the money for the down payment on a townhouse when I first moved to the city. At the time, I thought the retro artist's loft development was a bohemian dream come true. But Leo's endless jabs about how fake it was had taken the joy out of ownership before the ink was dry on the deed. His opinion? A cardboard facsimile of what an industrial artist's space looked like and was. Bought from a catalog. Erected on the razed site of the real thing. Now, when he came over, all I felt was embarrassed. Never mind that there were practically no real artist warehouses left in San Francisco. There may have been a few illegal ones in Oakland or Emeryville, but fires over the years had brought the Department of Housing down hard on any live/work holdouts left in the city limits.

The heat of the sun and the smell of earth from the planter boxes that lined the front walk permeated my skin. My hangover and the blowout of raw emotion made normal sensations intense. I unlocked the door with my Cuff and crossed the threshold to the vaulted great room inside. The entire front wall of the condo was panels of glass. The platform loft where I slept hung in the middle of the 30-foot height with a ceiling of faux corrugated aluminum high above. *Cat on a hot tin roof*, I thought to myself.

"You want something to drink," I asked Leo.

"Yeah, I'll have a beer."

I grabbed a couple from the fridge, popped off the caps, and joined Leo on the sofa. "Hey, I'm sorry I called you a slut. I know you're not sleeping with Evan," he said, visibly calmed from a sip of his beer.

"It's okay, it was a long night. I was as upset about the investigation as you. I don't know why we agreed to go to that stupid party in the first place. But, Leo, that you said the Freeschool is a joke, that hurt. You know how important the school is to me."

"I know, Lydia. You know I respect the school. The office on California Street, that's the prank. I assumed you understood. I never thought I'd have to explain stuff like that to you."

Making me feel stupid was a sport of Leo's. That I failed to read his mind was what he was insinuating. I didn't get the joke and that marked me as inferior. But how could he think I would go into debt for multiple six-figures for irony's sake? The afternoon sun streamed through the glass, a wall of heat. I swiped the windows icon on the SmartHome app to darken the glass.

Leo pulled me toward him, cradled my face in one hand, and began kissing me gently on my closed eyelids. I gasped from the delicate passion of it. He leaned in to suck in my breath. The kisses were soft, then hard, then furious. His hand was behind my head, pulling me down to the couch by my hair. He stripped off the stupid orange yoga pants in one motion and thrust into me with a violent sneer. I felt his rage burning into me. The rage of what happened today, but so much bigger. Anger over neglect and loss. All of this entered me with him. He came, but he kept going. I was a vessel for his pain and it felt amazing. Fucked-out and in a heap, I reveled in the smell of us. Leo's eyes were closed. He finally looked peaceful.

"Leo," I said.

"Mmm. What."

"What are we going to do?"

"About what?"

"The money. The building. Evan."

"What we've been doing all along. Who cares if we can't afford the office? Money is just a symbol. Risk and failure, it's what makes things happen. You're too tied up in goals, Lydia. Anyway, credit cards and loans are free. If you're given money, it's yours. Right? Why pay it back? Also, you and I are going to plan a big event. One that will bring in enough cash to keep us going and make those HERE fucks wish they had succeeded in tempting us into their pockets. Any attempt Evan, or Jol, or any of those Silicon Valley assholes try to copy what we do will come off as the plastic butt plug of consumerism that HERE is."

"So what is the next big thing then?"

I felt buzzy and sated lying in Leo's arms. He had let me in, really let me in. We were a team. I had passed the test, but just barely.

"To start, we should ask for more money from our members. You know, to support our actions, " he said.

Sometimes Leo was extremely articulate, and sometimes he wasn't, but I didn't want to ruin the moment by asking too many questions. That would reveal that I didn't totally understand him again. I had already been chastised for that.

"Um, you mean crowdfunding or Patreon?" I asked.

"Yeah. You know, the art of asking."

Evan had suggested crowdfunding several times when we ran low on cash. Most of the time, Leo wasn't receptive at all, and Evan ended up paying out of pocket. Leo said he didn't know how these platforms worked, or it was too commercial, or he had some other reason why it didn't mesh with our culture. With the fallback of Evan's money gone, Leo freely appropriated the idea.

"Okay, sure, I can set that up. We don't need Evan for that," I said. "We ask for a contribution for each thing we do or produce. A caveat is our supporters can't dictate what the project is or when we do it. They'll have to trust that our art will be disruptive and spectacular. We stay in control. The Order has enough credibility to get a few thousand supporters. Fort Point, the HERE billboard, our show, the Embarcadero Pie Fight, Rincon Reign of Meat, and everything else this past year—that's proof enough. But, Leo, our office rent is $12,000 a month. That is a fuckin' shit ton of money. Will membership and patronage be enough?"

"Well, you could start charging for your goddamned classes," Leo snapped.

I drew back, surprised momentarily by the whiplash of his mood swings. Freeschool was FREE, that was the point. My mistake was suggesting that Leo's crowdfunding solution would not solve all our problems. He was recoiling at my contradiction and doubt. Shit, shit, I knew I had been walking a thin line with this conversation. And I still didn't know where we stood when it came to the school? Leo's priorities seemed to change moment by moment.

Evan had handled the business side of things for over two years. Leo was the showman, not the implementer, not the fundraiser. I wasn't bad with computers or business strategy, but Leo was a misogynist to the bone. Women were never Leo's counsel.

"Wait, Leo, hold up, hold up. We're going to do something huge. We don't need to monetize the school. You'll see. I have an idea for an event so spectacular that people will donate hundreds, no, thousands each to support and see it. If we can raise over $100,000, we'll be in the clear for a while. After the event, we can ask for a membership of like $20 per month and grow from there. Then we can cover our expenses and expose HERE for what they are."

I got his attention. He knitted his hands behind his head and relaxed back into the sofa, tight-lipped and thoughtful. The self-censorship and second-guessing that Leo was forcing on me tore me in two. I walked on eggshells one moment and embodied the brash, punk persona that Leo wanted the world to see in the next. Problem was, Leo wanted both from me. Which and when, only he knew.

13

THE CAMPUS

Evan

Watery light from the private courtyard of the HERE campus bathed my office in serene reflections. When they assigned me this office, the desk had been oriented toward the door. I shifted everything around so I could look out at the gardens while I worked. Topiary shapes and manicured greens stood as silent and motionless as if they were in a painting. Occasionally, someone would sip a coffee on one of the cement benches. But mostly, the open-air grounds were empty of human life. My new workspace was the antithesis of the grungy tin ceiling, book smells, and peeling paint of Rain Dogs. HERE was all clean glass and echoing tiles. Sterile, efficient, uncanny.

My signing bonus and salary had been more than enough to pay for a day manager at Rain Dogs with plenty more for building improvements. The game design work was interesting and suited my talents and training. However, the futuristic environment was a constant reminder that Lydia and Leo were out of my life and that I was the one who made the separation more and more permanent each day. Jol actively worked against Leo now, and I was her accomplice. I'd feel fine, fully immersed in work, when a memory of Lydia and Leo would trigger a wave of nostalgia and heartbreak.

Jol and I had accomplished a lot in the past months. We scored the top floor of Sentinel Building for the HERE Urban Playground indoctrination center. The Victorian flatiron sided in patinated copper panels had been purchased by Francis Ford Coppola and George Lucas and converted into the film studio, American Zoetrope. Their company had occupied the location since 1971, along with tenants like NPR and Pixar. Formerly owned by the Kingston Trio, the building was the original location of the Hungry I, a famous strip club and music venue. The space was an arts and innovation icon.

Jol went after the lease as a direct response to Leo's appropriation of the Financial District. The Sentinel Building was clearly more surreal and historic than California Street. However, I might argue that Leo's space had the advantage of being something that didn't belong. The Order's location downtown was meta and ironic. I hadn't shared those thoughts with Jol because it would have frustrated her. This type of nuance escaped her and the situational design team's capabilities. Any suggestion that Leo had outdone her, Jol would take as an insulting reminder that she wasn't as creative as him. She no longer admitted that she had pursued him for this type of insight.

The secret launch of a real-world scavenger hunt, HERE Urban Playground, or HERE UP for short, was Jol's top priority. I worked with development to code crossover gateways from the physical terrain of the city to the virtual landscape of HERE UP. Players would be able to walk in and out of the game—extended reality portals triggered by cutting-edge headsets. The work was revolutionary and challenging. My team included the best Young Turks from Stanford, Berkeley, and MIT. I adored working with Jol. Yet...

"Fucking Leo!"

I sat bolt upright and swiveled my chair around to face the door. Jol swept in like a tempest. I could feel the radiating power of her anger from across the room. The clack of her stiletto heels reverberated as she planted herself squarely in front of me. With one hand on her hip, she slammed her other fist down on my glass desktop. In protection and concern, I grabbed both of her hands. They felt smooth, small, and warm, like river stones plucked from a sunny bank. My touch abated her storm, but she was still dangerous. It flashed in her eyes.

"Leo sent out a newsletter to the Chaos Order with insider information on the HERE UP launch! Did you leak the release date?"

"No! Absolutely not. How could you accuse me of

that? I haven't talked to Leo since the morning after the party. I haven't spoken a word to anyone outside of the company about the drop. You know I barely leave your side. It wasn't me."

"Listen to what he said about us—ersatz art, black hat marketing, stolen audiences—he's calling for a boycott of the release," Jol paraphrased from the scrolling text on her Cuff.

"He is making us look like idiots. Like monsters capitalizing on the stolen creativity of starving artists. This is bad, Evan."

Jol shouldn't have been surprised. We knew Leo would do everything and anything to fuck with us. This attack was not unexpected, and I anticipated more and worse to come. I wanted to tell Jol to roll with it, to treat Leo's sabotage as part of the game itself. From my perspective, he offered us opportunities in disguise. That mindset was how I kept sane, but the same would not work for Jol. Leo's actions were deeply personal to her.

"Listen, Jol. Leo is unpredictable and extremely volatile and he is waiting for our counter move. You have to understand. This is fun for him. Money, threats, public disgrace, these are his playthings. Conventional morals and social norms that most people value or assume are inviolable human laws are repulsive and mocked by him. You can't win if you react with anger to what he's done. Jol, listen, you can't outmaneuver Leo until you change the way you think. Really, for the time being, we should just keep in our own lane. You're not equipped to battle him on his turf."

"How can you stand that man? I don't understand why anyone cares about him at all. Who would be attracted to such a fool? How does he have thousands of devoted fans who would dive off the Golden Gate Bridge if he thought it was a nice day for swimming? How can I work with that, Evan? How did you do it?"

"It's hard to explain. Maybe he's a father figure to people who had totally crap parents? I don't know. I guess, for me, he is the symbol of a different kind of family. One that accepts me for who I am, not what they think I should be. Or, at least I thought he accepted me for who I was before all this happened. Does that make sense?"

"No. It doesn't, Evan," Jol said, the beauty of her face was stained by a scowl.

Jol didn't understand how I could be sympathetic to both her and Leo. She looked at me, looked deep. Her judgment felt right, like home. Yet the same kind of judgment from my mother would have been unforgivable. Jol and my beliefs were on the opposite side of the spectrum. She needed me as a guide when it came to the arena she was forced to play in.

Still holding her hand, I reassured her. "I'm not sure how Leo found out about the launch of the game. He may have paid someone off. More likely, one of our employees got wasted during happy hour and Leo's spies extracted the game drop plans. We need to hold another company meeting about the importance of confidentiality. Any further breach should result in termination. The staff needs to understand how serious this is. As for Leo, let's switch everything up so what he said has no truth at all.

We'll ruin his credibility. That way, he won't be taken as seriously in the future. "

"Yeah, it is early enough to move things around on our calendar. It will be expensive, though. And what about the Order's competing events? Stunts all over the city. More bad press directed at us. There's a big buzz."

"Jol, honey, we can't play on their field. It's a waste of time to try. What the Order is doing is completely illegal and dangerous. No permits. No waivers. And that's not the half of it. There is a good chance that someone will end up in jail, or hurt, or dead. We're corporate, we have to follow all the rules and cover our asses, legally. We're already dancing on the line of what our investors will accept. Comparing HERE to the Order is an exercise in frustration. I know how competitive you are, Jol, but you gotta let it go for now."

"Well, fuck." Jol said.

She rolled a chair over to my desk and sat, her rage somewhat abated. I sighed.

"Okay, fine, we needed to go back to the drawing board then—change the dates—we needed to up our game. Our Urban Playground experience has to be so surreal and immersive that it surpasses the culture jams the Order has been promoting around the city. We have our spies too. Chaos Order is about spectacle and danger, but HERE is about radical inclusivity. Anyone can safely experience our adventures," I told her.

I gambled that our budget, mystery, and accessibility would trump the showy stunts of the Order. HERE UP would be different, better, not be the exclusive domain of misanthropes with death wishes. HUP was a game anyone could play.

Jol and I agreed on the new schedule. Leo's hullabaloo about our November release being a Christmas consumerist ploy would come to nothing. We'd push the launch out past the holidays and shoot for the following spring. Our plans would become more confidential than a political conspiracy.

§

THE COPPOLAS AGREED to a year's rent on the penthouse floor of American Zoetrope. The extension was a blessing in disguise. We needed more time to turn the empty offices into our indoctrination center. Jol scheduled a meeting to tell the set designers and the development team that they had an extra quarter to polish up their work. Advertising, marketing, sales—everyone got an extension. Most of the company, minus the board members and investors, would be relieved. To say the previous timeline was aggressive was an understatement.

Rent at Sentinel Building was a mosquito bite compared to the cost of the Transamerica use contract. A floor of Coppola's flatiron was a 10th of the price of the top of the Pyramid—San Francisco's most iconic skyscraper. That the Tran's property management company even considered our original offer was a miracle. Another half-year agreement for the use of the spire was out of the question. It would have cost millions. However, unlike the Sentinel Building, the Trans needed little to no modifications. That meant we could just shift the dates.

Likewise, the actors hired for the HERE UP waypoints throughout the game could be rescheduled through the casting agency we retained in L.A. It would be a scramble. The money that Leo cost HERE with one newsletter blast was massive, in the millions. I should have been furious, but instead, it made me nostalgic for the freedom I had under Leo's paranoid, underground, no-paper-trail way of doing things.

14

CHAOS ORDER

Lydia

I clicked through my emails. Mostly overdue bills demanding my immediate attention. All the utilities, subscriptions, the office lease, and everything having to do with our new location were under my name. Leo made sure of that. After paying off our maxed out business card with my personal credit card, I busied myself handing out course syllabuses for the 5-MeO-DMT Death Doula class.

A line of students signed-in at the front desk. The Freeschool's end of life series was a popular one. How-tos for the dying, human composting, and Buddhist palliative care were among our most popular offerings. Death was a booming business in 2032. Maureen's classes in urban clowning had become a staple too, and Weather Girl's filmmaking and gender transition courses always sold out.

The problem was, it didn't matter if we filled every class we offered, the sliding-scale tuitions did not make a dent in the astronomical lease. Yet, affordability was the foundation of the Freeschool plan. Leo ignored or was blind to how desperately I tried to hold our sinking ship together, even if I explicitly told him how bad the situation was. His ability to slip the noose of any ultimatum or responsibility amazed me. I longed for the days of free space at Rain Dogs and Evan's expert help. Back then, the whole thing worked. Now—

"I fuckin' nailed 'em," Leo called through his office door.

Leo's priority was the Order's mobilization against HERE. He had emailed our inner cabal ordering them to attack the game company any way they could. He advocated gathering confidential information, computer hacks, and acts of physical sabotage with extra points for creativity and press coverage. War had been declared, and from the sound of it, we had just won ourselves a battle.

Seeded at the bars surrounding the HERE campus were Freaks with code names like Sexy Sonia and Nerd Bait. Their jobs were to cozy up to HERE employees after hours and pump them for information.

"What's the news?" I left the stack of syllabuses on the reception desk for the late students to pick up, walked across the lobby, and stood on the threshold of Leo's door. It didn't matter how many times I saw Leo sitting at his office desk, he always looked like a boy on Take Our Sons to Work Day, framed by skyscrapers in his work boots, Carhartts, and a grungy t-shirt.

"I got info that HERE moved their launch to spring of next year. I haven't got the new date yet, but I've got them on the run," he told me with glee.

Leo's obsession with thwarting HERE took vital time and energy away from the planning and fundraising that we desperately needed to keep bankruptcy at bay. The year-end event I had masterminded would be elaborate and expensive. Crowdfunding had gone well, but we need a much bigger push to raise enough capital to keep the lights on. I had designed a production more outrageous and more public than anything we'd done so far— costumes, a food fight, an aerial show, and that was just the beginning. It would all take place during peak holiday shopping traffic in a guerrilla takeover of the cable car turnaround between Ellis and Market.

The spectacle revolved around a skywalk. I hadn't walked the high-wire since my junior circus days. I desperately needed to train for the headlining act that I had orchestrated, but the demands of running everything consumed most of my time. My coach at the Circus Center saw my face once a week, at most, and I hadn't lost any weight. I'd actually gained a few pounds and was drinking and smoking as much as always. Time was running out.

"That's great news! But I need you to focus on making those videos for Patreon, and we need to book more live shows. Leo, your commitment would be a huge help right now. We need money. Seriously. Our income from the classes and the weekly take at The Box isn't nearly enough. It's the same crowd week after week. We're not broadening our reach. Our existing members aren't going to donate over and over again," I pleaded.

"Yeah, all right, all right. Book some more shows for us at other clubs," he said with a dismissive wave of his hand, as if booking new venues was an easy feat to accomplish. He didn't convince me that his priorities would shift, but at least he threw me a bone, even if pitching our act to clubs was a huge amount of extra work I didn't have time for.

"Okay. I'll make the calls. Book some dates. Send out more emails," I said, exasperated.

"Lydia, you're doing a great job. Thanks," Leo said.

I hated myself for breaking in two for a simple thank you and a smile. Leo's acknowledgment made me tingle and blush. It sickened me, how he twisted me around his finger and how much I wanted to please him.

A riff from an old Clash song filled the room. I hadn't heard that ringtone before. Leo's eyes went cold.

"Hey, close the door behind you. I have to take this call. It's important," he said.

I sat back down at the reception desk wondering who merited a custom ring when Leo's office door flung open.

"Hot shit! I told you Sonia is banging some girl in HERE's human resources department? Well, get this, that same chick is also in charge of their corporate events. HERE is renting one of the Blue and Gold commuter ferries for a company wide team-building! Guess who's catering the party?"

It was us, of course. A way to attack HERE. A prank. Half-heartedly, I raised my hand to receive a high-five. Leo slapped my palm harder than needed. Catering an event sounded like an unnecessary distraction and a lot more work on top of booking more shows, planning the holiday event, and running the school. Furthermore, it would cost money, not raise it. I sighed. We'd have to get food, staff, and uniforms.

Plus, clearly, Leo had been fucking Sonia? I mean, Leo and I were polyamorous and all, but the custom ringtone, the door-closing business, what was that all about? While Sonia was slutting it up with Leo, I was left with all the work. I slumped, curling in on myself. The exhaustion was becoming unbearable.

"Did she get an advance for the food, at least? We're going to need that money up front," I asked with a heavy sigh.

"I don't know. I didn't get details like that. Call her yourself," Leo said.

He retreated back to his sanctum as I sat, dumbfounded. Desperate, I sent out a call for help through an emergency newsletter blast to the Freaks. Luckily, Cara, a new convert, wrote back minutes later.

15

JOL WEELE

Evan

I called up the stairs to Jol. "Candice and Tom are on the phone. They want to know if they can crash here."

"Don't yell. Come up here and talk to me like a civilized person," was Jol's response. I noted the hypocrisy of her yelling her reprimand back down to me and smiled.

"Tom, I'll call you back," I said and tapped my Cuff to disconnect.

Nothing had prepared me for dating Jol. No. Maybe that's not right. Come to think of it, Jol had many of the qualities of my mother, both good and bad. Mom was strong, some might say willful and stubborn. So was Jol. They were both conservative, ambitious, and family-minded. Jol's most irksome quality was her strict adherence to the rules of social conduct. Things like, addressing people by Mr., Mrs., or Dr. Those types of rules really made my skin crawl.

Leo, on the other hand, insisted that everyone be called by their first names regardless of their title—doctors, professors, lawyers, the President of the United States. To Leo, they were all equals. Academic achievement or honorifics were tools of oppression. He claimed he knew a garbage man who was smarter than those who held the highest offices in the country. I knew exactly which garbageman he was talking about. He was right.

I climbed the stairs and stood at the door of the bedroom we shared. Since I joined HERE, my apartment had become a collection of dust bunnies and a death camp for house plants. I could have sublet it out, but I had no monetary reason to do so, and it was nice to have a safety net if things went sideways.

Jol sat by the window. She, by all measures, was stunning—upturned eyes and perfect skin. Like my mom, Jol also had an impeccable fashion sense. Her caramel satin blouse shimmered, the full sleeves draped over the arms of the chair where she sat. I thought I would end up with someone like Lydia; the polar opposite of Jol. No, not someone like Lydia, I thought I would end up with Lydia. Clearly, she had a thing for Leo, but I assumed no love affair with Leo could last long. Yet, Jol was the woman I loved now.

"Jol, Honey, my sister, and brother want to stay with us

for a couple of days. They are sailing up from Dana Point for the Rolex Regatta. They could stay on the boat at the marina, but they want to get to know you better."

"Oh! That's nice. What kind of boat do they have?"

"It's an Oyster—50 feet, I think. A very nice boat. Do you want to go on a sail?"

"I've never been! That sounds lovely," Jol said.

I called Tom to let him know that he and Candy were on for the guest rooms for the following week. My sister and brother had treated me differently since I got a job with HERE and was dating a woman that our mother approved of.

§

Tom's Oyster was a dream boat; porn for the sailing connoisseurs. A sleek vessel by any measure. He gave us a tour of the spacious galley, more like a chef's kitchen; the comfortable cabins; and the state-of-the-art electronics. I started craving a boat of my own. Jol and I could afford one now, and a Sausalito slip would be a great way to decompress when the specter of burnout threatened. Tom didn't have a snowball's chance in hell at winning the Rolex. He was a hundred percent a weekend warrior, and clearly, his boat was not outfitted for racing. In my opinion, that was Tom's overall personality—in it for the show, not for any true achievement.

The day before the race, Tom offered to take us on a fun run. Crisp winds made for perfect conditions, clouds on the horizon shot through with fingers of sherbet light. The gentle roll of the boat, sounds of clanking halyards, and squabbling gulls reminded me of my childhood. Sailing camp had always been a retreat from the demands of my mom. It was one of the activities she and I could agree on.

Tom motored past the jetty. "Okay, I'm going to turn into the wind so we can raise the mainsail. Jol, you take the wheel. Hold this setting here until the sail is up." Tom pointed to the navigation display. "The sail will flap, expect it. Don't try to change course to fill it with wind," Tom said.

Tom was trying to woo Jol to the ways of the sea. To her credit, she accepted the challenge and took the helm without hesitation. The big sail inched up the mast. Tom regained the helm and set a course while Candy started the automatic winch. She cautiously eyed a nearby pile of line at her feet. The headsail ballooned with a loud fwomp. Lines, canvas, and steel vibrated with tension as we skimmed across the bay. With the sails filled, the boat tilted at an alarming angle. Startled, Jol grabbed my knee.

"We're heeled. Sailing is on a slant most of the time. You'll get used to it," I told her.

"Wow, I couldn't have imagined this feeling. It's amazing," Jol said.

Jol was usually the dominant person in any room. I took guilty pleasure in showing her a world she had no experience with.

"Yeah, this never gets old. Funny huh? So much power just to move at the pace of a fast run. It feels intense, but we are only going about six miles an hour."

"Really? Are you serious! It feels more like seventy."

I loved skipping like a pebble to the line of the horizon. My thoughts turned deep blue. Jol nestled in my arms while Candy delivered a pitcher of margaritas from the galley. Tom busied himself around the boat.

"So, Jol. You have designs on my brother," Candy said, ponytail whipping in the wind.

Candy's hair was bleached blonde now, like my mother's. Her colorist was top-notch; it looked natural, but it was weird that my sister was turning into Connie.

"Yes, he fits nicely into my plans for world domination," Jol said with a wink.

"Wedding bells then?" Candy asked.

"Cut it out. You're so rude," I said, feeling familiar irritation cross my face. Tom, Candy, and I had squabbled throughout our childhood. I didn't like them in my business then, and I didn't like it now.

"What? You were hanging out with a bunch of losers before. Your new girlfriend here is a Cornell MBA that was featured in Forbes's 30 Under 30. She's a big deal. We all want you to snap her up."

"You're annoying, Candice. Why would Jol want to marry into a family like this? You're a bunch of rude twats."

Tom and Candy had always advocated for the school/high-yield career/pragmatic marriage/kids/death plan. They pushed me away from Cloe and Rain Dogs toward the conventional path that they deemed incorruptible. It made me want to do something unexpected and unacceptable. It didn't make me want to marry Jol.

"I'm flattered," Jol said. "Really, I am. But, Evan and I haven't even discussed marriage. Furthermore, I believe it's a private matter. So, Candy, tell me about yourself. I understand you're an attorney like your mother."

Candy, pleased to have been counter-stalked by Jol, launched into a long account of how she became an associate at a prestigious firm. Tequila induced, she babbled on about the cases she was working and how many years it would be until she made partner. I gazed at Jol, proud that she could turn a conversation in any direction she pleased. Jol had far more class and guile than Tom and Candy.

We pulled a Crazy Ivan to head back into the marina. The boat came up into the wind and inched forward until it nearly bumped the mooring ball. Tom threaded the anchor harness through the chocks and cleated the lines. The boat drifted back with a tug, then relaxed to a comfortable roll. Tom's sailing skill had improved.

16

BLUE AND GOLD

Lydia

After weeks of planning, the day of the HERE corporate party arrived. Gleaming stainless steel walls lined Cara's commercial kitchen. Counters, sinks, ranges, ovens, and salamanders were all polished to a high luster with lemon oil cleaner. The unmistakable citrus scent tickled my nose. Despite the large space, there was a lot of intentional bumping and jostling among Cara's army of earth-mamas and Herb's biker buddies manning the prepping table.

I had asked Herb to recruit servers out of his heavies. He knew a lot of big guys because he belonged to a biker club and was a professional bouncer in addition to being one of the first Chaos Order Freaks. Leo's vision for the prank included the beefiest and most rough-hewn of our crowd. A visual joke, but it was for our protection too.

Herb's guys and Cara's staff worked together arranging trays of hors d'oeuvres. I videoed the pixie-hens ordering around the towering, heavily-tattooed men. Pure comedy. Between scoldings and food prep instructionals, tastes of wonton spoons and Caprese bites were doled out. A Tolkien vibe, for sure.

At prior meetings and events, I had dismissed Cara as a plain Jane, maybe a little too spiritual for my taste, but she ripened under Herb's attention. He handed her spices while she stirred a copper pot with a long-handled wooden spoon. In the glow of the hearth, I witnessed Cara's goddess awaken. Herb was clearly smitten.

The other cooks also transformed from homely to enchanting among their elements of alluring scents and tasty delights. The bikers, bouncers, and other tough guys turned tender under the tutelage of the coven of kitchen witches. I felt a little left out. Clearly, I wasn't an object of adoration. No tastes and tickles for me.

§

WE PULLED up to the dock in Cara's pink and white van. Our paperwork was in order. The security guard found us suspicious, but she was powerless to do more than a scowl. Technically, we checked out.

Half-dozen bikers wearing ruffled pink aprons over leather jackets and greasy Levi's boarded carrying boxes of food and drinks. The boat's first mate escorted us to the galley where Herb started his guys on unwrapping and garnishing the trays the way they had been shown at Cara's. Leo, Sonia, and I took the liquor crates to the lounge. In less than an hour, the passengers would be arriving.

I had taken the commuter ferry across the bay on a couple of occasions, but this particular boat was far larger and more luxurious. It must have been reserved for weddings and parties.

I got to work setting up the bar while Leo installed a bypass router for the video display wall. Sonia stood over him giggling like a nit. A low growl escaped my throat. I hated that she was prettier than me. I mean, if I was objective about it, she stood six inches taller, her natural red hair fell in long waves, and her features were straight off the cover of a magazine. Plus, she should be the one stocking booze, not me. I guess Sonia thought flirting with Leo was a more important skill than actual bartending.

"Lydia, come over here. Log in to my computer so we can test this setup," Leo said.

Ha! He didn't trust Sonia with his password. I bumped her aside roughly and signed on.

"Okay, Lydia, change the WiFi. Look for a connection called SpaceGhost."

"Found it," I said.

"Okay. Good, now turn on the camera, hit the red broadcast button, and give me a test."

Leo reached up to turn on the display. My eight-foot-wide face appeared on the presentation wall. I grimaced and bit viciously at Sonia like a junkyard dog—joking but not joking. She laughed, and I had to admit, she looked cute cowering from me.

"It works," I said and grinned across the wall at Leo.

"Great!" He got off his knees, wiped his hands on his pants, and kissed me.

Take that Sonia. I'm his number-one, I thought. A twinge of shame crept up my spine. Still—she was too blatant with him. Despite our polyamory, some respect was called for.

When the HERE guests started to arrive at the dock, Leo and I spied on them through a porthole in the bulkhead between the kitchen and the lounge. Dweeby coders with good looking dates mingled awkwardly. From among the lesser crowd, Jol stepped onto the boat from the gangplank in a red, sleeveless sheath. She was radiant. Evan looked damn good at her side too. It was less what he wore, but more how he seemed—confident and strong. His hair was cut shorter, he had shaved off his beard, and he rocked the geek-chic look. He had the aura of a leader.

Leo tensed at my side. His eyes trained on the enemy. I believed Leo didn't actually hate Evan, but a malicious spirit seemed to rise from him like heat. Maybe it was focus, or obsession, or even forbidden jealousy. Whatever it was, it was intense.

I sent Sonia to open the bar. Her human resources girlfriend approached looking adorable in dark-rimmed glasses and a 50s-style circle dress. Cruel, the way Sonia used her. This hapless pawn would probably lose her job over the prank. I struggled more and more these days to suppress my empathy for the sake of the big picture and the Order's mission.

With a roar and rumble, the boat set off on a party course to Angel Island. Once the engines settled into cruise, Herb grabbed trays of hors d'oeuvres and distributed them to the other servers. Ready for showtime, they ducked through the low galley bulkhead into the lounge. At first, Herb and the others were simply clumsy. Herb's buddy with the lumberjack beard and rabid eyes pushed and bumbled into guests. He mimed a nautical roll and pitch that didn't exist. Funny, this guy didn't strike me as a clown, but he pulled off the act perfectly. The others followed suit. They daintily selected foie gras medallions and mozzarella balls from their trays, studied each prize in their bare, paw-like hands, then squished the morsels into the palms of partygoers with menacing smiles. No one was about to complain about the horrible service or the mess for fear of being squashed like a bug. The marks just wiped their hands the best they could, no napkins to be found, and tried to steer clear. I spotted Evan scanning the crowd, already suspicious.

Tears of laughter rolled down my face. Leo tried to shush me but he was practically pissing his pants too. Fucking funny. I heard a high-pitched screech. An animated argument had erupted between Sonia and her HR girlfriend. It was clear that Evan was certain a prank was afoot now, and I was sure he knew who was behind it. He made a beeline for the kitchen.

"Quick, hide!" Leo said. He shoved me toward the pantry and barred the door behind us so Evan couldn't get in. Leo had installed cameras on all decks and an extra handful in the party lounge. He booted up his laptop and activated the spy cams. The picture quality was low, but Evan's anger was obvious. He headed for the galley, burst in, and searched the empty space. I jumped when he rattled the locked steel door of the pantry where we hid.

Leo switched camera views when Evan, frustrated, returned to the lounge. A wonton whizzed by his head. Cheese balls and duck livers were flying like paintballs. Sonia's girlfriend pulled at her once carefully coiffed hair like a lunatic. Leo and I collapsed into a puddle of laughter on the cold metal floor.

"Get it together. Lydia. Stop laughing," Leo said, poking me in the ribs with a finger and gasping in hysterics.

"I'm okay, I'm okay, really. Ready, let's do this," I panted, finally catching my breath.

Leo grew calm, steeled his face, and clicked the red button on his laptop. I monitored the cameras in the main lounge from my Cuff. The wall-sized display sparked to life with a multi-colored test pattern. Leo's face loomed, hissed, and swept across the huge screen with a glitched vertical hold. The effect was a filter the tech guys from the Order had loaded on Leo's laptop.

"We are everywhere," Leo boomed Wizard of Oz style. "HERE, you are parasites feeding on the lives of artists. The death of this city is entirely your fault and the fault of your capitalist brethren. You cannot control the chaos. Chaos will destroy you. Your time is at an end!"

That was Sonia's cue. She clicked a detonator. Glitter bombs went off in a shimmer of iridescent dust. Microsparkles wafted down to gently coat the food and drink-covered nerds in a dusting of bling.

Leo was already stuffing his laptop into the dry bag he brought readying for the getaway. He rolled the yellow vinyl top and clipped it closed. A lifejacket from an oversized duffle came sailing at me. I put it on and followed close on Leo's heels as he pushed his way through the crowd to the exit. Herb's crew played defense, blocking any attempt to stop us. The jump into the bay had always been part of the plan. Now, I had second thoughts, but there was no other way out. It was a high drop—twenty feet into icy, angry water where our chase boat would pick us up. Leo went in first without hesitation. Then Herb. I didn't want to be last, but I was glued to the deck with fear. My cold sweat froze in the whipping northerly wind.

Boat security, now alarmed, rushed toward us yelling and clattering like apes from down the narrow gangway. The dread of my capture broke the trance. I leaped over the rail. Stars streaked across my vision and wind slapped at my cheeks before I hit a floor of water. I plunged into freezing black. Bubbles pricked my skin. I sank down like a bullet. Liquid was forced up my nostrils by the impact. Finally, the downward momentum stopped and I swam toward the moonlight, broke the surface, and blew jets of ocean out my nose.

I bobbed on the choppy bay. Shapes floated in the darkness. I could see Herb in the moonlight a dozen feet away. Some of the other bikers swam up to me and we linked arms. Leo found the growing island of Freaks and clasped me around the shoulders. We huddled together with the floating vinyl bags, waiting. A cheer rose to the sky when rescuers came alongside. But where was Sonia? Was she still on the ferry? She wasn't part of the floating island of Freaks. Leo climbed aboard the small sports boat, followed by Herb. I maneuvered to climb up the rear ladder to the back deck. Still no Sonia. I wished I hadn't been so mean to her. I hated to admit it, but I was beginning to like that girl. One of the Freaks helped me out of the water and threw a thick blanket over my shoulders. My skin burned with cold and my teeth chattered.

"S-s-s-s-o-nia isn't here," I said, shaking.

"Shit, she's not. You're right," Leo said.

"SONIA!" He called over the water.

The rest joined in, "SONIA!"

"Where are you?" I shouted. My throat was tight.

"Shhh, listen, can you hear her?"

I listened over the howl of the wind and the boat engine but heard nothing human.

"She must have jumped late. She's probably up further," Leo said.

We motored in a slow zig-zag to avoid sucking Sonia into the prop. Poised like a Tahitian spearman, I held a boat hook in my hands with intense focus. Nothing. No head above the water or flash of an orange vest. *Did she jump? Was she behind me? Did security grab her?* I searched my memory for signs. It was a blur. The plunge, the icy water, everything happened too fast to know.

We swept back and forth. The wave chop slapped at our craft as I scanned across the surface of the water. My hands were so cold, I had no sensation in my fingers. Still no sign of Sonia. Leo became unconcerned, impatient even.

"We're all going to freeze to death out here. She's fine. Either, they caught her on the boat, or the Coast Guard will find her," Leo said.

"Seriously, Leo! You'd just leave her out here?" My words were barely comprehendible, hypothermia becoming a real danger.

"Lydia's right. We got to find her," Herb said.

"Sonia's alright. You two are a couple of bleeding hearts. Look, the Coasties are coming now. We can't stay here. If we don't leave, we're getting caught," Leo said.

Fuck if Leo was right. The searchlights of the approaching Coast Guard swept the water less than a mile away. They would see us any minute if we didn't make a fast break for shore. If Sonia was in the water, I had to trust that search and rescue would find her.

17

DOWNTOWN

Evan

Blue and Gold had caught one girl—the red-headed bartender. Sonia. I hadn't met her at any Chaos Order events, but she knew me. Of course, she knew me; I was the target. Security didn't get much information out of her, only that the others had escaped in a speedboat that had been trailing the ferry. I should have realized that every detail was planned, including the getaway.

It came out that Poppy from HR had booked the Order to cater the party, but I knew that she wasn't intentionally involved. She had been conned at a bar near the HERE campus. Sonia confirmed that it had not been an inside job, that she played Poppy. Regardless, security breaches like these could not be tolerated, we made that clear at the last town hall meeting. Poppy had been warned.

Jol wanted Sonia to be held on charges, but she respected my wishes to not make a big deal out of what was obviously, at least to me, a harmless prank. The ferry company also wanted to push for criminal destruction of property. I lied and told them I had no idea who would crash our party to start a food fight. It didn't help that the captain had overheard me questioning Sonia about Lydia and Leo by name. Finally, I threw in an extra couple thousand to cover damages and keep the incident out to the press. Five hours passed at the port office before Jol and I could finally go home. We got back to the house at sunrise.

"Look on the bright side. It's good for morale. I mean, having an enemy can be very motivating. Right?" I tried to smooth Jol's ruffled feathers.

"I don't care about your stupid bright side right now. I fucking hate Leo. My vintage Valentino is completely ruined. I had to throw it in the garbage."

"At least we rooted out the leak. I'll have the HR girl terminated on Monday. Plus, these are the kind of games you signed up for. This is exactly the kind of creativity you wanted from Leo, but when it's directed at you—"

"Whatever. Who cares? I wish you'd stop making excuses. Sometimes I wonder whose side you're on," Jol said, angrily pushing eggs around a frying pan. She set a mug of decaf on the kitchen island.

"Jol, come on, don't you want to know if they're all right?"

"See! You do care!" Jol screamed.

"Somebody could have died, for all we know. Of course I care," I pleaded.

Jol had been totally irrational since the party. My initial anger had given way to admiration. Now, I thought the incident was funny—beyond funny, it was genius—but I didn't expect her to understand. She never had. The reason HERE tried to recruit Leo in the first place was precisely because Jol and the others were so clueless about these types of things.

To Jol, what the Order did was unfathomable. Public nudity, accosting strangers on the street, and disregard for law and order, Jol would never view what Leo did as an exciting form of protest or of high art. Irreverence and disrespect were pathological in her eyes. Her values were strictly conventional, Jol believed anomie would cause the downfall of civilization. I was on the other side of the fence. Insanity was a mutable social construct in my opinion. Crazy was in the eye of the beholder. Weaned on postmodernism—good, bad, they didn't exist.

"Jol, calm down. Leo, Lydia, and I have been my friends for years. Put yourself in my shoes."

She gave me a withering look, slammed down a plate of eggs, and stomped up the stairs. Unlike Leo, who could hold a grudge for a lifetime, Jol's moods were like passing clouds.

"Jol, Honey," I called up the stairs.

The slam of the bedroom door reverberated through the house. I shoveled some eggs into my face, took a gulp of coffee, walked up to our room, and knocked sheepishly.

"There could be injuries, or someone could have easily drowned," I said through the closed door.

I needed to go check on Lydia and Leo, but Jol needed me to comfort her. If I took off now, there'd be hell to pay. Jol was family. Leo and Lydia had abandoned me, they would have to wait.

"Don't come in. I locked it," she shouted through the door.

"Please. I love you. Can we just talk?" The 'I love you' part was new. It felt a little awkward but it also felt true. Her footsteps approached the door, I heard the lock click, some more steps, then nothing. I waited a minute, and tried again.

"Can I come in?"

"The door's unlocked, suit yourself," Jol said. Her voice sounded calmer now.

I opened the door gingerly. Jol sat cross-legged on the bed. Her feet were bare. She had on fuzzy drawstring pants and a pink camisole top.

"We've had a long night. Let me rub your legs for you."

All she said was, "Fuck you," but she lay back on the bed. I pushed up her sweats and rubbed her calves. Dark skin, silky smooth, glowed like mahogany warmed from the inside. I kneaded my fingers into her legs and feet. She sighed, and I did too. This war with the Order was far from over, and it set everything on edge.

I eased off Jol's pants and kissed the tight coils in the tiny triangle of hair between her legs. I admired how impeccably she maintained her body. She sighed again, but this sound was deep with anticipation. I spread her pussy and licked and probed. Going down on Jol was a wonderful thing. I lapped like a happy puppy. When she started to writhe, I circled my tongue around her clit. She grew wetter and wetter. I was incredibly hard under my pajama pants, it was painful, but I wanted her to cum in my mouth before my own pleasure. Jol lifted from the bed and pushed her pelvis against my face. She moaned and released with a glorious gush.

Readier than I've ever been, I slid into her. Our rhythms synchronized like waves. That we were exhausted, that this was makeup sex, that I confessed my love combined into a buzzy release. I sank into the enjoyment of her. Jol came again, this time, I joined her. We climaxed while our bodies pressed together. Now spent, she nuzzled in my arms, but it wasn't long before I checked the time. I still needed to make sure Lydia and Leo were alive and not rolling in the currents at the bottom of the bay.

"I'm going to go check the Freeschool downtown—make sure no one is hurt," I said.

Jol didn't respond, she just pulled the covers up and turned her back.

"I love you," I said, again. "But I have to go. They are my friends regardless of what they do."

"Fine, I'm going to get some sleep," Jol said. "I love you too."

§

THE FINANCIAL DISTRICT was a hive at 8 a.m. Industrialists hadn't changed a bit in over a hundred years. I could smell the cortisol rising off suit-covered men and women like auras of power and ambition. They walked with stiff purpose to their meetings, flowing around the wrongness that was me with rebuke aimed at the non-belonger.

I craned my neck to gaze upward at the glass giant that now housed the Chaos Order. Blazing light bounced back to space off the mirrored flank of the building. The rotating door at the skyscraper's base made a pneumatic suck each time it presented a human-sized compartment for me to step into. I let three openings pass before pushing in. I never liked revolving doors. Since I was a kid, I imagined them as mechanical people-crushers.

Inside the lobby, my steps echoed off the glass walls of the atrium. I signed in at a granite desk and was directed to the 42nd floor. The elevator doors slid wide, emptying me into a corridor of yawning indifference. Wood-paneled doors were all the same except for the raised brass lettering announcing each entity within.

Chaos Order > Freeschool

Strange—these words spelled out between the doors reading Sherman Brothers and Levy and Associates. Lydia didn't see or hear me when I pushed into the Freeschool reception area. She was plugged into AirPods behind her cheap IKEA desk.

"Lydia," I said over the clicks from her keyboard.

Shock washed over her face. She yanked the buds free from her ears.

"What are you doing here! If Leo sees you, he's going fucking shit a brick."

"So, you're both all right. Herb? Everyone else? I was really worried. I stopped by your place but you weren't there," I said.

The sight of her reminded me of how much I missed her, the culture of her. Worn loose, her hair hung in a fall. Her lacy blouse clung to her breasts, nipples showing as clearly as if she were naked. High and tight black jeans accentuated the smallness of her waist and wide hips.

"I got a call from Sonia. She said security grabbed her before she could jump off the boat, and you covered for her, for us. You didn't have to do that. I'd hate to ruin things for you at HERE," Lydia said.

"It's all good. I bribed a few officials at the ferry company. Even if the higher-ups at HERE found out I knew who crashed the party, and I do mean crashed, they'd probably be cool about it. Really, unless they are completely stupid, they know it's you. HERE might even see it as a win. They still hope you and Leo will join the project."

"Not a chance on the Leo front. To him, this is not a friendly game. It's personal. He thinks you stole from him. What you stole, I'm not totally sure about," Lydia said

"Where is he, by the way?" I asked. Not knowing what to do with my hands.

"That's top secret." She gave me a wink.

"More pranks, then?" I asked.

"Something like that. He had to go to Oakland to pick up some gear."

"I see. Well, I'm glad no one was hurt. Brilliant, by the way—the food fight. No one had a clue. By the way, I have your cameras and the stuff you left behind. They're kind of expensive equipment, and they're evidence, so I thought I'd get them back to you. Stash them somewhere, that way Leo won't know I was here."

I reached to drape the messenger bag I carried over her shoulder—HERE conference swag. I thought that would add a cryptic touch. A hint for Leo to find.

As I leaned forward, Lydia kissed me. Her lips were soft and lip-gloss sweet. The scent of peaches and clean sweat enveloped me. I pressed into her and felt her tongue push into my mouth. I didn't resist, instead, I joined the play of it for a sweet moment. I slid my hand from her hip to up under her top and cupped her breast. Her skin was dewy and soft. I thought about how Jol seemed the opposite of Lydia.

That thought, the comparison, jarred me to my core. What was I doing? Fuck! I had just been with Jol. Told her I loved her. I pulled away.

"Oh, god, Lydia. I'm so sorry. I don't know what came over me. I just... I miss you. Or... I don't know. I've got to go," I stammered.

Lydia stood her ground as I wheeled back toward the door. The bag with the cameras and gear now hung from her arm, the joke of the HERE logo no longer funny, instead, it seemed territorial and wrong.

Jol was right, I shouldn't have come.

"Hey, Evan. It's nothing. Don't worry about it, I won't tell Leo," Lydia called through the door.

Did I come here hoping to catch her alone? I felt unsure of myself and my motivations. No, I was sincerely worried about her... them... and the others. The faceless accountants and lawyers hidden behind the walls laughed. I hated downtown. I hated myself.

18

THE FALL

Lydia

L eo and I surveyed the high-wire and the traverse lines at the far end of the Powell Street cable car turnaround on Ellis.

"The wind's strong. I'm glad we went with the tightrope. A slackline would have been impossible in this weather," I said.

Very few of the preoccupied holiday punters noticed our calculated behavior. A few looked to see where I was pointing, but the rigging meant nothing to them—power lines, ethernet cables, they didn't know. Leo and I pushed through the gaggle to where Herb had set up the decoy hotdog cart. It had been easy to pay off the regular vendor to not show up today. We just doubled his usual daily take and he lent us the cart and space.

Herb, our ersatz hotdog man, stood behind rows and rows of condiments. The sight might have been considered suspicious by the frantic-eyed shoppers if their myopic attention hadn't been on their Cuffs, devices, and shopping lists.

"All set?" Leo asked.

"All set, boss," Herb replied, sliding open the compartment of his cart to reveal bags of fun-sized candy, Chips Ahoy, and frozen foot-longs.

Bell ringers would signal the melee in less than an hour.

"You better get up there, Lydia. You still need to get into costume. I'll call you from the BART station when we're ready," Leo said. I watched him descend, bounding down the escalator two stair steps at a time, into the belly of Powell St. Station.

In the temporarily subleased 5th-floor office of the Urban Outfitters building, the aerialists crowded the windows to catch some of the action before the sky show. Opera glasses in hand, I pushed through to a prime vantage. Our phony Salvation Army ringers sounded their bells furiously as they tried to hand out dollar bills from their donation pots; try being an understatement. As we anticipated, none of the passersby took the money. Unexpected role reversals were a staple of the Chaos Order's repertoire and, as a whole, the public never accepted switching places with the needy.

I laughed aloud as I scanned the budding confusion.

Men and women looked to their herd for reassurance. *This is wrong, I'm not poor,* I imagined them thinking. *Bell ringers are supposed to ask for money, not give it out.* The skittish movements broadcast the signs of fear. So far, so good. I trained my binoculars on Herb and waited. Leo, in his Santa suit, swaggered towards him. The sight of Leo had me swooning. He was so cool.

The next part of the plan unfolded quickly. An over-animated exchange between Santa and Herb turned into a wrestling match, then to blows. Leo and Herb rolled onto the ground, letting loose. To me, it was clearly a mockery, full of partially pulled punches and pratfalls, but the crowd around them scattered. A wide circle formed as Herb leaped on top of the cart and grabbed a ketchup squeezie in one hand and a mustard in the other. Leo's jolly suit turned into a squishy Pollock painting of yellow and red. The goop dripped puddles onto the cobblestones. He blew a whistle around his neck to signal the backup forces.

Dozens of elves streamed out of the BART station, screaming, running, and jumping on any nearby garbage can, utility box, or planter. Rabid as gremlins, Herb chucked bags of cookies and frozen hotdogs from the cart to the waiting elves. They tore open the sacks and pelted the crowd in a frenzy. Great gouts of ketchup and mustard fountained into the air.

Stampede! The shoppers, now in pure panic, rushed away from the cart toward what appeared to be a way out at Ellis Street.

"That's the cue! We're on!" I hollered.

The aerial elves climbed to their places on the ledge. Three were set to traverse, six would repel, and I would skywalk. I inched my balance pole out the window, took my position. The sound of zipping across the gap and down the building prompted me to step out over the oblivious shoppers. The screams and yells of the spectators were peripheral in my bubble of pure focus. One stockinged foot crossed in front of the other again and again. My heartbeat pounded against my skull. I had cleared the first line of trees and was approaching the second when a shout boomed out. The sound came again, loud, amplified this time.

"Stop! You're under arrest!"

I looked, partially because I wanted to see what kind of idiot cop would tell me to stop in mid-air. To my horror, the moron was reaching for my line.

"No!" I cried.

My attention drawn up, I found myself wobbling. I tried to regain my balance, but my vision was full of grey flapping knives. Pigeons, startled by my yell, burst from the tree below. Wings buffeted my face and body. I dropped my pole. In a split second, it was over. I was falling, the pole crashed to the ground with a reverberating ring. Bursts of white and red light exploded through my eyes. I heard a sickening crack as I felt a branch strike the middle of my back. The bricks rushed up. Then there was black.

PART III

19

GIRLFRIEND IN A COMA

Evan

Dumbstruck, I stared at the supermarket bouquet—a peppery smell wafted from damp carnations. Who were the stupid flowers for anyway? Lydia couldn't see or smell them. She was in an induced coma. One vertebra pulverized, two others fractured. The doctors needed to keep her completely stationary until they could cement up her spine. Even with a medical scaffolding erected inside her body, Leo told me she would probably never walk again.

Leo's back was turned to the half-open door. He sat in a visitor's chair surrounded by a sea of unforgiving fluorescent lights. Hunched over, he studied the limp hand he held between his own. The room held no words or movement, only beeps and hisses. I wanted to turn around, walk out, run out, try again another day. My heart pounded. *Did Leo know that I had kissed Lydia? Stupid to wonder now. What did it matter? Lydia could die.*

"Leo." My voice hitched in my throat.

"Leo," I said again, more loudly this time.

It looked like he hadn't slept in a week. His eyes were red and his chin stubbled.

"Ah, it's you. Where's Grace Jones?" he asked.

Leo's sad smile may have been the most sincere expression I ever saw on his face. Nothing Machiavellian in him now, just a bad joke in a bad situation.

"We decided it would be better if I came alone." I lied. Jol had no idea I was here.

"Yeah, Jol hates me. I don't blame her. I would hate me too," he invited me to sit next to him with a small gesture.

"God, she's so tiny," I said.

Lydia looked like a little broken bird. Her arms and shoulder were crossed on top of a pale blue blanket. An orderly must have cut her hair. *Monstrous*, I thought to myself. There were so many tubes—one in her mouth and a cannula in her nose, electrodes threaded under the sheets, and cuffs clipped to her fingers and arms.

"Have her parents been here?" I asked.

"They have a hotel nearby. They don't like me much. You know, Lydia may be the only person in the world that likes me for real. Most people are afraid of me. But, Lydia, I think she loved me."

"She does love you, Leo. She loves you. She's not going to die."

"She might, Evan. She really might. And what did her love get her? Elves, fucking elves, falling from the sky. It's not funny now. What the fuck were we thinking?"

Leo dropped Lydia's hand for a moment and slammed his fist down on the metal railing of the bed, then he fell silent. He took her hand up in his again and touched it to his cheek. Silent tears rolled down his face. Leo was crying. Something I never thought I'd see. I rested my palm lightly on his shoulder.

Leo spoke quietly. "You know, my dad was the only person I ever admired. I felt about him the way you felt about your aunt. I told you he died, but I don't think I ever told you his overdose wasn't an accident. He loved me, but he killed himself anyway. He abandoned me with a monster for a mother. She wore him down. Gave him no choice. He should have killed my mom. She'd just dig into him with a knife; she'd dig into me too. Maybe I'm more like her, and not like him at all. Maybe he saw the same monster in me and that's why had to leave us. Had to leave me with her. My kind. He couldn't win."

"Leo, if it means anything. I'm covering all the medical expenses. Whatever you need, I'll help."

Anger flashed in Leo's eyes.

"Fuck you, Evan. Throw money at it, why don't you? That's who you are now. You and your company sicken me. Quit HERE. That's what I need from you. Do that." he demanded.

"What would that do for anyone? How can I pay her bills if I do that? You want me to be a gutter punk like you? Some joke of a vigilante artist. For what? Why?"

Dammit. He sucked me into a fight as usual. Why did I always step into his traps?

"Jol would leave you if you quit your job, wouldn't she? That's it. That bitch has got your balls in her handbag. Does she know you've been sneaking around behind her back fucking Lydia? Hmm?"

She *had* told him! I should have known. Lydia told Leo everything. They probably had a good laugh over it. Cold sweat prickled over my skin.

"It was a kiss, Leo. And that was an accident. It happened once. I didn't fuck her. But you, you fuck anything that moves. I know you and Lydia aren't exclusive. You could never make a commitment like that. No ties for you. Why would a kiss matter to you?"

"You're a fucking cunt, Evan. A pansy, little, fucking cunt." Leo stood up. "You don't understand me and you never will."

"Please, Leo, come on," I backpedaled, "I'm sorry. I don't want to fight. I never lost respect for you."

Leo sat back down. He looked exhausted. His power, unplugged.

"Respect, huh? I don't need your respect. I'm just a loser gutter punk. You better go, Evan. I'm not in the mood for this right now. I wish I hadn't called you. You don't deserve to be here."

"Okay, Leo. I'm sorry. I meant what I said, I am here for you both. Call me if you need anything."

I laid the flowers on the tray table at Lydia's side. I had to get away on weak legs, run away from this horrible tableau.

20

WHERE AM I?

Lydia

Lines. A grid of intersecting lines. Texture like birdshot through fine white paper. I moved my eyes. The glare was blinding at first. Blue sky and the leaves of a tree resolved through a window. *Where am I?* I thought.

My breath sounded mechanical, like a pump filling a tire. Woven in between the whooshing sound and the beep, beep, beep of my heart, I heard my name. I turned my head to the sound. It was Leo's face. He looked sad and pale.

"Eee—" I tried to use my voice. But I couldn't form an L or move my throat around the O. Something hard and choking was preventing my desperate need to say Leo's name. Coughing was excruciating. I bucked as I tried to expel what was lodged in my esophagus.

"Nurse!" Leo yelled.

I saw Leo reach over me to press a red button on a plastic pad by my side. All hell broke loose. Within seconds, doctors and nurses swarmed like bees. They checked screens and shone lights into my eyes. One doctor finished the job of extracting the transparent tube out of my mouth. It was wet with snot. I coughed, then screamed. The beeping ramped up to double time; an alarm went off. I swatted at the doctor who was hurting me.

"Sedative!" I heard someone yell.

A nurse with a syringe pushed into the growing crowd of medical staff. I thought she would stick the needle in my arm, but instead, she inserted it into the tubing of my IV bag and pushed the plunger. Warmth spread up my arm and hit my body like a cresting wave. The beeping slowed and I began to float. My body dissolved away, weightless and buzzing. I heard someone speak to Leo, but I didn't understand what they were saying to him. The world shined in the light of the love and concern in his eyes. It felt like Leo had created me. But he faded back and away.

"Leo," my voice was dwindling and hoarse, "I can't move my legs," I said weakly as I fell under the power of the Fentanyl.

"It's all right, my love. You'll be alright."

He stood and kissed my lips and eyes.

"I love you... too," I said, and drifted into a dark, dreamless sleep.

21

WAKE

The sun felt like nothing. On my arms and face, sublime warmth penetrated my skin, but my legs had no feeling. I could stab a needle into the limbs and not flinch. I knew. I had tried. That's not to say my legs were dead, not exactly. They jumped and twitched when I least welcomed their disembodied company. Pain followed the dance, but with a vagueness. More like a memory of pain that floated and itched, not in my legs, but elsewhere.

In the gardens, brine mist hung in the air. Waves crashed at the far edge of the property. The breeze chilled the trails of my tears. Bamboo tubes clattered like bones. Under normal circumstances, this garden would be a peaceful retreat, but Leo and I had lost everything. The office. The school. Leo had even let his sublet studio go.

Despite Leo's protests, HERE did pay for my

treatment. The Chaos Order was also generous with donations of money and food. They had crowdfunded nearly fifty-thousand dollars. A community of cooperation and kindness bloomed in the wake of my accident. I wanted that to make me feel better, but honestly, it didn't.

"Hey, Lydia," Leo called.

I wiped my eyes and swung my wheelchair around in a jaunty arc to face his approach. I had mastered maneuvering the chair in therapy and took some pride in that.

"I brought you brownies and some other goodies," Leo said. It was odd to see him out of his element. He appeared spectral in the bright colors of the garden.

I knew the brownies were his special brownies. Perfectly legal, but not allowed in the hospital. No intoxicants except for the ocean of drugs they fed me from plastic cups twice-daily. A hypocritical rule in my book— and one I didn't follow.

"Let's go to our spot," Leo said.

He kissed the top of my head as he pushed me down a sun-dappled path that led into the woods and away from curious eyes. The nurses and therapists didn't wander far from what their jobs demanded, and they never mentioned the mud-covered wheels of my chair.

Out of eyesight of the staff, a creek rippled musically over smooth grey and black rocks. Leo and I had claimed a wide swathe of loamy forest floor over our many visits to this hidden spot. Our passing was marked by a Turkish carpet of stones, sticks, and flowers pressed into the firm mud. Leo parked me in the shade and unfolded a nylon camp seat that he had stashed behind a tree on a previous visit. Sun filtered through a canopy of eucalyptus.

Cooking, I hadn't got the knack of yet. Leo held his lighter under a spoon. Brown sugar, a squirt of citric, and the water bubbled like an angry witch's brew. Bubble, bubble, toil, and trouble. Yeah, trouble. But it was mesmerizing. He rolled a little ball of cotton between his fingertips and added it to the mix. When he drew the liquid into a syringe through the cotton filter I vibrated in anticipation..

"All I could find was some shitty Mexican brown. I need to see my man in the city for the good stuff," Leo said.

He had been hanging out on the Pacific Garden Mall to score from runaway teens and lowlife hippies.

"Ready?"

"As I'll ever be," I said.

I loved him most during these forbidden trysts. I got legitimate injections and an assortment of opioids in pill form at the hospital, so Leo only needed to find the existing tracks to hide the illicit augmentation of my already heavy drug regime.

Leo had been a junkie since he was fourteen. That's what he had been hiding all along—the constant long sleeves, never spending the night, or even time in bed with me. He had been hiding his deeply scarred arms. Since the accident, Leo had opened his whole history of pain. Something shifted and he let me in. I felt like the first person to really know him, but maybe I wasn't. Leo had a way of making everyone feel special.

As the H entered my arm, my love intensified. It spread from my body to the softly speaking creek, into the leaves, high into the clouds, and back to these stolen moments. But love glowed most brightly for Leo. He was my dark angel, my bad boy, my broken heart. Leo injected himself and we lolled in our chairs. We sat apart but our essences mingled in the cool, pulsing sounds and the texture of the wind.

Sex would be possible, later, maybe—but I wasn't ready for it. Sex reeducation was part of my occupational therapy, but I hadn't started intermittent catheterization yet. The permanent tube and bag embarrassed me. Leo said he didn't mind, but I hadn't reached the same level of acceptance for my new body that he had. He adapted, even embraced my vulnerable condition, and that was astonishing to me. Shooting up together was more intimate than any sex act anyway. Leo shared his pure contentment and the orgasmic release that the drug gave. That meant volumes more than cumming.

When my free hour was up, he wheeled me back across the lawn and to the patio of the dormitory house. I watched him backtrack to the trail and disappear into the woods. He'd return tomorrow. And every day. Back inside the group living quarters, the winter sun streamed through the windows spinning dust djinns in the air. It smelled of cinnamon, peppermint, ginger, and biscuits. A black cat poked through the spokes of my wheels, a cheeky little thing named Camilla. She jumped to my lap for a scratch and a ride to the kitchen.

It was lunchtime. After that, my grueling schedule began—six, sometimes eight hours a day. I was in great shape except for my legs, those hung as limp as rotten bananas. Surprisingly, my new addiction made the physical therapy routine easier, not harder. It eroded my resistance, procrastination, and boredom. It was top-notch here—electro-reflex machines, warm pool, game room, a railed track with a suspension harness system, and OT for cooking, laundry, and driving. Greg, my trainer greeted me with my cup of meds—oxycodone, blood thinners, beta-blockers, antidepressants, vitamins, and God knew what else. Little gems in a multi-colored pile.

"Bottoms up," he said.

"My bottom's down, for good, dude," I quipped back with a sly smile.

I grabbed the water cup from the holder attached to my wheelchair and downed the pills in a gulp. I was glad for the oxy. I was coming down a bit and needed a bump. Greg had me stretch and practice some transfers. I could move from a bed to my chair, but a floor transfer, not even close. To move from lying on the ground to seated in my chair was the gold standard, and I felt like I'd never be able to do it. Greg assured me I was wrong.

"You were a professional aerialist and free-solo climber, girlfriend, and you're young and strong. You can do this. I know you can," he said.

I liked that Greg was tough on me. After the warmups, I asked to be put on the recumbent electro-reflex bike. That always cheered me up. For half an hour, I could pretend my legs worked again. The electricity channeled through electrodes caused an automatic reflex that made the legs push and pull the peddle. A little trick of science. Sadly, the magic of working legs couldn't be conjured in everyday life. Neuralink implants and stem cell therapy held some hope. Bionics were widely available. But those treatments weren't within my grasp. They cost a fortune.

Night was when the reality of my loss seeped deepest into my heart. The tempest of the Pacific out my window, she a soulmate in the dark, turbulent killer of ships and men. The ocean had no legs, only her buoyant body, and foreboding miles.

Leo and I planned to go back to SF. I wanted to stay in Santa Cruz with my mom and stepdad, but for Leo, that was out of the question. He'd been living in the little art shack I had built as a teen on their acreage on Highway 17. He argued that the redwood paths and steep terrain of my parents' property were unnavigable on wheels. The real and unspoken reason was he wanted to get away from their scrutiny and judgment as soon as possible. My SOMA loft stood empty and waiting for us.

Every other day, I saw my psychologist. I didn't tell her much, but I did tell her I was scared to go back to San Francisco. The environment of old school friends and family in Santa Cruz might be more supportive to my adjustment, she said. When I told Leo that my shrink had recommended transitional housing near the rehab hospital—that San Francisco was full of hills, traffic, old buildings, triggers, and trauma; that it was not good for my recovery—he went ballistic.

"You can be a cripple here or you can be my queen in a throne. It's your choice. Stay with these bliss ninnies or come home and restore the Chaos Order with me. I'm all you need, Lydia. Anyway, who will love you in that chair but me?"

He was right. Who would love me?

22

GOING HOME

I grabbed Leo's knee so hard he yanked away. Strapped into what looked like a jet fighter harness, he sat perpendicular to my forward-facing wheelchair. A barf bag would have come in handy. My stomach lurched. Leo looked as green as a stagnant pond.

"Going home—" he said, but he couldn't get out the rest of his sentence as we swung around another corner. None of this would have been so terrifying if it weren't for the fact that the route from Santa Cruz back to San Francisco was over 17, one of the most twisted and bloodcurdling highways in the United States. The violent sway of the van felt like tumbling off a cliff each time the vehicle slingshot around a tight turn on the redwood-lined road. Affectionately known as Blood Alley, this highway was fraught with sharp curves, blind spots, narrow shoulders, and erratic changes in speed limit. The auto-driving van calculated these things but that didn't make it any less scary.

On the occasional peaceful straightaways of the mountain crossing, I willed myself to relax and enjoyed the scenery of the familiar mountains. This was a shadowy fairyland set among giant red girdled trees. From the windows on the side of the van, my eyes reached back into the clearings, searching, expecting to spot the flicker of a sprite or a gnome in the morning light. One of California's evergreen forests, these peaks were an environment totally unique in the world. Odd that this wonderland would seem alien to most people. I didn't realize until young adulthood that redwoods only grow in California, Oregon, and a Southern province in China. A verdant stitch between the two continents from when they were connected in the primordial past.

We crossed through the colorful South San Franciscan sprawl that signaled the nearing SOMA exit to home. Back in the safety of the flatlands, Leo's manic well of words bubbled back to the surface.

"You're going to like what I did. Of course, you can't use the hanging loft, but it's like the kitchen and ground floor were designed for—um—for you."

His awkward hesitation charmed me.

"Lydia, how do you want me to, you know, talk about your legs when we get back home?"

"It's fine, Leo. I'm not sensitive about it. Call me a gimp or a cripple for all I care."

He chuckled low in his chest. I could see delight

sparkle across his eyes. I knew he was entertaining the idea of calling me his "gimp girlfriend" in public and imagining the outrage it would cause. Shocking people was Leo's bread and butter. The fantasy passed and he looked up.

"So, I'd like to have a welcome home party soon. The Order can't wait to see you," Leo said.

"We'll see. I need time to settle in. I'm feeling tired already."

"Oh, um, they're already coming over on Friday."

"I see— well—don't cancel on my account. It's fine. I'll be fine by Friday."

I didn't feel fine or like I'd be up for a big social event at all. In fact, I was pretty irritated. Since the accident, I kept my own company. Me and Leo was what I could handle, not a crowded party the same week as my homecoming from the hospital.

"Really, it's nice that you planned a party."

I could see in his eyes that I wasn't convincing. He let it pass, but his mood darkened.

"Look, here comes our exit," I changed the subject.

His mood flipped again.

"Right, as I was saying. The kitchen didn't need much work. You have a roll-in shower now. The loft, I turned that into my office. I didn't think you would mind since there's no way you can get up there."

My parents had paid for a top-of-the-line home modification. They hired a specialty outfit that adapted homes for the disabled. They also let Leo supervise the job. Maybe to get him out of their hair. Leo loved bossing around contractors, and it kept him busy, so it worked out well. He had commuted back and forth to SF once or twice a week to monitor the progress and order the laborers around.

The van pulled up at my condo and Leo walked around the back to operate the lift. He swung the cargo doors open with a clatter and the machinery whirred to life. I rolled onto the platform while he gathered up our bags. The contraption swayed and stuttered as it lowered me with agonizing slowness to the street.

The front steps had been replaced with a long ramp. After three months away, home seemed both familiar and exotic—glinting walls of glass, the little squares of lawn, my neighbor's yard littered with brightly colored plastic toys, the weirdly empty street. It felt unreal, like boarding a UFO. Leo chatted nervously, but I hardly noticed what he was saying.

"The ramp is ADA compliant. It had to be thirty-six inches minimum width between the edge of a ramp's handrails. It's one foot in elevation for every twelve feet—"

I let Leo's words crest over me and fade into a background of foreboding. My body, gross and heavy, churned with vertigo. The workman had left the place immaculate. However, the polished, spotless floors and freshly-made bed did not calm me. I felt adrift and lonelier than I had ever felt in my life. Leo could always read my thoughts. That I wasn't overjoyed would normally infuriate him. Today, he was more sympathetic.

"See, Lydia, I put in an adjustable bed. Zoop, zoop, and you can watch the sunset or work on a laptop or XR set. It's your command center. Fire the missiles!"

He played with the little remote. The head of the mattress went up and down, up and down. That the bed was in the middle of what had been the living room is what freaked me out. Really, the open plan of the condo was ideal for me and my new condition. Rationally, I knew I should be grateful. The large ground floor seemed custom-made for the spacious accessibility remodel—a multi-purpose room. Sure, the first thing I saw when I rolled through the door wasn't normal—this wasn't normal; I wasn't normal, and never would be. The new Amish farmhouse dining table would be easy for me to roll up to, and despite the missing chairs, it appeared to seat eight. There were conversation groupings for guests with soft brown leather club chairs and mission-style side tables. The aberrant bed beckoned to my tired body, covered in a satin spread and jewel-colored pillows. It was a thoughtfully designed space, but all I could do was wipe away the tears of loss and grief that welled up in my eyes. I couldn't see new beginnings here, only an end to my old way of life. After months at rehab, I had looked forward to this, and yet I was broken and dependent.

Leo stood frozen in place, as cold as a marble statue, watching me cry. The tick of the kitchen clock resounded loud as a funeral drum. Its sound wove through the spiraling motes of sunlight streaming from the bank of windows behind me.

"Shhhh, shhh, shhh, my angel. It's going to be just

fine," Leo said, breaking his rigid pose and coming toward me, his voice tight. I mourned the boyish playfulness of a moment before. I had disrespected his work, but he suppressed his usual lashing out.

"Look, I'll get you your shot and you'll see. It's wonderful. This is our home. You and me, we aren't like other people. So what? Fuck em, Lydia. Our difference is our strength."

Leo could be a callous bastard, but he always knew what to say to bring me around if he needed to.

"I'll be right back," he said.

I watched him clatter up spiral stairs to his spider's lair. It hurt how inaccessible the loft was to me now. A forbidden country. Leo disappeared from view, then reappeared on the stairs with his gear.

"Help is coming," he called, his cheerfulness returning.

He folded down the bed cover and adjusted the headrest.

"Alright, here we go." He swooped around behind my chair and lifted me into the bed.

His spell began. A sprinkle of this and squirt of that, the alchemy of fire, and the potion was complete. Leo kissed my brow as he tourniqueted my arm. The pain of the needle bit, then the ecstasy of the glowing liquid bloomed in my veins and lit up my cheeks. The velvet-covered pillows cradled me and the doom and hush of the room dissipated into bliss. My condo transformed into a shimmering palace, a sanctuary, a fortress for me and my lover. Leo gave himself his shot and flopped down on the bed next to me. We lolled in pure pleasure for a few exquisite moments, then he spoke.

"See, everything's all right. You're home."

23

THE PARTY

In the mirror, tears carved fiery paths down my cheeks through freshly applied makeup. A silvery hail of breaking glass skittered across the tile. I watched with detached curiosity as if I wasn't the one who pushed the jar off the counter.

"What happened?" Leo called from his perch above.

He clattered across the catwalk and down the stairs appearing at the bathroom door. My ruined face, the shattered mess, and makeup brushes strewn across the floor told the tale.

"Call them, tell them it's canceled. I don't want a welcome home party. Say I'm sick." The quaver in my voice humiliated me further. "I can't see anyone like this. Why did you invite them, Leo? I can't be a part of the Order anymore. I can't be a part of anything. "

Teardrops rolled off of my chin and splashed against

the bare skin of my ruined, skinny legs. I felt nothing. No warmth or wetness registered.

"You don't need to do anything, Lydia. Come on, baby. Everyone wants to see you, walking or not. Plus, they gave us money for your recovery. Do you want to seem ungrateful? Show them what they paid for. Show them the new Lydia."

"God, Leo, only you would tell me not to be an ungrateful coward so we can keep our cash cows happy. I'm a fucking paraplegic, not a show pony. Give me a fucking break?"

"We need the money, there's nothing wrong with that, and I didn't say you were a coward. So what if your body is different? The Order, they're all freaks. That's what we have in common. Look, let's get you calmed down and cleaned up."

Leo disappeared from view. I listened as he climbed the rickety metal stairs back to his office. Thoughts of the party disappeared as I imagined him in the quiet huddled over a small flame. Then he reappeared. In his hand, Leo had the same cure he had for everything. The change in him was obvious—a dopey half smile, his frame slack and liquid. When he bent over me, his pupils were tiny pinholes. He wrapped my arm with the loving embrace of the tubing and flicked at the soft bend in my elbow. I hated it, but he was right. He changed my channel from hopeless to euphoric with a jab. There was no repairing my ruined makeup. I had to redo everything, but it didn't matter.

"Let's get you cleaned up," Leo said.

He helped me into the shower chair and swept up the jagged debris of my tantrum with a broom. I watched in numbness for a moment, then unhooked the detachable sprayer, turned the water to scalding, and scrubbed the wrecked cosmetics from my face. Calmed by our cure-all medicine, I painted myself for a party. Leo helped with my outfit. He bunched up my pant legs and pulled them over my feet, calves, and knees. Once I could reach the waistband, I wriggled into my slacks. He zipped on a pair of black leather boots and handed me a slim-cut women's tuxedo jacket with white satin lapels and a plunging neckline. I rolled to the mirror. Shockingly, I looked elegant and put together. Beautiful even.

Herb and his entourage roared up on their motorcycles as Cara's catering vans pulled in at the curb. Cargo doors slid wide and a flurry of Cara's Kitchen hens emerged laden with platters and bowls. Smells of roast meat and garlic wafted through the early evening air. Herb's big guys helped the girls unload. In my time away I forgot how huge Herb was—a moose of a man, whereas Cara stood scarcely taller than me in my wheelchair.

It would be hard to maneuver around the condo when it was full, so I mapped out a strategy to park myself at traffic points, at least until everyone had a chance to see me.

"Herb! You're so much bigger now that I'm so much smaller. Come here and give me a kiss," I said. His presence calmed me. Herb was a big beacon of compassion and equanimity.

"Hey, little darlin! You're more beautiful than ever. I've

missed you. Everyone has!" He planted a smooch on the top of my head like a bomb.

Herb's buddies stood behind Cara with kegs of beers and heavy trays. The smiles that beamed through the door were so genuine that I felt ashamed of my earlier outburst about the party. Weather Girl's hair glowed radioactive green in the setting sun as she peddled up the street. Maureen, Sonia, Chauncey, and Peaches tumbled out of Ubers. These were my people. I had nothing to fear or prove. Well, maybe—

"Nice set of wheels," Sonia said as she crossed the threshold.

"Hi, Sonia. Yeah. How 'bout I change my name to Hot Rod?"

I tried not to glower at her. She and Leo had spent a lot of time together while I was in the hospital and in rehab. That she was intimately familiar with my condo, I had no doubt. Leo didn't hide his relationship with her or his random sexual exploits. I encouraged his trysts because that was our agreement and I didn't feel capable of sex in my condition. Although I wanted Leo to myself, we never talked about closing our relationship. After the accident, it didn't feel like the right time to declare my insecurities and desire for monogamy.

It would have been admirable if Sonia had dressed down for the party. After all, it was my welcome home. My mother always said, don't outdress the bride. But no, she radiated mystic beauty in a beetle wing green dress. Her plump lips were glossy and kissable. Long red hair fell in a turbulent river down her back and she smelled like a paradise of sin—vanilla, leather, and night jasmine. The real turn of the screw was a short skirt that revealed the longest legs I had ever seen. Beautiful, functional legs— what I wanted more than anything else. She popped the bubble of my growing confidence. Polyamory was the accepted norm in my community, but my useless legs and the lack of sensation in my pussy made me feel sexless and incapable of satisfying Leo, much less myself. Sonia drifted into the crowd. I balled my hands to force down queasy tears.

The condo filled up with crazy hair colors, roller skates, and lab coats. Outfits ranged from homespun prairie dresses to latex suits. Tall, short, big, small. Some of the girls were already shrieking and hanging over Leo's balustrade with dangerous abandon. Funny how I thought of my old bedroom as Leo's space even though I had only been home a couple of days now. Herb tapped the keg and the room broke into a cheer. Pop tunes and the mouthwatering aroma of Cara's food on the long farm table filled the room.

"Hey, darlin', drink up!"

Herb brought me a beer from the keg. I downed it in four gulps.

"Can I get you a plate of food? I'm happy to, but you might want to roll over there for yourself. There's a lot to choose from. Cara outdid herself."

"Thanks, Herb. This is all so amazing. I'm grateful."

My words, flat and formal, hung in the air. Herb brushed aside the awkwardness and took charge of my chair. In the age of synthetic convenience food and nutrition pills, Cara's wholesome, locally-grown cuisine was the antidote. The spring rolls caught my eye. Delicate in their translucent wrapping, herbs and flowers were just visible under the surface like small works in stained glass.

"You want a couple of those?" He asked.

"Yes. I'll take some of that kale salad too."

Paw-like, Herb reached over my head and scooped up a heap of glittering green ruffles with a serving spoon.

"What else, darlin? How 'bout some meat? Build up your strength."

The Korean kalbi looked good, so did the chicken satay.

"It's so hard to choose. Beef's a treat, but the chicken is healthier."

"Both it is," Herb said, and heaped it on.

"Alrighty, then. We'll get you set up. Your beer's about gone. Can I get you something more to drink? Do you want another brew or some of Cara's punch? It's like peach, mint, and vodka. It sounds gross, but I tried it, and it's amazing."

"Punch," I said, at ease under Herb's gentle care.

He parked me by an empty club chair, placed a setting and napkin on the side table, and went to fetch some more cocktails. I took a bite of kale. Cara's food made me feel better from the inside, and it was delicious and wholesome. She had sent casseroles and pies to the rehab with Leo. I felt the love baked into each dish. I'm sure her food cut my recovery time down by weeks.

Leo flopped into the chair next to me and stretched out his legs.

"Things are getting wild, right?" He said, clearly pleased with himself.

I looked around. Sure enough, an impromptu open mic was being organized by Maureen. Weather Girl swooped by on roller skates to grab a pan shot for her channel.

"I reckon so," I said.

I offered a smile. It almost felt warm. But not really.

"Well, see, you had nothing to worry about. Everyone loves you."

Instead of answering, I took another bitter bite of kale. I really didn't know what to say.

24

MÉNAGE À TROIS

Where is the goddamn hole? Trying to locate my urethra with a hand mirror five vodka punches and two beers later was nearly impossible. I took a breath, heaved my body up with the grab bars, and nearly ended up sprawled on the floor. Peach punch, the irony of it. The line of over-watered Order members outside the bathroom added more pressure I didn't need.

Normally, I would ask for help, but Leo had his tongue down Sonia's throat. What was I supposed to do? Roll over and say, excuse me, can I borrow my boyfriend back? I need help to pee. There was a real threat that I might piss myself. But there was no way I was going to leave this bathroom a broken, crying mess. Everyone would think that Leo had gotten to me. *God, when did I start caring what people thought? Had I ever really not cared? Was that all an illusion?*

It took every ounce of focus to still my hand and guide the plastic tube home. In my condition, I didn't trust that I'd stop at my bladder, so I fed the catheter slowly until urine started to flow. A millimeter more and the yellow liquid poured into the toilet bowl.

I tossed the disposable kit into the trash and cleaned up with an antibiotic wipe. Every shred of confidence was thrown into the garbage with the pee tube. Sonia had monopolized Leo's attention for the last three hours. My small bubble of hope popped, this party was a train wreck. At least it was for me.

In the mirror, I looked fine, if not pretty. A small victory. I expected to see some deranged zombie, but no signs of outward distress were visible. Shaking off my humiliation, I washed my hands.

"Sorry, everyone, this cripple stuff ain't easy," I said to no one in particular as I rolled past the line outside the bathroom.

My hair was ruffled along the way and I got a few air kisses. Fed up, I steeled my resolve. Leo's makeout session with Sonia didn't make my interruption easy, but I wasn't about to sit in my chair like a complete chump and watch. I cleared my throat. That didn't work. I tried a tap on the shoulder. Finally, Leo plucked himself out of Sonia's face.

"Leo, I'm tired. Can you please send everyone home?"

"Oh, good, it's you. We were just talking about you," Leo said.

"Sure. If that's what you call talking?" my words dripped with sarcasm.

"I'm done with this party. I need some sleep. This is too much, Leo," I continued.

"Sure, darlin'. I'll send everyone home, but Sonia and I have a proposal for you. I need you to think about it before you say no."

"No," I said, gripping the arms of my wheelchair until my fingers turned white.

"Listen, Lydia. This is important to me. Please hear us out. Sonia is a sex therapist, right? I mean, well, she has no formal training, but anyway, she is a sex worker. So, what do you think of Sonia spending the night with us? Don't answer. Think about it for a minute. Let Sonia give you a kiss to see how it feels, then you decide."

"Leo, really, I'm tired. I want—"

"Just do it for me! Please. Try. Kiss her. I'll send everyone home if you do that. See, I'm on my way! Believe me, this will be good for us," his words trailed off as he bounded out of earshot. I watched him begin to corral the herd toward the door. What a bastard.

"So. Was this your idea or Leo's?" I asked through a jaw so tight I could hardly speak.

"Look, Lydia. I'm no threat to you. Leo tells me you have been uncomfortable with sex since the accident. That's all. I can help you. I can help the three of us."

"Well, I can't goddamn feel anything below my waist, so yeah, it's uncomfortable. I don't see any point. I'm not into sex anymore."

I wanted to be open-minded, but loathing and embarrassment sunk me like a stone.

"Leo's the point. And you are sexy. Maybe you can't

feel your clit, but you can feel pleasure and love. He does love you, but can't you see, he's going to leave if you can't be intimate? I'm not a one-partner kind of gal, Lydia. You know that. I don't want Leo for myself. Honestly, I find you more attractive than him. Like he said, just let me kiss you. See for yourself."

In her own twisted way, Sonia was fucking Leo *for me.* She was saving us. She knew as well as I did that he was impulsive and childish. He changed allegiance when it suited him. The condo didn't hold him. Comfort was an embarrassment. I believed I could trust Sonia, but my heart hurt all the same.

"God, Sonia. I get it, but I don't even know what to do anymore," I said.

"This wasn't a spur-of-the-moment idea. You know, I work at Lusty's, right? The girls there are super, super cool. We Googled all about paraplegic fucking. It was fun, and we learned a lot. It's a fetish, you know? Look, lots of people in wheelchairs have fulfilling sex lives. We can do this. Listen to your body, not your fear," Sonia said.

"Fuck, Sonia, these are *my* sex problems. It feels so intrusive that you talked to a bunch of hookers about my personal shit. I'm not your research project. You should have asked first." The resistance was easing. An emotional wall crumbled. Sonia was cool.

"Don't throw shade. The girls at Lusty's are amazing people. Relax. They want to help too," Sonia said.

Leo's hand touched my arm from behind. I had half a mind to punch him in the dick. Problem was, sleeping with Sonia might actually be the right kind of solution. We were rule-breakers. That was our code.

Instead of punching him, I said, "Give us a few more minutes. There's still a bunch of people here."

"Sure, sure, I got it," Leo said.

Charged with new purpose, he walked toward the loft.

"Out! Out! Out!" He shouted.

Leo finished his sweep of the kitchen then rumbled up the stairs to the loft kicking over half-full Solo cups on the way.

"Get up. Get up. You don't have to go home, but you can't stay here."

Two topless girls appeared over the railing. They waved at me, then ducked down, presumably to get dressed. My sweet Cara was packing up the buffet, while Herb picked up cups and plates. *I should help*, I thought. Really, why had I been so hasty to get everyone out the door? Cara and Herb would have had a lot more helping hands to deal with this mess if it weren't for my selfish outburst.

"Cara," I called, "Please don't bother with that. I'll have help come over tomorrow to clean up. You've done so much. If you leave anything behind, I'll make sure it gets back to your shop."

A blanket of quiet covered the loft as Cara and Herb closed the door behind them. Sonia stood over my wheelchair and brushed the hair away from my face. Her gentle kisses started around my hairline. She kissed my ears and the back of my neck. It felt like butterfly wings. Despite myself, I enjoyed the physical attention. I ached for touch and sensuality. My arms and scalp tingled. When Sonia kissed my lips, she felt as soft as honey butter on cornbread. I'd been with plenty of women before. I knew the satiny feel of girl skin, the softness so different from a man's roughness, but Sonia's confidence was startling. She parted my lips with her tongue and kissed me. After a few moments, she took my face in her hands and looked into my eyes.

"Okay. We got the place all to ourselves," Leo said, taking in the sight of me with Sonia. "Look at you. See. Now that's beautiful."

Leo leaned down and kissed me wet and deep, lifting my chin as he bent over my chair. He took Sonia's face in his other hand and pulled her in. I watched their tongues connect. He broke away and turned to me.

"Good, now that's settled."

This was weird territory. I willed myself to relax as Leo rolled me to bed. With ritualistic care, Sonia built a nest of pillows. She supported my back and guided my knees into position as Leo placed me among the colored silks and velvets like he was arranging flowers.

"Go cook us some dope, and we'll get ready for you," Sonia said to Leo.

"Special sauce tonight. Pure White. It costs a fortune, but it's a special occasion. Right? It's my welcome home gift, baby." Leo said. I sighed. I felt like my life wasn't my own anymore.

Sonia laid out the remote for the adjustable bed, a silver hairbrush, some lube, and a box of condoms. The bed whirred as she raised the mattress and kissed my lips as the bed lifted me to her. I didn't realize until now that this kind of attention had been missing from my life for a long time. Maybe for as long as I could remember.

Leo returned and filled our veins. The shot turned me to syrup—numb and blissful. Leo's instructions were half-heard as the drug cocooned me in the warmth of Sonia's arms.

"Sonia, finger her. Now finger yourself. Lick your fingers. Kiss her." Leo's commands came in excited rapid fire.

Sonia moved around my body, her own form mesmerizing and elegant. The loose red curls dusting her shoulders and falling down her back matched the brighter coils around her pussy. Long legs and arms, so pale she would have been camouflaged in the white sheets, all but invisible if she hadn't been dusted with a Milkyway of warm brown stars. These freckles, cast so lightly across her nose, formed dense whirls and constellations on her calves, forearms, and back.

I watched with detachment as Leo unzipped his fly. He gripped his cock with controlled strokes as he continued to direct the scene. Sonia pulled Leo onto the bed and took off his pants. She kneeled and lowered her mouth to lick the pearls of pre-cum off the tip of his cock.

"You're a virgin again, Lydia," Sonia whispered in my ear.

"My girls, unique as snowflakes," Leo said as he slid into me. I didn't feel a thing below the waist, but it didn't matter. Sex was possible and it felt right because of Sonia.

I awoke with Sonia by my side. She normally worked

Saturdays at Lusty's, but she had traded her coveted weekend shift so she could come to the party and make love to me. My body melted when I saw her. I was spellbound by her. She wasn't sweet and kind like Cara, but she wasn't vicious like Leo either. Sonia had the power to shut Leo down with a word. Not many people could do that. At least not anyone that cared about what Leo thought of them. Maybe that was her secret, she didn't care.

25

PEEP SHOW

L eo's face was a mask of rage. His eyes, wide and unblinking. He was caught in a loop that I couldn't escape. I had no legs to run and nowhere to go. We were out of drugs and money. Leo wasn't junk-sick yet, but I almost wished he was. Then he wouldn't have had the strength to attack.

"I'm in a wheelchair. I can't walk. What can I do? You want me to turn tricks like Sonia?" I was cornered. No winning arguments like these.

"I already told you. Call your parents. Tell them we need more money for the business—for your school. You took my stash. We need MONEY!" The last word came out as an unholy shriek. My parents had already sent us three thousand this month. Plenty of money to live on. Plenty, if we hadn't been junkies with a fast-growing habit. Without his shows or the cause, Leo had grown despondent and aimless. Further investment in the school or the Order was a fantasy.

Sonia didn't help matters. She was a heavier user than Leo, but she had struck a balance in her life long ago. Sex work paid for her drugs, and the drugs made her sex work palatable. However, she wasn't about to pay Leo's way, or mine. She had boundaries with Leo that I didn't. I hadn't mastered the game and I wasn't sure if I wanted to. Not if it was like this. This was hell.

"Leo, honey, you keep everything upstairs. Think about it. How would I get up there to steal more than my share? I think you're the one that needs to get a job. You're the one who's been double dipping. And you can walk."

"Get a job! Get a JOB!" He lunged, his face was inches from mine. Sparks of spit hit my cheeks. I tried to roll backward, but Leo grabbed both arms of my wheelchair and dumped me over in a violent crash. The suddenness of my head hitting the floor. The shocking burst of light. It was like the accident all over again. Trauma ricocheted through my body like a bullet. The joystick jammed. Wheels whirred like the legs of an upended insect looking for purchase to flip itself right. I sprawled on the floor trying to claw my way back to the chair. Leo's boot connected with my gut.

Did that just happen? Would Leo really kick me? Did he kick me? My mind rebelled at the thought. I struggled for breath. Pieces of memory jigsawed together. Quick flashes of why I loved him and how each of those vignettes contained abuse.

I shouted for the automated home security system to

call the police. Alexa confirmed in her soothing accent. *Calling emergency services. State the nature of your emergency.* It was my voice responding, "Domestic assault!" but we didn't call the police. Not me. Not us. Yet —they were on the way. There was nothing I could do to take it back.

Calm descended out of necessity. Leo righted my chair. He bent down to speak a quiet apology and to help me up, but I pushed him away.

"Baby, I'm sorry. I don't know what came over me."

"Leo, you have to leave before the police get here. You need to get out. I can't do this anymore. Go!"

"If I leave, I'm not coming back," he said, but softly, his rage tempered by what he had done.

"I don't want you to come back. You're disgusting," I said, but I *did* want him to come back. I already wanted him to come back, even before he left. I wanted this to be a dream, or a nightmare. For this to all rewind to before the accident. To before the Order. To when Evan, Leo, and I were together. For the nightmare to be over. But this was unforgivable. I had called the authorities. Now I needed to leave too. I couldn't have the police poking around the condo.

"Out! They're coming!" I screamed.

I lifted myself into my chair and rolled through the door behind Leo, locking it behind us and changing the lock code with a few taps on my Cuff.

"Please, Lydia. I didn't mean to hurt you. It was an accident. I know you didn't— I'm sor—"

"Go!" I shrieked.

I didn't look but I knew Leo was still standing on the sidewalk with his hands in his pockets as I rolled toward the bus shelter. A lost boy. I could feel his eyes on me.

Need to see you, I texted Sonia, praying Leo wasn't heading for the same salvation I had chosen. Sonia's place. Sonia's arms.

Pitiful and limp, I let the bus attendant load me onto the Muni and secure my chair with nylon belts. I didn't have the strength to move, the shock of the kick to my gut and the thought that Leo was out of my life forever turned me to wretched rags. The city passed in a blur warped in time. When the lift lowered me to the street outside of Lusty's, I didn't know if I'd been riding for minutes or hours.

Birds chirped from the soot-clogged trees on Broadway. Streetwalkers wore their skimpiest tube tops, miniskirts, and ankle-breaking platform heels. Despite the blue sky's reassurance, the sun's warmth did not cheer me. I was boiling at my center, but my arms and hands were as cold as a corpse's.

Sonia had texted me that her shift was ending. I waited in bleak silence on the sidewalk unable to wheel myself inside the club. A passerby aired me a fiver. I wasn't offended. I felt like a beggar and I actually needed the money. When Sonia finally emerged, I held back my tears. She saw me before I said a thing. I had no words to give.

"Oh my god, honey, what are you doing out here? This is not good. You look like shit." Sonia rushed to my side. A gust of wind lifted her red silk robe, showing a glimpse of her freckled leg. I studied the embroidered cherry blossoms on her cheap Chinatown Mary Janes and shifted my gaze to my palms laying open on my lap.

"I don't know what happened, Sonia. Leo's gone. I told him to leave. Changed the door codes. I needed to get out of the house. The police were coming," I said, trailing off.

"So you threw him out for good?"

"I think so. I called the cops. He threw me down. He kicked me in the stomach. It was bad, Sonia."

"Honey, that's awful, just awful. Let's get you inside and warmed up. I'll get you right," Sonia said.

I saw her relationship with Leo for what it was, not something to be jealous of. She was a life preserver for Leo's sinking ship. His nonconformist idealism and art had become muddy and misdirected, violent even. His hatred had coiled back around on him like a serpent. Sonia had been trying to save Leo from himself. Get him back on track. Make him great again. Although, over the last month, she seemed to be letting go of that hope too. His absurdity had become desperate and lacked content and direction. He was unstable. The charisma was gone, replaced by rage, addiction, and frustration.

Sonia and I had the dressing room to ourselves. The girls on the day shift were either in the peep show booths or on stage. The smell of perfume, wet wipes, coffee, and ammonia from a cat box of an unseen cat was thick in the air. I parked my chair by a row of Hollywood vanities draped in scarves and lingerie. The surfaces glistened with bottles, tubes, and pots filled with cosmetics. Globe lights painted the room with a warm glow.

"Leo said I needed to get a job. He knocked me out of

my chair. He's out of his mind. What am I going to do?" I asked.

"That fucking bastard. I mean, like, fuck. Roughing up a girl in a wheelchair. That's the lowest of the low. Okay. Here's what you do. Stay with me at my place. Work with me here. You don't have to be alone for a minute. The girls will take care of you. This is a family. You'll see." She kissed my cheek.

"Let's get you in the shower. You stink, girlfriend." Her wink was that of a hustler, all stage and show, but full of love all the same.

Tears of gratitude rolled down my face and neck. Sonia offered an exit plan. A way to make money and a place to live without calling my parents or letting Leo know where I was. A way to hide from it all. She was willing to sacrifice her independence so that I could reclaim mine. Sonia was the antidote to Leo's cruelty. I loved her.

My hair still damp from the shower, Sonia rolled me to the office to meet Amber, Lusty's manager. Amber's room was a windowless cube with an antique desk at its center covered with flyers and disassembled electronics. I didn't know it yet, but when she wasn't wrangling strippers, Amber was an amateur electrical engineer on the side. Her dry, spindly frame housed a sharp mind.

"Hey meals on wheels," she said in greeting. "Sonia told me you want to do the nudie shows. Well, we don't discriminate." She gave me a thumbs up.

Amber started me in Private Pleasures—the peep show arcade. My new boss decided the five-foot by five booths would be the most comfortable transition for someone without use of their legs into sex work. Black curtains lined the gallery of booths and on-demand shutters opened for one-on-one shows. I was billed as The Paraplegic Nymphette on the sign above my preview window—an exotic novelty that no other sex club had. Maybe I was a sideshow freak, but I didn't care. In fact, it didn't feel very different from the performances I had delivered for years, privately or publicly.

Customers kept the sliding shutter inside the booth open with a flow of digital currency. A mic control let the viewers direct my digitally enhanced show. Guests could even purchase a remote sex toy interface from the gift shop, although most opted for old-fashioned manual masturbation instead of the expensive gadgets.

I moved my legs with my hands so the patrons had a good view of my pussy and ass. I didn't feel much as I fingered myself, but what *I* felt wasn't the point. This was show business. If I acted horny, my patrons were none the wiser. Funny thing, stripping helped with the pain. I was out of my body, disassociated, watching men and women on the other side of the glass. They were the curiosity, not me.

After a couple of weeks of pleading with Amber to let me dance on the group stage, she gave in. The group show was an Addams Family party filled with wild sexuality and play. The opposite of sci-fi isolation of the mirrored and screened Private Pleasures booths. Although my wheelchair made the cramped space even smaller for the others, the girls spun me around in my chair and positioned me at the viewing windows that lined the walls. Six windows for six girls. I could see the customers jerking off behind dark glass superimposed with a bright reflection of my naked body.

On stage, we sang and joked. Girls did handstands on the arms of my chair. I was a fully-capable-of-contributing actor in the show. My legs were unwieldy, but my arms were very strong. After a short while, pulling myself up on the dance poles became second nature. I choreographed my own legless floor act. Fetish or not, the paraplegic stripper thing became a big draw for customers and the press alike. Lusty's management was thrilled by the positive spin. It was right up their alley—diversity, inclusion, and sexuality for all. I needed that, empowerment.

Stripper star, or not, I still couldn't stay at my own place. It terrified me. Even though Leo was gone, the danger was still there. A galaxy of potential threats. I heard that Leo was couch surfing. Some of the Freaks were more honest with me about his state of mind. Maureen told me he was still obsessed with taking down Evan and plotting against HERE. She said it was all he talked about. The Order had become a revenge cult.

Word had spread about where I was working. Most shifts, familiar faces appeared like ghosts hidden in the dark, but the day the automated door slid open and Leo was on the other side of the glass hit me like a bucket of ice water. I reached for the alarm to ring for security but stopped myself. Leo had not done anything to warrant his ejection. He didn't even turn on the mic. He just stared at me. His face, a mask.

My life suddenly seemed like a pointless mess. The grungy, low-ceilinged club closed in from all directions and I panicked. My empowerment evaporated, turned into a desperate and toxic delusion by Leo's presence. The drugs were a rollercoaster of pleasure and misery going round and round. An endless spiral down a toilet hole.

"I want to get clean," I told Sonia after my shift. "I know I can quit now, but if I go on much longer, it won't be so easy."

"Honey, you, of all people, you shouldn't be shooting up. I told Leo that he was a bastard for getting you hooked. You need strong plumbing for this shit. It's poison —for you. Maybe for me too." Sonia trailed off as she cooked up a spoon for us.

She handed me a rubber tube and syringe. With the shot, the pain and hopelessness that Leo had triggered disappeared. All gone. I rushed into the floaty bliss. But I knew by now that this was a false peace, a shallow facsimile of happiness, a tacky copy of life. It was temporary and it was a trap.

"You know, I don't even get high off this stuff anymore. Don't feel a thing. Still, I use a ton and it costs me a fortune. It's part of my biology now. The point is, coming off of it will be utter hell for me? But I've never had a real reason to kick it. Not until now."

"Really, Sonia! Will you?"

"It's not going to be easy. I've tried before. It's the worst thing imaginable to go cold. It makes you want to shoot yourself in the head." She swept through the warmth of the dressing room where we sat. "We need a plan and a place to detox. We're going to need methadone too. I know *I* will. Quitting could kill me. Literally, kill me."

Tears streaked my face. My fiery angel was willing to go to hell with me to lift me up.

"I need you," I said. "Come here. Help me stand so I can hold you."

Sonia lifted me out of my chair and supported my weight while I embraced her. Leo never sacrificed anything for me. Sonia was a different animal. Wild and free, but also loving and kind.

26

COLD TURKEY

That night, we used the rest of our hammer in the age-old tradition of the last hurrah. We binged the latest Nextflix series as our heads lolled, chin to chest. Sonia's proximity and the flickering show, a Kirlian photograph display on the back of my closed eyelids. It's easy enough to vow not to use anymore when you feel no pain. It was all bright futures and new beginnings but tinged with the knowledge of a paradise lost. We drew closer to hell. I would never forget that this perfection existed, but the gates of heaven would be closed to me starting tomorrow.

When I could finally lift my head and maneuver my chair around the apartment, I grabbed a tall kitchen bag and scraped the picks and empty baggies off the counters, along with beer bottles and Chinese takeout cartons. I rolled into the hall and dumped the lot down the trash shoot before we could change our minds.

Sonia kept some dancing shifts, especially the 1 am to 3 am slot. For her, working at Lusty's took the same effort as walking down the street. She's been at sex work since the age of fifteen. It started when her high school boyfriend pimped her out for beer money. A joke and a dare, but Sonia's red-haired beauty and youth had an instant and profitable draw. The avalanche of cash was beyond either of their wildest expectations.

It was easy living at first—her boyfriend convinced her to recruit and turn out more girls. A year later, he demanded that she drop out of high school so she could work for him full-time. By the time Sonia's boyfriend turned career pimp and decided to move his entire stable to Los Angeles from Vacaville, Sonia had fallen in love with another girl and made her escape.

Sonia moved her business to North Beach. When her pimp came looking for her, she wisely found more protection in the strip clubs. Twelve years later, the work hadn't changed much for Sonia, but her mindset was different. To her, sex work was her art, and the drugs were as routine as eating and sleeping.

Whether the supply dries up or the funds do, no long-term addict is a stranger to withdrawal. Sonia included. She knew the horrors that were in store for us. I wasn't familiar with the physical mutiny of every chemical in my brain and muscle in my body turning against me, nor was I as strong as her.

For Sonia, the heebie-jeebies in her legs were the worst part, especially at night. If she wasn't working, the spasms kept her pacing in endless circles around the furniture and up and down the hall of our small apartment. When I massaged her feet and calves, the muscles under her skin felt like electrified steel cables, hard and buzzing.

My body violently rejected everything but sugar and basic carbs. Every muscle, even the paralyzed ones, clamped down like vices. One saving grace was we didn't have to spend much on food. The only thing I had an appetite for was donuts, and the day-olds from the bakery down the street were free and good enough if we didn't mind retrieving plastic bags out of the dumpster on the way to the Methadone clinic.

Our march down the trail of tears for Dixie cups of salvation happened twice a day. We waited with the other hookers. Their sweaty, mini-skirted thighs made a sucking sound as they rose from the vinyl benches when their names were called. The clinic was a hassle but a necessity. Without the heroin substitute, I doubt I would have survived, but it wasn't gear by a long shot.

My Sonia's already pale skin turned translucent like ice. Her lips cracked and bled and her bruised looking and sticky eyes sunk into the black caves in her drawn face. I avoided the mirror as much as possible, but I knew I looked as beaten, sad, and sick as she did. The girls at the club told me it would be like a bad flu, but that didn't even begin to describe the agony. A flu didn't come with a deep well of anxiety, shame, and the endless shits ranging from bloody black, sickly green, to glowing orange. Sonia popped Imodium to prevent crapping on stage.

Otherwise, the customers would have gotten way more than they paid for.

Ten days later we curled into each other like cats in a patch of late-morning sun thrown on a worn cotton quilt laid over Sonia's bed. Sleep felt better than anything except for maybe that first shot of H with Leo. We got up to brew tea and eat at sunset on the sixth day. The clink of dishes and the smell of real food cheered me as Sonia made noodles and peanut sauce. Chopping, cooking, cleaning—our humanity reemerging.

"We need to get out of town," Sonia said.

The drama hanging over us and the familiar San Francisco streets were triggers. Sonia reminded me that because we were feeling better, backslides were a constant threat, especially if we didn't change our daily habits. To see Leo, even for a second, would be a major setback for our recoveries. Mine, in particular. We needed a change of scenery.

PART IV

27

THE GAME

Evan

I had a few hours to myself before my morning meetings. A pod in the Nespresso machine hissed to life and the room filled with the bracing aroma of Bianco Forte.

Jol and I met with investors at nine; casting was at eleven. Hopefully, I'd have time for lunch at noonish. I'd been relying on nutritional injections far too often to be healthy. I hated all the conferences, but they were an unavoidable part of corporate life.

A carbon band held bone conductive electrodes comfortably to my temples. On my virtual desktop, I swiped through the meeting agendas for the day and checked the press for mentions. Nothing on the feeds about the upcoming HERE Urban Playground launch. Counter to most product drops, in our case, no news was good news. The headset I wore was a prototype of our breakthrough extended reality tech, and it needed to remain top secret.

Lydia's accident was terrible. I would give anything to reverse what happened. But having Leo occupied with Lydia's recovery was the best thing that could have happened from the perspective of the company. Leo's relentless drive to expose, sabotage, and slander HERE had taken a toll. Everything we planned was based on mystery and buzz. Getting HEREsets onto the heads of early adopters in an organic way was the top priority. If those influencer ears and eyes were connected to the arts and gaming communities of San Francisco, all the better.

Leo had been only partly right about our plan to sell ads—the means to deliver those ads was the real brass ring. In-app virtual billboards and branding of virtual spaces was already commonplace. HEREsets delivering a continuous augmented experience—AI avatars, indistinguishable from real humans, sharing word-of-mouth recommendations in virtual social situations—was the real revolution that only a handful of HERE insiders were privy to. Leo had grossly underestimated our scope. Billions of dollars were at stake.

We wanted the public's focus on the creativity of what we did, not on the highly targeted advertisements that would eventually stream through wearables that HERE hoped would become more ubiquitous than SmartCuffs. The world would be divided into those who were citizens of extended reality and those who were not. Even I had been distanced from the full truth in the beginning. I was only given security clearance once my friendship with Leo and Lydia was no longer seen as a liability.

"Hey, beautiful, you in?" I spoke through my HEREset's communication app.

"Of course. Meeting's in an hour," Jol answered.

"Right. Walk with me. You eat yet?"

"No, not yet. We'll grab croissants on the way."

"Sounds good."

I slid the door open to the adjoining office with a blink. HEREsets used neuromuscular signals as direct input, allowing for a frictionless interface with the surrounding IoT. New technologies had been implemented at break-neck speeds around the campus in the last year.

Jol's shape was framed by sunny gardens through her window-wall. She wore a form-fitting dress with a thin fur collar. The beige knit against her skin was smoke and incense, or like the dusty wings of a silk moth. Her HEREset's curved projectors looked like small iridescent wings sprouting from her head.

"You are truly beautiful," I said.

Her laugh echoed against glass and stone.

"Come over, I have something to show you."

She beckoned me in. A sillage of scent enveloped me from five feet away.

"Sit down. Here are the potential testers. Make sure you don't know any of them, even as acquaintances. If they recognize you, we're sunk. We'll lose their trust before we begin. Sit down, take your time. This is important."

I looked at holographs of ten potential players, four of whom would be selected for the first round of the HERE UP game. None were familiar. Still, we were taking a big chance.

"I don't know any of them. But they might know me. You know, I have some fame, at least with the Order. We still have time to hire and train someone from LA to lead the first test group. I shouldn't be the one to run this. I'm too high profile," I said.

"I think you are the only one who can, Evan. You know the game like your own mind. You wrote the immersive narrative. Who else can really understand if the game is working or not? You underestimate your necessity and your advantage, like it or not."

"I love it when you talk dirty to me," I said, rolling the Lucite desk chair closer. I ran my hand up under her skirt. She kicked me back with a playful click of her tongue. A habit that turned me on—half rebuff and half mischievous invitation.

"Let's go to the cafe. I'm hungry," she said, pushing me away for real this time with her jeweled hand.

We were the first to arrive at the nine o'clock meeting. Empty handed, I watched Jol stir her latte and nibble delicately at an almond croissant wrapped in wax paper. My breakfast from the lobby kiosk had been scarfed in the elevator. Jol teased that I had nasty American habits, one of which was gobbling my food. A criticism she delivered with affection.

Jol cleared away the remnants of our breakfasts as the HERE coders and marketers took their places around a conference table of polished blond wood. The potential investors and the C-suites were the last to arrive. We needed to move into mass production with the headsets right away, but our experiential marketing campaigns were unorthodox and proving to be indecipherable to the newest set of investment capitalists. I snuck a wink at Jol as I walked to the front of the room.

"Welcome. I'm Evan and this is my partner in implementation and release, Jol Weele. Today, we will discuss the rollout of the HEREsets through the medium of our XR game, HERE Urban Playground, or HUP, for short." Jol stood up, bowed, and retook her seat.

HERE's CEO introduced Donna and Graham—VCs from Silicon Valley. They were young and hip, but despite their trendy sherbet-colored suits, they gave off the weight of old Asian money. Billions were on the table.

I blazed into my presentation. "HERE UP is an XR immersive narrative game played in the streets of San Francisco. Players will be led by a HERE docent, known as the imposter. If any of the real players get stuck or try to divert play outside of the gaming area, the imposter's job is to redirect the game. The imposter is also responsible for the safety of the players. This type of game has a long history in the Bay Area, but our technology is all new. Our entry market is young influencers, artists, and techies. We know that this group will spread our message through word-of-mouth and social buzz if we succeed in making HERE UP mysterious and exclusive. A secret society, if you will. Of course, that exclusivity will vanish once wearable devices have wider adoption and penetration. But the cool factor will push our tech into the more wary markets. We hope to overcome the fears of less sophisticated consumers through influencer adoption— media stars, writers, musicians, coders, sports personalities, et cetera. The way we get HEREsets into the hands of style-makers is through the HERE UP game campaign."

"Does the game run continuously?" Donna asked through lips painted a vivid orange.

"That's a smart question," I responded, although I thought it was a stupid one. Had she read the brief? "No. The games are scheduled and will run two times a week for the rollout. Gamers have to be invited and register at our indoctrination center before playing."

"Just San Francisco? Isn't that rather a small target for a global rollout?" Graham asked.

"We plan to launch similar games to all US major metropolitan areas once we have beta tested here in San Francisco. Next up are New York City, Los Angeles, and Detroit. From there, international centers like London, Paris, Tokyo, and Bangkok will be hubs for new campaigns."

"Who will head up the international rollouts?" he continued.

"We plan to travel to each site and map the areas with experts. The youth culture of each location will be distinct, so we need to hire locally to make sure each game is effective. Our intention is to make our HEREsets the 'must-have' wearable accessory for anyone under fifty and for advertiser penetration to be complete. Other types of marketing will become obsolete over time. By leveraging pop and subculture references, we hope that a deep and passionate following will form before the mass rollout," I said.

Donna spoke up.

"It seems risky. Very risky. What if the game is not as cutting edge as you expect? Don't you believe traditional advertising and publicity will do just as well for us, if not better than this unprecedented experiential campaign?"

A murmur rose from the far end of the table.

"Good question," I replied again, "but let me answer you with another question. Should we advertise XR with conventional campaigns? Experiential and situational marketing is the wave we need to ride. It's what we are selling, so we have to use it ourselves. Headset technology so far has been clunky and uncomfortable. We believe HEREsets will raise our biologically integrated products above the noise. HERE will be the next Apple if we play our cards right. It might be safer taking the traditional, and frankly, outdated path *if* we didn't have a dozen competitors racing to get their XR hardware to market first. Like with Apple, one winner will emerge. Passionate brand loyalty will win the day."

"Okay. Sure. But how will we be protected legally?" Donna asked.

"During the initial rollout, the contract to participate will be tacit. To claim the headset and play the game, the agreement must be accepted. Of course, all legal requirements are met, but who reads those 'check this box' type of things anyway, right? Especially when that checkbox is floating in mid-air in front of you like a miracle. We expect the players will accept the terms without thought," I said.

"Yes, but tricking consumers into thinking HERE UP is an independent, underground art movement and not Big Tech in disguise is bound to backfire. Not to mention the bigger legal risk here—injury, even death. In your proposal, I see you have players in traffic, climbing ladders, in underground tunnels, and running in a staged chase through the city. Sounds like a recipe for disaster," Donna said.

I looked at Jol. She took my cue and answered.

"We have invested a great deal of time and money into creating an unprecedented experience. We believe the risk that our game is exploitive or dangerous will pale in light of the sheer ingenuity and fun of the real-world immersive narrative combined with our HEREset's near-eye display. This is king-making. It's a marketing gamble, yes, but one we insist on taking," Jol said.

I picked up where she left off. "Yes, as Jol said, the HERE UP game is designed to create an organic, grassroots promotion. I'm leading the first test group next month. The players will be selected by our psychologists based on profiling for the initial run, but after that, influencers and press members will be seeded into each group. The prototype headsets will not be given away to the players. In fact, they are programmed to deactivate outside the game area. If stolen, they are as useless as a paperweight. The best encryption available makes the software unable to be reverse engineered and furthermore, the essential code is locked in the cloud. The commercial release will be dropped at XR World next September. The buzz, by that point, should be earth shaking." I refilled my chest with air.

Everyone at the table sat up taller. Like me, they had forgotten to breathe. Donna began to speak, but Jol interrupted.

"Frankly, we are here to seek capital for the manufacturing of the headsets. We have investors lining up to finance us. We are not prepared to budge on how we will roll out HERE UP and HEREset. The question is, do you have the vision to invest in the next trillion-dollar company?"

"Fine," answered Donna. "But we'll only give you a five-hundred-million to start. After the American launch, we'll talk about the rest."

Jol wisely let Donna claim the last word.

Five hundred million—not bad for an hour of work.

28

FIRST RUN

You Are HERE gleamed off bright steel under pinpoint spots. The sculptural sign hung over a long, curved reception desk of polished copper and burl. Our casting office in Los Angeles had sent two receptionists. They looked like they had stepped off a slick, digital movie set. No office workers I ever met looked like these two. Dark-skinned Fatima was crowned with a shimmering firefall of rich-girl hair. A Bollywood princess with a musical accent—an affectation in the days when most people spoke with globalization's bland unity. Patrice, the lesser beauty, wore a smart DayGlo pink bob. Her full lips were painted to match her hair with the precision of a surgeon's knife. Their sleek, black skirt sets fit their slender frames like they were sewn into the suits.

Fatima lined up headsets along the polished counter for me to inspect. Inky black halos for wicked angels. In one of our first headset design meetings, Jol asked me to imagine a world where you never saw anyone's eyes again. Point taken. With aggressive convincing, we got a hardware budget big enough for a Mars mission and set a ridiculously aggressive deadline. The near-eye array had been developed at Stanford and perfected by our R&D department. The gist was it used electromyography to pick up signals from the electrical field cast across the wearer's skin and eyes to detect muscle movement. The visuals were refracted by a grid of intersecting beams with tiny prisms. A full virtual experience was achieved through a veil of light like a personal holodeck. To pry the technology out of the hands of academics had cost us billions.

HERE's signature rising tone enveloped me when I pushed the tiny power button above my ear. At the crescendo, a gong sounded and a woman's soothing voice said, "Welcome to HERE. I am Elyah. To commence, state your full name and repeat after me—I accept the terms and conditions of the HERE corporation."

Far too fast for any human to read, blocks of text scrolled in front of my eyes. I knew what they said, but the legal department hoped the players did not. The prototypes could potentially cause a host of health issues, motion sickness being the least dangerous, but most common. And we didn't fully understand the long-lasting repercussions of pumping 7G directly into the human brain.

"I, Evan Bouchard, accept the terms and conditions of the HERE corporation." I clicked a box that appeared to hover in front of me.

"Accepted... Evan... Please proceed to the indoctrination center. Green arrows will illuminate your path. A red crossbar indicates a wrong turn. Follow the arrows to the door scanner, take a seat inside the center, and wait for the remainder of your party. Thank you for playing."

The arrows appeared and lit the floor like a path pointing to the hallway door.

"Check," I said and handed the headset to Fatima. She replaced it on a charging pad and passed me the next one. Patrice and Fatima had done the gear check earlier, but I couldn't sit still. Over-caffeinated and vibrating with anticipation, time moved far too slowly. I needed to keep busy or I'd lose my mind.

"I'm going to run through the automation in the indoctrination center again," I said.

Patrice and Fatima rolled their eyes but nodded, humoring me, as I put the first headset back on. Their smiles were good-natured and sympathetic. Everything had been checked and rechecked. Really, I didn't need to do anything, but they understood this was a big day for me. HERE Urban Playground was my baby.

The corridor leading to the center was both futuristic and retro. The set designers had done an amazing job. They captured the exact vibe I requested in the style meetings: *Steampunk meets what people in the 1970s imagined the future would be like.* As a response, the distinctive features from the exterior of the Sentinel Tower were woven into the hallway design. Patina greens, glossy mahogany, and subtle nouveau elements laid into carbon black panels that seemed to suck the light out of the air around them—just the right balance between creepy, campy, and elegant.

My HEREset triggered the door of the indoctrination center as I approached. The door clicked, swung open, and the room whirred to life. Oscilloscopes and Tesla coils buzzed and snapped in recessed niches. The carpet was a thick shag. The entire back wall of the room rippled and shimmered to the beat of a heart. "Welcome, Evan," Elyah's voice echoed in my head. We'd given Elyah a punch of reverb for critical points in the game. Bone conducting tech on the HEREset vibrated the sound through my body.

The wall display changed, blurred at first. An image of the outside world zoomed from aerial into hyperfocus. My skin tingled and my stomach sank like a stone in a pond. I sat in one of the SOMA chairs facing the animated wallscape. The scene was so realistic I felt I would fall through to the street below.

"Evan," Fatima's urgent voice filled the room.

I inhaled sharply.

"Yes, what is it?"

"The first of our guests are arriving."

Shit. That I was supposed to be undercover gave me a real case of the heebie-jeebies. I was a miserable actor. Leo had reassured me my guile was completely lacking whenever I dared set foot on stage or tried to play a character at one of the Order's events. Stiff as plywood, he always told me.

I rushed down the hall and burst back into the

reception area. Patrice saw my panic and raised a hand to calm me.

"Don't worry. Fatima hasn't unlocked the door yet. Calm down. She's waiting until the coast is clear, then she'll let them in one at a time," she soothed.

I dropped my shoulders and pulled my best hangdog look.

"You'll be great, Mr. Bouchard. Break a leg."

Patrice's smile was warm. She took the headset from my hand and placed it on an open pad. Damn, when did I become Mr. Bouchard? It's not like I was much older than these girls. At Rain Dogs and in the Order, Mr. Bouchard would have been an insult. Something Leo might call me if he thought I was being stuffy and uptight. But to my staff, it meant respect. Was I on a higher level than everyone else? Did I want to be?

"Just call me Evan. I'm supposed to blend in, remember."

Being admired felt awkward. Isolation and loneliness were byproducts of my authority. By the time I realized my position separated me from the rest of the world, it was too late to do anything about it. Greatness is a trap, a seductive one. I slipped into the back office and closed the door.

29

IMPOSTER

HERE players were not accepted as couples or in groups, only as individuals, at least for the beta runs. This uneasiness was calculated by design. That everyone started off as complete strangers enhanced the novelty, cooperation, and strategy of the game. As the imposter, my responsibility was to keep the group safe and to create an environment of problem-solving and play. If a natural leader emerged from the group, I would simply stand back and allow the participants to work out the puzzles for themselves.

Invisible cameras cast a visual net across the floor of the indoctrination center. From the small office behind where the receptionists stood, I monitored and recorded every action of the arriving players. I didn't turn on the lobby mic to hear the exchange between the first player and Fatima, although the audio recording captured the conversation for later review. Instead, I watched the player's physical behavior. The girl was in her mid-twenties. She wore thick-framed SmartGlasses, stretch pants, trainers, and a black leather jacket. She took off her mixed-reality Ray-Bans and tuck them into her satchel. Walking to the full-length mirror, she admired the HEREset that Fatima had handed her, turning her head this way and that. I could tell she was pleased with the slight wing-like protrusions. When Jol suggested that the appearance of the headsets be a priority, I scoffed. Now, it was clear she was right. Wearing a HEREset would become a status symbol.

I knew that Elyah, our AI, had initiated the game sequence when the girl's posture became stiff and attentive. After a few minutes, she poked her finger into the air and exited through the hall. I could have switched cameras to follow her or changed to the multiple feed view, but didn't bother.

The next player entered—a tall man, slightly older, with a square jaw and sandy brown hair. If I had to guess, I would say he worked as a game designer or programmer. He had an awkward geekiness about him. I watched him listen to Elyah's instructions, but unlike the first girl, he walked back to the desk. Curious, I turned on my audio monitor.

"This legal agreement, it's a lot to take in," he said. His voice was deep but boyish.

"Yes. It's all standard though. A waiver of liability, confidentiality agreement, and an agreement to share your data with HERE. Nothing you haven't signed a million times before," Fatima said.

"All the same, I'd like to sit down and read this more thoroughly?"

"Of course, Greg, Take all the time you need. Well, within reason. The game starts in fifteen minutes." Fatima gave him a charming shrug.

Fatima must have known the man's name from his intake record. She escorted Greg to a small, separate lounge to the side of the main lobby.

Ha! Take that legal, I thought.

The legal department had been cocky about the whole matter of fine print. They insisted that no one would bother to read the contract. That 99% of people never read any online agreement. The lawyers were arrogant to the point of placing bets on it. I had just won a thousand dollars. Looked like this guy was part of the 1%.

Patrice announced the next name on her screen, "Inara," and buzzed her in. *Whoa.* Inara was goth to the extreme. Her face was painted a ghostly white and her eyes shimmered with purple shadows. It was hard to tell through the monitor, but she seemed to be wearing multiple layers of lace, gauze, and velvet in black and deep gem tones. On Inara, the HEREset looked natural, like jewelry. Black wings at her temples, a spooky crown. She inspected herself, agreed to the terms with a jab of her finger and disappeared through the door within minutes.

Daphne was the last. It struck me how different the players were from each other. I wouldn't have known if it weren't for Jol's fashion obsession, but I recognized Daphne's handbag as Chanel by the pastel quilting and the buckle of interlocked Cs. Everything she wore looked expensive, even if normally I couldn't tell which designer was which. Patrice seemed impressed too. She handed Daphne her HEREset. *Hmm.* I spoke a note into my Cuff. "Feminine color options needed." The grungy, punk look of the black winged headset was completely wrong on Daphne. She noticed with a grimace in the mirror.

They're all here—five total, including me. The psych report advised this number would create the right balance, or imbalance, really. I opened the door and bounded into the reception area.

"Great! Last but not least!" I said to Fatima and Patrice.

"Ahh. Mr. Bouchard. There is still a player completing the..."

Oh, shit! I forgot all about Greg! I was behind the front desk as he stepped back into the lobby. He eyed me suspiciously.

"Hi. My name is Greg. Did you ask to read the contract more closely too?" He asked.

I let out the breath I was holding. From the office door I left open and my familiarity with the girls, Greg had drawn the conclusion that I was also a stickler for contracts. Just another conscientious player. In my excitement, I had almost blown my cover.

"Yes. Hi. I'm Evan. Can't trust the lawyers, am I right?," I said, trying to sound natural. Out of the corner of my eye, I saw Fatima rushing to initialize my headset and bypass the setup so I could pass seamlessly into the game with Greg.

"There you go, Evan. All set. You two go on now. You're going to be late," she said.

"Thanks, Fatima."

Shit, I did it again. I said her name with familiarity. With a chagrined smile, I tried to communicate to the girls how grateful I was for their help.

"Ready for this, Greg?" I asked.

"Sure man, let's go."

"I'll be right behind you," I said.

Greg threw another suspicious glance over his shoulder, but walked through the door to the hallway. Fatima shooed me away. Anything I had to add could wait.

"Hey, Greg, wait up," I called.

Greg turned as he activated the door to the indoctrination center with his HEREset. IoT tech would scan us and trigger the start of the game as soon as a total of five players entered. At the far end of the room, Inara held an old-fashioned tablet so that it shielded her face. Someone without a SmartCuff was an oddity, especially in a beta test group. I turned to the girl in the trainers and introduced myself.

"Hi, I'm Evan. This is Greg."

"I'm Carla and this is Daphne."

Daphne, puzzled about why I didn't approach her first, moved to block sight of Carla, knocking into her with her expensive handbag. Clearly, Daphne was used to being the center of attention.

"Isn't this the coolest! Did you see all the weird stuff in the hall and around this room? We're the first group to play. Don't you feel honored? We're, like, the only people in the world to ever do this!" She said in a barrage of rapid fire chatter, making a point to touch my shoulder, then Greg's.

"Yeah, pretty cool," I said.

Inara held her device even closer to her face, but I could tell she wasn't really looking at it. Instead, she sneaked glances at us out of the corner of her eye. Before I had a chance to finish introductions, Elyah's booming voice filled the room.

"Welcome to HERE. The game is about to begin. Please take your seats."

30

URBAN PLAYGROUND

E lyah's digital avatar glided through the scenery outside. Dressed as an Egyptian queen, she walked toward us among the oblivious pedestrians. Trees and cars faded into mist as she rose on air and stepped over the wall's edge and into the room. Now with us, I could see the detail of her braided wig decorated in gold, carnelian, and jasper. Eyes of kohl burned as she observed us with slow sweeps of curiosity. A jeweled serpent wound around her head, hissing. Its ruby eyes seemed to track my movements. I knew each HEREset interacted with the wearer independent of the others in the group, so what I saw was slightly different from what Inara, Greg, Daphne, and Carla saw.

"Shhhhh," Elyah said. The snake hissed along with her as she drew a ringed finger to her lips. She had a riddle for us. The first clue.

"Sacred, majestic, great piles of stones, used to encase both

riches and bones. These bones, they aren't ancient, in fact, they wear suits. In honeycombs halls, they hide all their loot. Stashed hordes of gold in tombs are not locked. Instead, they are hidden in bonds and in stocks."

Poof. Elyah evaporated in a shimmering haze. The door clicked and swung open, and the green arrows reappeared. To my surprise, Inara spoke first.

"Oh my god, how cool! Well, a pile of stones. It could be a cemetery."

"Yeah, but she said it wasn't a tomb and the clue is inside with people," Greg replied. The group drew together until we stood in a circle.

"Alive and in suits," I interjected, not wanting to give away too much.

"Could be an office..."

Before Daphne finished her thought, a piercing wail filled the room. The sirens were real, but motion generators created the sensation of the earthquake. Mechanisms hidden under objects and countertops tossed coffee cups and potted plants to the floor. Lights flashed and the ground rumbled.

"Let's get out of here!" Carla yelled over the ear-splitting alarm.

I'd been through this earthquake simulation many times before but the panic of the players was terrifying. I made a mental note to tell the psych team to dial it down a bit, maybe add a trigger warning. We tumbled over each other into the hallway. The way to reception was blocked with whipping electrical cables. Sparks flew. The fire was augmented reality, but the danger certainly looked like the real thing.

"This way," I shouted and ran toward the emergency exit at the opposite end of the hall. I knew someone would have to break into the firebox to release the door. Carla read the sign, hesitated, then used the tiny mallet that hung alongside to shatter the glass. She chipped out the shards before pulling the lever. The door opened and we rushed into the stairwell. Once outside, the earthquake effects were generated entirely by the HEREsets. Even though the ground was not really moving, the quake seemed extremely realistic. My heart pounded in my chest.

The set design team had the foresight to set up a guardrail on the curb opposite from the emergency exit so players wouldn't rush into the street traffic. The peaceful outdoor diners enjoying their midday wine or espresso at Cafe Zoetrope leaped to their feet in alarm as we burst out of the tower shrieking and waving our arms. The simulation died away and was replaced by calm. Birds chirped and vehicles rolled by as if nothing had happened.

"That was a pants pisser," Greg said.

"Yeah, holy shit, it's gonna be like that, is it?" Inara replied.

"Let's catch our breath," I suggested.

"Do you see what I see?" Daphne said.

"Whoa, freaky," Greg said.

Bronze-edged thunderbolts laid into the decorative red granite and malachite sidewalk tiles under the historic cafe tables glowed gold, pointing the way to the two steel slabs in the sidewalk. The doors erupted upward as a cage elevator rose from below street level. We walked toward it as a group.

"Uh. Go ahead, Greg. You first," Inara said.

"Who's coming with me?"

"We should all go. The plaque says that the elevator is rated for 2000 pounds," I said.

Hesitantly, the group stepped onto the platform. Metal groaned under our weight as we huddled together and I punched the down button. The doors closed overhead and it went black. Machinery rumbled and we sunk below the street. Automatic lights flickered on as the elevator clunked to a stop, but after the brightness of the day, it took minutes for my eyes to adjust.

The cavernous wine cellar unfolded in a zigzag of cubbies filled with bottles. A cold, dank wind moved through the basement. It must have been from an air filtration system. Coppola wines, newer vintages, gleamed ruby and blond in the racks near the stairs leading up to the restaurant. Behind locked bars in the deeper recesses of the moss-stained cell, the rare, dusty, and old awaited the order of a moneyed celebrity or an opening night celebration.

"Party time," Greg joked. The others fanned out to explore. Down here it smelled of earth and cork mixed with a whiff of sour, spilled wine.

"Look! It's a coin with something on it," Greg called in excitement to the group.

He retrieved a glowing artifact from a wall niche and

showed it to us in his palm. It shone in the virtual incandescent light as we studied its design. American Spire appeared embossed under a triangle with two fins at the top.

"I knew it! Like I said, the pile of stones is an office building. A pyramid-shaped one. It's the Transamerica!" Daphne exclaimed victoriously.

"You're right! That's only a couple of blocks away. Let's go," I said.

"You found a clue," echoed in my ears. It was clear from how the others jumped that they heard Elyah's voice too. The holographic display flashed 'one artifact found' in the upper right edge of my vision and the stairs up to the cafe lit up with green arrows like the ones from the indoctrination center. The gamers raced across the confetti-colored carpet inside the cafe. Hastily, I glanced around at the framed vintage movie posters as we passed through. Back outside, our mid-city mountain was within visual distance. It loomed over us. We drew to the foot of the skyscraper as mysterious as the pyramids of Giza. A honeycomb of limestone-white I-beams led to the entrance through a plaza of miniature redwoods and shadowy ferns. Sculptural children of bronze played in the shade. The brickwork, a cryptic puzzle under their forever still shoes. The sunken asymmetrical fountain pulsed with light, enhanced by the AR of our HEREsets.

"Let's go sit in the shade. I need a breather," I suggested

I led the group to a circle of seats around the fountain.

"Do you see that?" Daphne said.

The water glittered gold around lily pads. At the heart of the fountain, a sphere of blue shone. The gurgle was peaceful.

"Whoa, freaky. I guess someone should wade in there and look then," Greg said.

"Go ahead, Greg. You do it. You're our man of action," Daphne said.

Greg walked to the edge of the pool, took off his loafers and socks, and rolled up his pants. He stepped in and moved across the algae-covered tiles with care, feet clearing a path through a layer of submerged coins.

"Hey, guys. There is something rectangular in here. It's a keycard!" Greg said as he came up with his dripping prize.

He dried the card on his khakis and walked back to us. We passed around the artifact. I turned it over in my hand even though I had seen the item many times before. The flat rectangle of hard grey plastic was embossed with an eye-topped winged pyramid and the words *Elevator Pass*.

"Well, we've got an elevator card. Pretty sure that means we go inside," Daphne said.

"She's right, guys. Let's go in. You lead the way, Daph," I said.

A sign above the bank of kiosks read *Virtual Observation Deck*. The digital viewing stations allowed the general public to manipulate the cameras mounted 800 feet up the spire to see spectacular views of the city without ever leaving the ground floor. One viewing station radiated light just like the other clues had. As we approached, a tiny Elyah waved at us from the monitor.

She spoke from the screen, but her voice came through the headset as clear as if she spoke into my ear from inches away.

"To see the view they pan and zoom. The lower types can't leave this room. Through lift, and stairs, and spire you hop. VIPs, straight to the top."

A loud ding caused the group to turn in unison to an elevator that opened behind us.

"I guess we're supposed to get in," I said.

Inside the lift, Carla studied the panel of numbers.

"Looks like the top floor is the 27th. But it seems like this building is way, way taller than twenty-seven stories."

"Well. Push the top one then," Inara said. "Let's see where that takes us."

Girl from Ipanema played faintly through my HEREset. The musical selection, a tiny private joke for me. Retro-pop culture references were my thing. The elevator opened on an old, abandoned viewing floor. Placards describing various points of interest stood dusty in front of walls of sun-hot glass. The city below us lay in crops of cement and steel. Cargo ships crept across an angry bay filled with stormy chop. Still further, Mount Tam shrouded in fog to the north, and in the opposite direction, South San Francisco and the arteries of highways leading to Silicon Valley.

"Hey, look at this, it does higher. It says *Private Highrise* by this set of elevators. There are no buttons, though, just a keypad. Do you think our key will work?" I said.

"Let's try it," Greg pulled the card out of his pocket and swiped it. The doors slid open with a ding.

"Cool," he said.

The building was much narrower when we exited the second elevator bank. Logically, this made sense, considering the shape of the Transamerica. However, something about the shrinking rooms was disconcerting. This room was no bigger than an apartment, liminal in its windowlessness, and full of heating and cooling equipment. It was nerve-racking to be so high up, yet in such neglect.

"On shit. Look at that."

Greg pointed up into the spire. An actual ship's ladder led to a hatch-like door. It glowed gold.

31

TRIAD

Carla's yoga-pant-covered ass wiggled above me. Unlike the other girls, she had worn sensible shoes for urban adventuring. Daphne and Inara stayed below in their high-heeled boots. They could have climbed, but I discouraged it. The legal department in my head told me to keep them out of harm's way. Despite the prep of the HERE crew, plenty of hazards still threatened to break ankles or skin on climb up to the point. Carla was at the viewing rail when I pushed through the hatch. Her jaw literally hung open.

"Move up, bro. I want to see too," Greg prodded with his voice from below.

I climbed into a dome. Greg clattering in behind me. A new clue sat on a circular dais in the center of the spire, ignored. The view was too otherworldly to pay attention to anything else. It was like standing in a lighthouse 850 feet tall. The city and bay spread out in all directions with nothing but a circle of reinforced safety glass that was little more than six yards across between us and the sky and the clouds.

"Wow," Carla said.

I had flown in small planes before, but this was surreal. We floated in mid-air. I could have spent all day taking in the view. However, Elyah, immune to human wonder, had a stricter agenda. On the dais, she was flickering like a tiny holographic Princess Leia. Elyah was all business. She had on a pinstripe suit and red bottom stilettos.

"The loot reclaimed from corporate heights. A gold-filled case is in your sights. But in this tower, it is not locked. Instead, it's time to exchange your socks."

"Did she say socks?" Greg asked.

"I think she did. Let me check. Rewind clue. Display as text," I said.

Elyah's words appeared to hang in the air.

"Cool trick. I didn't know these things had voice command," Greg said.

His eyes narrowed. I knew things that only an insider would know. Greg's suspicion of me had only grown since we met at the indoctrination center. If Greg or the others had figured out that I worked for HERE, it was a minefield. I straightened my shirt and directed his interest back to the game.

"Let's go down and share what we've found with Inara and Daphne. See if they can help us figure out the new riddle," I suggested.

"I wanna stay a few more minutes. I'd wager that less

than a hundred people in the world have ever seen this view. It's amazing," Carla said.

"Let's Gram it. What do you think?" A video share made for a great diversion.

"Yeeeah!" Carla said.

I extracted a selfie drone from my pocket as we posed against the view.

"Watch this," I said.

"Three-sixty," I commanded. A little pod camera lifted from my hand and flew around us taking a video of the entire scene. I airdropped the 3D media file to Inara and Daphne and queued it to play through their HEREsets. A notification sounded below and the women exclaimed "Wow!" in unison.

Once the group was reunited and back among the tourists in the ground floor public observation area, a coffee break animation walked through our displays. Another iconic nod to the past, a coffee cup with legs, arms, and face sang "Let's go out to the lobby," to claim free drinks from the Starbucks kiosk of the Transamerica. It was one of the two test ads scheduled to run during the game. The commercial application of the HEREsets would be rolled out slowly. We didn't want to overwhelm the first uses with the AI avatars yet, but the test coffee coupon was a hit with everyone. Who would complain about free Starbucks?

We sat in the shade of a flowering gum tree covered in brilliant red flowers with our lattes and iced matchas. Long, red petals waved in the breeze like the tentacles of anemones. Greg relayed the clue from the observation bubble to Inara and Daphne and the group mulled it over in silence.

Daphne blew a hole in her coffee foam. "Isn't the stock exchange a few blocks away?" she said.

"Yeah, that's right. The Pacific Stock Exchange. I mean, Stock Fitness. It's a health club now. That's a good guess. Stocks— socks. The sock exchange," I said.

We walked with our insulated paper cups among the purposeful business people, idleness clearly belonging in another part of town. A few blocks down Sansome, the Stock Exchange rose unmistakably. Parthenon-like columns bound by tall stone figures of men, women, and children. It surprised me how Soviet-style art still dominated the public spaces in the city, especially around institutions of past and present capitalism. I admired Diego Rivera and his ilk for their enduring subversion. *Groups like the Chaos Order have been around for a long time,* I thought.

When a twelve-foot girl holding a cement sheaf of wheat winked at us and pointed toward the door, it was clear we were in the right place. Inside, the old trading floor was now a biohacking gym. Only glass walls stood between visitors and the elite professionals subjecting themselves to cryo-immersion, infra-red, and other brutality in the name of longevity and beauty.

Grunts and primal yells echoed in the vaulted space like a torture chamber. The long marble reception desk was populated by chiseled men and women dressed in spandex that showed every inch of their smoothed and sculpted bodies. At the farthest end, a woman who clearly didn't belong among the fitness army stood at a computer terminal. Instead of six pack-baring LuLu Lemons, she had on the exact same pinstriped suit Elyah's holograph wore at the top of the Transamerica. Next to her, a display card read Sock Exchange in looping gold letters against a background of royal blue.

"There it is!" Daphne said.

"Which one of you is willing to sacrifice your socks for the greater good?" Inara whispered, her discretion was unwarranted and unnoticed by the busy fitness fanatics.

Carla pushed Greg forward.

"Me again? Geez. Alright, I'm on it," he said as he sat on a padded bench and peeled off his loafers and green and black Argyles for a second time today. "These are silk. Cost me eighty bucks. Forty a sock. I have a feeling I'm going to have to give these away," he laughed good-naturedly.

Greg approached the woman in the suit with his balled-up socks. I knew she was a real human—an actress sent by the casting agency. We still needed actual people to manipulate real-world objects. Holograms could not do that—not yet, at least.

In exchange for Greg's expensive socks, he was handed a hard-sided briefcase. He brandished it in victory as he returned to the group. It looked like a relic from an old James Bond movie.

"Look. It's locked," he said.

We bowed our heads together to study the cylindrical dial embedded in the case.

"Any idea what the combination is?" Daphne asked.

"I asked the girl at the desk if she knew," Greg said.

"Well?!"

"She didn't. But Evan might—" Greg chuckled to himself. He was on to me and he was letting me know it. "But she did say I was to deliver this case to Big Louie at The Buddha Lounge," Greg finished his thought.

"Oh! I know that bar! It's in Chinatown," Inara said.

This was as exciting for me as it was for the players. Even though I designed the map and knew the answers to the riddles, the game was fun all the same. Over the last two hours, the group had bonded. No outlier or pariah emerged as the HERE psychologists had predicted. Inara became more dominant than I expected. Daphne, smarter and more cooperative. Carla and Greg were our action takers. The different personalities worked in concert.

Buoyant from our success so far, we walked down the sidewalk, the sun's glare wrapping us in shine. Greg swung the case from one hand to the other. The salty smell of elote con cotija from a food vendor cart on the corner filled the air. All around us, the XR headsets painted the urban streets with living art. A chair and desk crawled out of a fifth-story window to chase each other across the facade of a four-story office building. The occasional passersby sprouted wings, horns, or a sexy red dress. This was like the real world, but more surreal. Better. More fun.

It was obvious that we were approaching Chinatown from the morphing graffiti and the Chinese characters on the storefront signs. At Grant Street, the augmented reality went into overdrive. Glowing red silk lanterns adorn the street poles and a painted dragon came to life, tumbling from a brick wall and spiraling into the sky.

"There it is," Carla pointed with excitement.

The lit neon of the sign was muted in the daylight. A martini glass with its glowing olive and buzzing Buddha had been unchanged for nearly a hundred years. The lounge was a historical landmark. In the days of microdose pharma bars, we stepped through a portal to the time of Bukowski. Naugahyde stools lined a brass-rimmed bar. Dusty Christmas lights twinkled in the artificial evernight of the tiny dive bar. Unexpectedly, the place was packed, and not with your typical day drinkers either. These were grizzled Asian men in tar-black suits and dark sunglasses. They scrutinized us in unison as we took our stools.

"Suspicious. No, creepy," Inara said.

"You Big Louis?" Greg asked the old Chinese man tending the joint. He wasn't physically big, but his cantankerous mood sure filled the room.

"Who's asking?" Louis said, squinting his hazy, cataracted eyes at the row of us.

"We got something for you."

"Yeah? What is it?"

Greg set the briefcase down on the bar.

"What do you want me to do with that?" Louis asked.

"Well, don't you have the combination?"

"Nah. You're looking for my brother. I'm Little Louis. You just missed Big Louis. Too crowded in here, if you know what I mean." Louis tipped his porkpie hat toward the attentive group of gangsters, "Here, Big Louis told me to give this to whoever showed up with the case."

Louis slid a folded square of paper across the bar.

"Don't read it here. Prying eyes."

"Sweet!" Greg said, "We got the next clue. Let's go."

"Thanks," Daphne called over her shoulder and we stepped back out on the street.

My eyes adjusted as we walked toward Market Street. I couldn't help but think about Lydia. We were headed straight to the site of her accident.

"Hey, don't look now, but those Triad-looking guys are following us. Quick, let's duck in here," Inara said, pointing to a window filled with shiny, white-bellied lucky cats. Their cheerful line of waving paws transformed into beckoning hands through the magic of the HEREsets. Inside, we threaded our way through the crowd of tourists and racks of postcards. Silk lanterns hung low over densely packed displays. A tall shelf of jade dragons and incense burners gave us cover when the men in black peered through the window.

"I don't think they saw us come in. Let's read the note before they spot us."

Greg handed the briefcase to Carla and unfolded the plain paper square.

Fools will win a state of grace. A quest's end found within this place. Walk the maze one by one. At the center, the game is done.

"Maze! Grace! Clearly, that's the labyrinth at Grace Cathedral," Daphne exclaimed triumphantly. Her quick thinking impressed me once again.

"I think you're right, Daphne. But that's blocks away and we've got a tail. I know those guys are waiting for us outside. You think this place has a back door?" I asked.

"Ask that storekeep if we can cut through the back room. I think she's the owner. Maybe slip her a bribe," I suggested.

"Expense it, Evan," Greg hinted again. He was having fun with his suspicion, but the others hadn't a clue that I was an inside man despite his veiled quips.

The transaction went quickly. The grey-haired Chinese woman led us to her stockroom.

"That's a secret underground exit. Go through here," she told us and pointed to a low cement door with shallow steps leading into a dank tunnel. The passage smelled of old, leaky pipes—iron, sulfur, and wet. I thanked her, airdropped a hundo, and clicked the flashlight app on my Cuff. The others did the same. Multi-colored scrawl covered everything except for the damp floor. Tags were everywhere - RAT 2020, Ghetto Boy, Loquacious. Works of neon abstraction faded into black as they stretched into the recesses of the dark tunnel. The HEREsets animated the art. Shapes and letters ballooned, melted, sparkled, and pointed the way. The tunnel let out onto the street at the base of Old Saint Mary's Cathedral—the two hundred year old all-brick church was closed for restoration.

"Let's walk fast and keep some distance between us and them. Grace Cathedral is a few blocks up that way," I said.

With no sign of the gangsters, we hiked up Nob Hill. Historically, this had been the home of barons of industry and gentlemen's clubs—not the stripper variety, but elite escapes for those with means and old family money.

A spectacular advertisement unfurled all around us as we walked past the Fairmont. Transposed over the real city street, the interior of the Fairmont's paradise themed bar, The Tonga Room, glittered to life. A translucent image of the indoor pool and floating stage encircled by drinks in coconut shells, pineapples, and fishbowls appeared floating in midair. *Free to all HEREset wearers! All you can drink cocktails from 5 pm to 6 pm!* scrolled across my vision.

"What?! Abort mission! A free booze spree. What time is it?" Greg asked.

"It's almost 3:30. I think this coupon is for after the game, Greg." I winked at him.

"We're almost there. Let's get to Grace first, then we will drink ourselves blind once we win," I said. It didn't matter that I had designed all of this. The nerve-racking game had me ready for a drink or six.

The ad faded as we walked toward the Flood Mansion. On the far side of the rolling lawn of the estate, a row of black Lincoln sedans crouched like stalking jungle cats. As planned, the Triad had intercepted us. A driver's door opened and one of the leaders of the black-suited men stepped out.

"Shit. They're blocking the only way to the church unless we circle all the way around to the other side. The finish is right there. Spitting distance. But how do we get past them?" Inara asked.

"I have an idea. Carla, you hang back behind this

hedge. Stay out of sight. The rest of us will rush them. When we have them occupied, you run as fast as you can for the steps of the church. If the gangsters see you, go inside and hide. There are all sorts of spots to duck out of sight in there. Are you ready?" I asked.

I didn't give anyone time to think. I knew what we were doing wasn't actually dangerous, but the anticipation of engagement sharpened my focus.

"Go!" I yelled.

Inara, Greg, and Daphne rushed at the men in suits as they poured out of the parked cars. I stood my ground to make sure Carla was in the clear.

"Cào nǐ zǔzōng shíbā dài!" One of them flung insults at us in Chinese. That, or he was giving us directions to Walmart. None of us spoke Chinese, so who's to say?

The gamers engaged the line of suited men, blocking and corralling the gang members. Carla saw that we had subverted the Triad and started to make her break for the church. With the briefcase like a football under her arm, she dashed down the centerline of the street. One of the gang members tried to redirect his group, but the players continued to block their progress. Carla was athletic and fast, certainly the right choice for the final sprint.

I was about to join Inara, Greg, and Daphne on the hill when I noticed the passengers of a van parked on the corner were studying me closely. The panel door slid open. I separated myself from the group and walked down the hill to ask them to park somewhere else while the game was going on. I hadn't noticed at first, but now I saw the Order's logo painted on the matte brown flank of the vehicle. My mind glitched. Vans were not part of the game? Why was the Order here?

Yeti-costumed Freaks emerged for the cargo compartment, long brown fur trailing in the wind. A group of six yetis seemed to go straight for the Triad with the goofiness I would expect from a Chaos Order event. However, the shortest yeti did not advance with the trajectory of the group. I couldn't make out the eyes through the rubber slits in the mask. But I knew it had to be Leo. His small stature and strong-shouldered authority gave him away. *Why was he carrying a cane? Was he hurt?*

Fun fur, tailored three-button suits, and girls in skirts rolled down the lawn of the Flood Mansion in a jumble. They laughed and shouted to Carla, "Run!"

Leo strode toward me without any hint of the playfulness happening in the near distance. His steps were purposeful. He pulled off his mask at three paces, eyes wide with hate. Cords stood out on his neck and forehead.

I looked at the tangle of gamers on the grassy knoll thirty yards away. No safety there. They were too far away to see what was going on. I didn't yell for help. Leo and I were as good as alone.

"Leo, what are you doing here," I asked. Blood pounded in my ears. The air was thick with danger.

"You did this," he growled, electric with aggression.

"What, the game? It's my job," I asked, sincerely confused, "Leo, I— I really don't know what you want. This is the corporate launch. You shouldn't be here."

Before I could ignore him and turn back to the crest of

the hill where the game was unfolding, Leo's eyes narrowed. He crouched low and lunged. His cane arched and swung across my vision in a humming blur. There was a blunt thud. Searing white stole my vision, and a pop from my knee triggered an animal groan deep from my gut. Then the real scream erupted—rage and panic poured out like vomit. Crushing pain consumed me as I fell to the ground, panting.

Leo's engineer's boot hooked under my chest before I could beg or huddle to protect myself. He flipped me on my back and pushed down on my chest with the sole of his shoe. I lay flat in the grass. It took all my willpower to inhale enough breath to keep conscious. It might have been better if I had passed out.

He threw the cane into the grass and fell to straddle me, arm cocked back like a hammer. I tried to lift Leo off, pushing up with my good leg, but I was too weak. A sharp crack from inside my head sounded, and the taste of copper and iron washed my mouth and clogged the back of my throat. I turned my head and spit. When the aurora of animal fear cleared, I saw a pearly tooth in the grass in a spew of dark blood. In a moment of clarity, the tooth came into crisp focus. My senses were strangely heightened and dulled all at the same time.

"Leo, what are you doing? Please," I rasped and gurgled, my voice like frying bacon in a pan.

"I'm not crazy! You did this!" He roared and pounded his fists into my face again.

Warm wetness spread from my groin and down my thighs. I smelled piss.

Madness and rage painted a wide moat around the irises of Leo's eyes. Spittle dripped onto my already blood wet face. The matted fur of his yeti suit and the red dripping from his Cuff, my blood, seemed unnaturally crisp.

"Please, Leo—" I gulped.

Leo twitched in confusion when he heard sirens.

"Leo. Run, now!"

32

CONNIE'S DEFENSE

I was sure that Leo had suffered a severe mental breakdown. That had to be what led to the attack. My mother said Leo never took responsibility for anything. What he did, he did on purpose—a common behavior of psychopaths.

The suggestion irritated me. I couldn't believe Leo had conned me from the first day we met. That he never cared about Lydia or me. If you analyzed it rationally, he had kicked me out of the Order long before any of this had started. To believe what my mom said was paranoid. If Leo had been playing a long con on me, what outcome did he hope to achieve? It made no sense.

No, Leo's agenda never matched my mother's worldview. Therefore, she judged him as insane. Typical. Anyone that didn't agree with mom was either nuts, immoral, or stupid. But I knew Leo. He invested his life in the emancipation from fear. Cultural conditioning, he said, was a filthy lens with which to view the world. Rules of society were pointless if your ultimate goal was seeing the truth. People's lives were controlled through the hot buttons in our DNA—fear of ridicule, avoidance of pain, need for validation, and the chemistry of our pleasure centers. He wanted everyone to see through the veil and choose reality for themselves.

The idea that I was Leo's chosen opponent in a chess game played ten moves ahead just didn't fit. Why would it be personal? How would Leo have known that HERE would recruit me, or that Lydia would fall from her highwire? To break Lydia's back intentionally, to cripple her, someone he loved, that would be unfathomably evil. Leo wasn't evil. Or was he?

I untethered the rental car from its dock at the Santa Ana Airport. "Mom's house," I said into my Cuff. The cast that hugged my leg from thigh to ankle made it hard to get into the small Econ vehicle. The 3D printed contraption banged against the door frame. A road flare of pain shot through my knee. Leo's cane strike hadn't broken any bones, but the soft tissue damage throbbed under an itchy spider web of the carbon fiber armature. I adjusted the dial on the side to bend my leg enough to fit inside the car.

No, Leo wasn't evil. He didn't have godlike powers over cause and effect. His game was chaos for chaos's sake—to shake the snow globe of the world and see where the glitter settled. He was an unstable genius, and I couldn't have him go to jail. That's not where he belonged.

If I didn't care about my popped ACL, black eye, and

a missing tooth, why should the State of California? Fifteen years was the prison time Leo could serve for aggravated assault, and I had a bad feeling that the prosecution would push for the maximum penalty. He was a public enemy. But I still thought the world needed his message.

"Hey, mom. I'm down the street. I need to talk to you." I spoke into my Cuff.

"What! What do you mean you're down the street. You called me from the hospital yesterday. Where are you, Evan? Is this a joke?" she asked.

"No joke. Like I said, I'm a few blocks away. I hopped on a flight. I need to talk to you. I'll be at the door in a few minutes." I disconnected before she could protest.

At the front door, tapping an acrylic nail against the frame, Connie said, "Evan, this can wait. You're injured. You should be resting."

"I'm fine and it really can't wait, Mom. The court will appoint an attorney on Monday. That, or I'll have to hire someone else unless you agree to represent Leo. Please, let me in."

"Honey. I'm happy you're here. I mean it, but I'm not pleased about the circumstances. Look at your poor face. I hardly recognize you. How can you care about that man? He's a monster."

I followed my mom to the kitchen.

"Where's dad?" I ask.

"Sleeping. He naps now. We're getting older, you know, Evan."

"Nah, Mom, you don't look a day over twenty-four.

You're a superhero of justice," I joked, deflecting one dart of micro-aggression, but bracing for the barrage.

"Yeah, well, a little nip and tuck does wonders on the outside, but on the inside, I'm tired. And this business with you and Leo exhausts me. I thought you had moved on with your life, a steady girlfriend, a job worthy of your talents. Candy and Tom say Jol is lovely. Honestly, I think they both were jealous of your new home and office. They said this Chaos Order business was over—that you had moved on from the garbage ideas that Cloe put into your head."

Coco burst in, strafing me like a hummingbird.

"Later, Coco," Connie shooed. My mother never had time for me when I was young. She was too busy and too posh to parent. In a way, Coco was my real mom.

Coco was going to feed me, hell or high water. She couldn't be brushed off that easily. Instead, she busied herself making espresso and heating some empanadas from the freezer. The smell of frying oil and the clatter of spoons was familiar and comforting.

The memory of the last time I was home with Cloe surfaced. During that visit, I hated everything my mother stood for and everything she was pushing on me—school, career, marriage to a girl she had chosen. My life choices had soured Connie against Cloe even more. It was unfair. Cloe had lived authenticity.

Since then, my respect for my mother had grown. Or at least my compassion for her had. Being in a high position at HERE helped me realize why she had been away from home so much and why she feared that I would never find stability. That kind of fear was knitted into the bones of corporate life, but a purpose and meaning was the anchor against her judgment. We were becoming equals.

"My association with Leo will be over, forever, I promise, if you do this one more thing for me. I will dedicate myself to my career and family, retirement funds, grandbabies, the whole package. Please, represent Leo. No matter what you think, I know he doesn't deserve to rot in jail. He was out of his mind when he attacked me, but it was just one of his episodes. His methods are unorthodox, but I believe that his brand of a wake-up call is one that many people need. Represent him, and I'll break ties with the Order altogether," I said.

"The world doesn't need Leo or his ideas. I also know that if he is in prison, it's less likely he'll be a part of your life, not more. However, I trust you'll do what you say. I'll take the case if this is what you really want."

That Connie would do the unthinkable for me eased the tension. She invited me to stay with her and Dad to convalesce, and shockingly, I said yes. I needed to show my gratitude. Jol supported my decision to take a week off to patch things up with my mother. She had her own fires to put out.

HERE's board of officers wanted me out of the public eye until the trial's outcome was known and they could mitigate the damage from the press. Journalists had spun Leo's assault in several directions, but many chose to villainize HERE. Images of blood, the ambulance, and Leo in handcuffs were all over the headlines—*Dangerous Game Ends in Injury and Arrest.*

I realized that mom hadn't changed. That she couldn't. It was too late for that. She still criticized me with every breath. Her compliments had barbs. But unlike before all this happened, I saw the puppet master holding the strings—her pain, her fear, and the expectations of her own parents.

"Evan, you're so weird, but at least you found a good-paying job." The next day it would be, "Evan, you're crazy. Thank god Jol has a head on her shoulders."

In the past, these backhanded comments would have piled on my chest like boulders until I couldn't stand it any more. The rage and confusion would be unbearable and drive me to leave in the night without a word. This time, I saw through the posturing to the hurt little girl she was. In a flash, all she had done to prove herself to the world was revealed—her powerful job, her desperation to accumulate great wealth, her need for accolades. These were armor. Still, the week at home was hard.

I had chosen her sister Cloe over her, just like her father and mother had chosen Cloe over her. Cloe, the piano prodigy, the dancer, the artist. Cloe had been pretty and feminine. Connie had been loud and bossy, a bully in school, a tomboy. Cloe had been the favorite because Connie's and Cloe's parents thought that masculine qualities in a girl were something to be hidden away.

My grandfather, Connie's father, had died of cancer before he could be witness to my mother's perfect L-SATS score or Cloe's rebellious defection into the punk scene.

Connie never felt acknowledged or seen, just like I had never felt acknowledged or seen at home. Frozen in amber, Connie was forever flawed, and Cloe was always perfect. It was a legacy of absurd emotion. One I would stop here and now. I didn't need to react to Connie. Nothing she said was even about me anyway.

Pretty gardens, sidewalk cafes, girls in flowered dresses, and the sunrises and sunsets of a California beach town—I saw these things for what they objectively were for the first time. The lenses of hurt fell from my eyes. Shame that Leo had ladled over me for my privilege fell away, too. Even my parents softened to each other. Now, I could sit with my father in the yard and have a beer without anxiety forcing me to fill the silence. By the time Connie and I boarded the plane back to San Francisco to build Leo's defense, she and I were on the same team.

33

THE TRIAL

Commotion from the protest was visible from across the city block of Civic Center Plaza. Through the corridor of squat, club-like trees, I strained to see who was there, but I couldn't make out what was going on. A whistle escaped me as the car pulled around to the courthouse at City Hall. Order members had mustered in the shadow of the pale blue and gold gilt dome.

"Leo still has his minions," I said to Jol, who rode in the backseat with me.

"So help me, Evan, I don't know what he's done to deserve anyone's loyalty, including yours."

I kissed the furrow out of her brow as I autopaid with my Cuff and stepped to the curb. Jol and I pushed through a small crowd of press and picketers. The trial was news, but not big news. Neither Leo's nor my notoriety were mainstream, but we were followed by a minority of art nerds.

Maureen, in a rainbow wig and clown-white on her face, held a spray-painted sign high above her head. It read, "Boy, my arms are tired." Others flashed equally Dadaist messages. I laughed even though it hurt my heart. Absurdity in the name of reality checks was the signature of the Order. Nothing was sacred. And if it was sacred, it was a target. Leo's remaining Freaks weren't on my side, despite the fact that I had done everything humanly possible to help them and their leader, but I was pretty sure they didn't hate me either. They just didn't trust me.

Inside, the courtroom atmosphere pressed down like the deep sea. This was the nexus of all the Order stood against—rules by force. Leo sat by the side of my mother at the defendant's desk. Their backs were turned to a packed gallery that included Freaks, the odd spectator, and journalists from the Chronicle, the Guardian, SFGate, and the SFWeekly.

An American flag hung flaccid from its pole. The walls were painted over with so many years of rusty-brown polyurethane the surface looked wavy. Kinky Lady Justice with her blindfold stood and watched, unseeing, in a haze of lemon furniture polish.

I had urged the district attorney to follow my lead and not pursue a criminal case. My suggestion was ignored. Too many witnesses. Too high profile. Leo was a hero to a rebel few and he was an enemy of the state—a nuisance, a terrorist, and a source of property damage and copy cats vandals. The Chaos Order threatened the established social order. This could not stand.

My face, now a gradient of green and yellow, had healed during the time it took to get Leo to trial. I looked less like a hideous zombie and more like an unripe pineapple. I paid Leo's bail in addition to the considerable extra expense for the monitoring service for his house arrest. Lydia's condo was on the record as his address. The loft had been empty for months.

I had asked around when Lydia disappeared, so I heard she was living with Sonia, but I had no contact information. She had changed her phone number and none of the Freaks would give me specifics. My mother finally persuaded me to hire a private investigator. The P.I. told me Lydia had become a sex worker and addict and tracked her down to her mother's house in Santa Cruz. I called the number in the investigators report. When Lydia's answered, her voice felt like home.

I asked Lydia if Leo could serve his house arrest at the loft. She refused at first, but texted the next day with the door lock code and gave her blessing. All the comforts Leo could need were taken care of. Cara and Herb dropped off ready-made meals for him every few days. No drugs though, he was tested daily. Really, he was living better than he ever had before. But to Leo, incarceration was worse than death, even if it was in a fancy condo.

"It's starting," Jol said as the door to the chambers opened.

"All rise. The honorable Judge Powers presiding," rang through the court. The crowd rose with a clatter. Powers' robes dragged like a black train behind him when he climbed the steps to his stand. He had a grim, jowly face. Mother hauled Leo to his feet to face the charges.

"He looks mean," I whispered to Jol as we retook our seats with the rest of the gallery.

"Good," was her curt response.

No matter how much I wanted Leo acquitted of his charges, Jol still wanted him punished. Who could blame her? He ruined her career, beat me up, crippled Lydia, and got her hooked on drugs. A real douche by most measures. Jol's righteous presence burned like coal at my side. That she was here at all meant the world to me.

"Leo Gault, you stand accused of aggravated assault. If you are found guilty, you face a maximum penalty of fifteen years imprisonment and the maximum fine of $20,000. Do you understand the charges against you?"

"Yes," Leo replied.

Mom whispered in his ear.

"Yes, your honor," he corrected.

"Ms. Bouchard, you may now give your opening statement."

"Thank you, your honor." She studied the jury and glanced into the gallery to catch my eye for a moment. Then she began, "Good people of the jury, what I'm about to say is not a presentation of the facts. For that, you must rely on the testimony of the witnesses and the admissions of evidence later in this trial. Think of my opening statement as a picture of the events that led us here today. For now, I want to tell you this young man beside me, Leo Gault, is a leader in his community. He is a respected artist and a talented and intelligent man. Mr. Gault also suffers from drug addiction and mental illness. His father is dead and his mother is incarcerated. Leo's life has been one of constant struggle. He is the product of abuse and a foster care system gone wrong. Before the incident, Leo was evicted from the home he shared with his girlfriend, Lydia Boleyn. Desperate and heartbroken, Mr. Gault turned to his community for shelter and solace. However, in a manic state, unable to buy the substances he relied on, and in madness and pain, Mr. Gault committed a crime of passion. My purpose today is not to disprove that Mr. Gault attacked Mr. Bouchard, but to prove that his actions were not premeditated and that the cane Mr. Gault carried was not a deadly weapon."

The prosecutor, Mr. Tor's statement was less kind. If I were honest with myself, both arguments seemed equally true. Leo was out of his mind, yes, and a victim of circumstance. But he was also a long-standing enemy of law and order. Today's proceeding was balanced on two simple things.

"The prosecution calls Evan Bouchard!"

I walked to the witness stand in answer to the clerk's booming call. The spectators rustled like children rolling in fall leaves. A few in the jury box noticed that my last name was the same as my mother's. Eager to share their observation, they whispered among themselves excitedly.

"Order!" demanded Judge Powers with one sharp gavel crack.

I did my best not to limp to the stand. The pain from

the injury to my knee still sent jolts of electric pain through my body, but I did not wear my brace today.

"Please raise your right hand."

"Do you swear to tell the truth, the whole truth, and nothing but the truth?"

"Yes, I do," I replied.

I scanned the room from my new, higher vantage. I hadn't noticed the Freaks in the gallery had on bright yellow name tags. Nothing too outrageous or noticeable. I puzzled over what they could be planning when Mr. Tor snapped me out of my observation.

"Mr. Bouchard?"

"Yes."

"Mr. Bouchard. Can you tell us what you were doing on the lawn of the Flood Mansion on May 10th, 2033?"

"I'll do my best. It may sound a little strange. I was leading an immersive narrative adventure... so... um... an augmented reality game in real life."

"Please explain an immersive narrative adventure in further detail."

"An INA is an adventure game set in a real-world environment with computer enhancements delivered through an extended reality headset. In HERE Urban Playground the IRL environment was a two-mile-square area of downtown San Francisco. The preplanned course led through the Financial District, Chinatown, and Nob Hill. HERE UP has riddles to solve, clues to find, and a choreographed chase. The environment is augmented by a new kind of holographic headset that overlaid maps, characters, clues, and more over the top of the physical terrain."

"And ads!" Leo blurted from the defendant's desk.

Murmuring rippled through the audience and the jury alike.

"Ms. Bouchard, please control your client," the judge ordered, "Mr. Tor, continue your questioning."

"Mr. Bouchard, can you describe your relationship to the defendant?"

"Yes. He is my best friend and my former business partner."

Leo shifted in his seat. His eyes darted to the doors. His movements were reminiscent of a caged dog.

"Why do you think Mr. Gault attacked you?"

"Objection! Hearsay. Mr. Bouchard's opinion on what provoked Mr. Gault is irrelevant!" my mother called out.

I looked over my shoulder at the judge. The knuckle of his first finger was pressed to lips. Owlish eyebrows knit together. He took his hand away from his mouth to speak.

"Sustained, Mr. Tor, please adjust your questioning."

"Was this game organized and financed by you?" Tor asked.

"No, I am a designer, coder, and marketer, the game itself was created by the HERE corporation as an application for their extended reality headset."

"Extended reality? Can you please explain what that is?"

"Objection. This was adequately explained."

"Mr. Tor, is there a reason why we need a further definition of XR technology? It is a concept that is generally understood and Mr. Bouchard has described his company's advancements in this regard."

"No, your honor, other than the jury may want to know more about the nature of the game."

"Sustained. We've covered the technology, Mr. Tor. Please stick to the events that transpired."

"Yes, your honor, I'll restate. Mr. Bouchard, can you continue with the events of that day from where you left off?"

"Yes. Ten of the actors hired for the game were waiting in ambush for the group of players I was leading."

"How many players were you leading?" Tor asked.

"Four. Five, including myself."

"Thank you. Please continue."

"The hired actors were dressed as Chinese gangsters and were seated inside cars parked at the Flood Mansion on Nob Hill. The role of these men was to try to intercept a prop briefcase from our group before they could make it to Grace Cathedral and the finale of the game. The briefcase was needed to achieve the main objective, which was to reach the center of the Labyrinth inside the church. The Triad members, I mean the actors, were supposed to get out of their cars and chase us. The main object of the game was fun and the actors were instructed to let us pass after a game of Red Rover. However, a van pulled up near to where I was standing. I didn't recognize the vehicle but I did recognize the Chaos Order's logo. A set of people dressed in yeti costumes got out. I didn't hire them. It crossed my mind that HERE could have added a twist to the game that I was unaware of, although I believed that was unlikely.

Most of these people dressed as yetis headed for the group of players on the hill, but one yeti, one who walked with a cane, came toward me. That was totally unexpected."

"Did you know who was in the costume?"

"I suspected, but I didn't know who it was until he took off his mask."

"Who came toward you in a yeti costume?"

"Leo."

"Leo who?"

"Leo Gault, the defendant."

"Why did you suspect it was Mr. Gault before he removed his mask?"

"His height and his movements"

"Mr. Gault is 5'7"; an average height, not unusual. Especially if the costume hid the individual inside. There must have been other reasons you thought the assailant was Mr. Gault."

"Objection! Leading the witness."

"Sustained. Please strike the last question from the record."

"Why did you think it was Leo?"

"Because I knew his girlfriend had kicked him out. I also knew that he thought I was having an affair with her, which I was not. But I was told that he was acting crazy; that he was paranoid and obsessed with sabotaging the game. That he was after me."

"Who told you this?"

"Cara Walters. Others in the Order told me this as well."

"So, you believed that Mr. Gault arrived at the Flood Mansion with the intent to harm you?"

"I didn't say that!"

"Objection! Your honor, please," Connie said.

"Sustained. Mr. Tor, you know better than that. I've warned you already," Judge Powers said.

"I apologize, your honor. That's all the questions I have for now."

Mr. Tor returned to his seat. My mother gave Leo an affectionate squeeze on the shoulder as she stood. I suspected her kindness was an act. That she had no real warm feeling for him. On the other hand, her gentle smile felt genuine. Maybe I was wrong. She approached the witness stand clasping the locket she wore around her neck.

"Mr. Bouchard, can you tell me who hired Mr. Gault's counsel and paid for his defense?"

"You know that I begged you to take the case, Mom. You're defending Leo for me."

"Objection!" Mr. Tor bellowed.

The room erupted. Judge Powers pounded the gavel for a good minute before the audience quieted down.

"Are we asking for a mistrial, Ms. Bouchard? I warned you in chambers that your relationship to this witness is not relevant in the testimony. I allowed you to represent Mr. Gault against my better judgment. Do not pull another stunt like that," Judge Powers turned his attention to the court reporter, "Strike the last question from the record."

"Let's try that again, shall we," Judge Powers concluded.

"Evan, can you please tell us what you recall about your physical engagement with Mr. Gault on the lawn of the Flood Mansion?"

"Of course. Well, Leo got out of the van. He was walking with a cane. He had a mask on, so I wasn't 100% sure it was Leo at first, but I was fairly sure. He hit my knee with a cane, knocked me down, sat on my chest, then he punched my jaw with his fist. I got the air knocked out of me. We wrestled and fought on the ground. When I heard sirens, I told him to run."

"You told him to run. Why?"

"He's my friend. I knew he wasn't in his right mind. I could tell what was going on with him was a lot worse than just a bad breakup. Leo wasn't himself. He was practically foaming at the mouth. I didn't want him to get caught. I didn't think he'd do well in jail in the state he was in."

"So you were protecting your friend even though he attacked you?"

"Yes," I answered.

Leo's testimony wasn't mandatory. In many cases, having the accused speak would be a disadvantage. However, my mother had told me that she felt that Leo's manic state would illustrate that he was incapable of premeditating what he wanted for lunch, much less an attack on me. It was a risky move. He was uncontrollable and therefore unpredictable.

To my mother, if Leo got the maximum penalty, it

would not be a tragedy. But she would do her utmost to get the best outcome for Leo. She was a high-principled professional. However, the unusual circumstances allowed her to take some chances. Personally, I doubted Leo would make it through the swearing-in without adding contempt to his list of charges.

"Mr. Gault, what were your plans for the day on May 10th?"

"To destroy HERE! Those exploitative fuckers are trying to put chips in our heads. Control the artists. Program us. Manipulate us to do their dirty work. Influence the masses."

Judge Powers' gavel sounded like a rifle.

"Ms. Bouchard, control your client! Profanity is not allowed in my courtroom."

"My apologies, your honor. Leo, please answer the questions without swearing. I know following the rules goes against what you believe in, but for a fair trial, you must calm down."

"Sure, Connie. Anything for you," Leo said.

Leo winked at my mother. She smiled despite herself. He was so completely inappropriate.

"Like I was saying, HERE is exploiting the arts community. They tried to hire me as a frontman. They failed, but those corporate fu—phonies ruined my life. HERE wants advertisements to stream across your every waking moment. A slave class of cyborgs. They are probably working on ads in your dreams too."

"Objection. Hearsay," Mr. Tor finally spoke up.

"Sustained," Judge Powers said without any enthusiasm.

"Mr. Gault. You were asked what your plans were on May 10th, not why you are opposed to HERE's products."

"That HERE wants to change the world for the worse seems relevant to me. I planned to sabotage the HERE Urban Playground game launch and to film the outcome."

"So, your intention was not to assault Mr. Bouchard?"

"No. It wasn't. I saw him. He ruined everything. He's a sellout. I'm homeless because of him. He crippled my girlfriend then he fucked her."

Crack! The gavel came down again.

"Mr. Gault. If I have to warn you one more time, you will be held in contempt of court."

"Yes, your honor. I have poor impulse control. I will try harder."

The judge and prosecutor were playing right into the hands of Leo and my mom. Leo's diatribe seemed like a manic monologue, but it was chock full of hidden messages—that he hadn't planned to assault me, that he had poor impulse control, that passion drove his actions, that he *lost his mind*. It was a brilliant performance. What Leo had planned and had not planned would forever be his knowledge alone.

The final gloss of varnish on the portrait my mother had commissioned and Leo had painted was the cane. True or not, she proved through witness testimony and evidence admission that Leo had been using the cane because it had a secret Go-Pro camera hidden in the handle. She showed that he had recorded hours of undercover footage with the same hidden camera. In California, aggravated assault had to be committed with a deadly weapon. A cane was considered deadly only if it was weighted or altered to be an actual weapon. Leo's was modified, yes. But it was a standard medical-variety walking stick with a camera installed in the tip. Even I wondered if Leo had ever really planned to hit me with it.

After lunch, the arresting officer was called to the stand. Leo's state of mind and his multiple charges of civil disobedience, trespassing, and vandalism were admitted. By 4 pm, the evidence of the cane and camera, Leo's bloody yeti costume, and photos of my injuries had also been presented and reviewed.

Pride lifted my chest and brought tears to my eyes when my mother delivered her final argument. On that day, I lost all the rebellious hostility I held against her. She had come through for me without question.

"As you have heard, Leo Gault is a very disturbed young man with strong opinions about how things should run. These opinions may or may not be shared by you, men and women of the Jury, but the opinions on how society should operate are not on trial here today. What we are deciding on is if Leo Gault, in his right mind, planned to attack my son with a deadly weapon on the day of May 10th, 2033. I am not trying to prove the attack didn't take place. What I aim to show is that Leo Gault, in a flight of mania, diverged from his plan to disrupt the inaugural game launch of HERE Urban Playground and film the players to create anti-HERE propaganda. In a fit of rage, he turned away from the group targeted for a playful intervention to the solitary Evan Bouchard. If I have succeeded in proving that the altercation between these two young men was not a premeditated plan to cause harm or death, then you must find the defendant *not guilty* for the charge of aggravated assault. I leave that decision for your capable and intelligent voices united as one to decide."

After the statements, the judge explained to the jury that they must make their decision based only on the facts presented and not their feelings. The adjournment lasted less than an hour.

"Leo Gault, please stand for the verdict," Judge Powers commanded. The verdict was read.

"Not Guilty."

Leo timed his signal to Freaks perfectly. As he was escorted out of the courtroom, he raised his hand. The Price Is Right regalia that had been hidden under chairs and in backpacks was displayed in joyous celebration. Leo knew exactly where the line was at all times. When the trial was concluded, and Judge Powers had left the courtroom, and contempt was no longer a threat, music rose from hidden speakers and the Freaks roared, "Leo Gault, come on down!" in unison. The press ate it up with a spoon.

34

FOOL ON A HILL

Lydia

When we had arrived with our bags in the Santa Cruz mountains, Mom cooed and fawned over my exotic lover. While she reveled in Sonia's beauty and me being alive, I refamiliarized myself with the house. An A-frame, but no cabin, Mom's house was a palace. The ceilings peaked at three stories. The windowed walls brought the redwoods and Zen rock gardens into the beautifully furnished greatroom. It felt unreal, almost virtual here. Fine art that my mother had claimed in a string of divorces from tech billionaires made star appearances in high traffic areas. She had a real Rothko above the fireplace.

Sonia and I claimed my little art shack outside the

main house for our stay. I had built the cottage when I was sixteen, mainly to escape my mother. It had a deck and a working kitchen. To be fair, Rudy, her fourth and only poor husband, helped with the construction, but I built a lot of it myself. After an early dinner, I took Sonia to my teen sanctuary.

Daylight dipped below the tops of the towering trees. The slanting rays found an occasional straight shot into our private sanctum. The warmth of the sun released a pine incense that enveloped us. In the Santa Cruz mountain and in the arms of the woman I loved, the lightness of girlhood returned. This didn't feel like weakness; it felt like reclaimed power. A wildness. Sole to sole, Sonia and I played footsies with our bare feet. She laid on her back and pushed my paralyzed legs up and down. Her hair, a bucket of new pennies, spilled on the sun-warmed wooden planks of the deck. We had changed into loose-fitting cotton dresses washed so soft and transparent, we were as good as nude.

The smell of the hot land was a catalyst for earlier memories. As a girl, I ran through these woods. Banana slugs dabbed on the ground like spoonfuls of bright lemon curd, both delightful and disgusting. Bird calls. Gnats. Grasshoppers that appeared and disappeared like magic.

I squeezed lemons from a garden tree into a plump-bellied pitcher and mixed the juice with honey, well water, and ice. Sonia and I sipped the tart results through striped paper straws. Billie Holiday poured her throaty longing and melancholy out through the crackling ruts and grooves from an old phonograph. I dwelled in my thoughts for long, lazy moments.

The phone rang.

"It's Evan," I said to Sonia.

"Well, get it before it goes to messages."

"Evan?" I answered.

"Lydia, Leo got probation for two years and a $2500 fine. No prison time. It's not aggravated assault. No premeditation. No deadly weapon. It's what we hoped for. I know you were on the fence about what should happen to him, but this is great."

"Not guilty," I mouthed to Sonia.

I finished up the call with Evan. He was on the hunt to find a new place for Leo to live. He had a few good leads. My loft would be empty again in a week, or two at the most. Evan said he would let me know as soon as the details were final.

"Do you want to go back to the city when Leo moves out?" Sonia asked when I told her Evan's plan.

"God, I don't know. It's easier to stay clean when we're away from all the grit and stress. But even here, I think about shooting up every day. There's no escape from that. I don't know, Sonia. What do you want to do?" I asked, not knowing which side of the argument I wanted to take.

"Back in the city, what did we have? Bad habits. A love triangle with a psycho cult leader," Sonia said. She laughed and continued. "Mmm. You know what? We can't just retire and live off the grid for the rest of our lives. We're too young for that. I'm already getting bored."

Sonia's loving gaze was reassuring.

35

EXIT INTERVIEW

Evan

Freedom won disappeared as soon as I stepped foot on the HERE campus. Uncertainty crashed over me in an avalanche of cold eyes and silent lips. I didn't know what my colleagues were thinking, but I did know that years of collective work had been destroyed on the lawn of the Flood Mansion. True, I had warned HERE's board that courting an artist like Leo was a deal forged in hell, but only a few people knew that I had fought that unholy union. Most of the employees at HERE thought Leo and I were a package deal.

Jol had called me daily with updates on what was happening in the marketing department while I was recovering at my mom's. She told me that the launch of the HEREset would be shifted to conventional campaigns —ads, press outreach, social media, and virtual launch events.

I swung by my office, expecting to find a locked door. But no, everything inside was cared for as if I had never left—no dead plants; my personal things had been dusted but untouched. My headset sat waiting for me. I hadn't wore it since the attack. I triggered the HERE virtual home screen with a blink and groaned under the weight of a thousand pending messages. Notifications rang endlessly like a doorbell gone haywire.

The emails and messages would have to wait. I had ten minutes to get to the main conference room; the same room where I raised billions in capital and planned our revolutionary game launch. Now, I expected my walking papers.

A lightness of being overcame me—a new bearing I had tired on when I finally stopped blaming my mother for my trauma. She had been the root of my fear. Now, no one had dominion over me.

Through the window, I saw Jol in profile. Her familiar beauty sent tingles of warmth across my face and chest. She sat at the conference table, sipping from a paper cup, while she chatted with our CEO, Jessica and Tobey, her boss, the CMO. Harry, the head of Legal, sat across the table, observing. I nodded to activate the door with my HEREset and it slid open.

"Hey, Evan! "Welcome home. How's your mom?" Jessica said.

Tobey simmered at me like a caldron.

"Jol, Jessica, Tobey. Hello! Hi, Harry." I addressed the room in a friendly tone that was as tight as a drum around the edges. "My mother's well. Thank you for asking," I said.

When I sat, Jol's hand clasped mine under the table in reassurance.

"So, Evan, first I want to apologize. What happened was completely our fault. As you know, HERE is covering all of your medical expenses and will continue to do so. Consider any future therapy, physical or emotional, paid for. I know, knees are the worst injury to recover from. I blew mine out training for the Boston Marathon." Jessica never missed an opportunity to mention her passion for running. Harry and Tobey grunted in sympathy or annoyance, hard to say which.

She continued. "What we asked you and Jol to do was misguided. Marketing can be cutthroat, but there's no justification for targeted exploitation. It was manipulative to try to steal an audience from the Order and trick the arts and tech community. We had no right to commodify sincere protest and artistic expression. Right, Tobey?"

Tobey was Jol's boss. I never got to know him well in the year I had worked for HERE. Whenever I was in a meeting with him, he was too busy railroading everyone in the room to his point of view. Jol held her own with Tobey, but barely. Today, he was uncharacteristically sullen.

"Yes, what we did was wrong. People's lives aren't marketing assets. I'm sorry, Evan," Tobey said like a robot.

Jessica sat back in her chair listening to the script she

orchestrated delivered through another's mouth. Tobey's body language said he wasn't sorry at all. Regardless, I had expected to be the scapegoat. Tobey's humble pie was an unforeseen treat.

Jessica rested her elbow on the table and tented her fingers. "Evan, Jol. We are dissolving Situational Design. Jol, as you know, this means you will be absorbed back into marketing. You've been doing a bang-up job back there already. You'll keep your directorship and your salary. Tobey is writing a new job description for you, but you'll have input on your responsibilities. Evan, I'm moving you to development. As you know, your job was created for the release of HERE UP and the HEREset. The job was a hybrid straddling marketing and dev. You're a visionary for the coding and terrain departments, so you'll be a director in that capacity."

"Thank you, Jessica. That's very generous of you. But I have to ask, what if I don't want to stay? I joined HERE because I was interested in situational design and extended reality narrative, and it sounds like that's gone. Corporate management may not be for me."

Tobey stood and started to pace. Jessica motioned for him to retake his seat.

"It's your due diligence to ask that question, Evan. I would have been disappointed if you didn't explore all of your options. We are prepared to offer you a sizable severance, if you choose to leave," Jessica said.

Jol finally spoke. "I'd like to know what my severance might be too."

Larry's deep voice interrupted the moment of silence

Jol's unexpected request caused. "You'll both have to sign a revised non-compete and non-disclosure agree—" Jessica held up her hand.

"The board has agreed on an offer. We have prepared a figure for both of you," Jessica said.

She rolled a diamond-tipped pen across the desk toward a small pad of paper, wrote one long number, folded it, wrote another. She slid the offers to Jol and me. I watched Jol lean back in her seat and open the note like a poker hand. I did the same.

The agreement that I made with my mother nagged at me. I promised her that I would prioritize my career and family if she agreed to represent Leo. To her, the choice would be obvious—take the job in development. However, the generous severance could be put toward a new future that met my intrinsic goals and gave my life meaning. To quit would be a betrayal to her. To continue to work for HERE would be a betrayal to myself.

"I'll take it," we said in unison.

Jol beamed at me like we were eloping. She surprised me once again.

36

THE OCTAGON

Lydia

That Evan decided to leave HERE didn't surprise me. But when I learned that Jol decided to quit too, that came as a huge shock. They weren't forced out. On the contrary. Sonia thought they were insane to refuse nearly a million dollars annually, each! But I understood. Evan never wanted to conform in the first place. An office job for the sake of work and a salary was meaningless to him. That he didn't want to be a part of someone else's machine drove Evan's life, and mine, and Leo's. Jol... well, Jol loved Evan and that was enough.

My place was haunted. After Leo's house arrest was complete, Herb and Cara took him away to their farm in

Marin. Regardless, Leo's presence lingered, even when all traces had been diligently wiped away. Despite the ghost, it was good to be home among the dust motes.

Cara's kindness overwhelmed me. I found my kitchen freezer loaded with ready-made casseroles and frozen smoothies. Beyond the windowed wall, Sonia unloaded our bags from an Uber sedan. She looked pretty, shining as she does in the late morning sun. Sonia strained under the weight of our two giant backpacks. She passed by me and dumped our luggage on the bed.

Wind chimes rang in the faint bay breeze out the open front door. On top of the key table was a handmade paper envelope. Mysteriously pretty. No stamp. I sliced it open. Real, pressed violets and bits of silver confetti spiraled to the floor as I yanked free the tightly packed invitation.

"Hey, look, Herb and Cara are getting married," I said.

"That's no surprise," Sonia said. "A match made in Middle-Earth. We're not going to the wedding though? I mean, I don't have to tell you, Leo lives at Cara's and Herb's now," she said.

"I know, but it seems harmless. I mean, it's the Marin Hills. Cara's place must be a fairyland, knowing her. And the food! You know it's going to be amazing. It says hot tubbing with friends. It's an overnight," I waved the invite over my head like a winning lottery ticket. "Everyone will be there."

"Yeah—our enemies included," Sonia said.

"Come on, it's a sleepover. Should we really miss out because of stupid Leo? I need this. We need this."

"Good point. I do hate wasting energy avoiding someone. I've done *that* before and it's an awful way to live. You're right, why should we miss out? But, honey, don't decide yet. We just got back. Give it time to breathe. Let's unpack first, at least," Sonia said wisely.

Evan wanted to see us as soon as possible now that we were back in the city. He even offered to come to the loft to help us move back in, but I insisted on meeting him at Rain Dogs. The remnants of the Chaos Order, or whatever they called themselves now, were headquartered in Evan's building. I was surprised that the Order welcomed Evan as a leader, but I would have done the same. Leo had become a liability and a drain on the group.

On the way to Rain Dogs, Sonia and I stopped to have a real club-kid breakfast. Irish back bacon, greasy hash browns topped with poached eggs and hollandaise sauce for me. Tofu scramble for Sonia. And all of it chased down with thick cups of Philz coffee slicked with real cream. Sonia may have preferred our Santa Cruz quinoa and organic super-greens diet of the last two months, but this bacon was my idea of heaven.

I missed the old comic book store terribly—it was the origin of everything, my home away from home before weakness and pride cast us in three directions. Maybe the magic of our recondite family was still held there like an insect in amber. I'm sure Evan felt the magic returning now that the oppression of Leo had been lifted.

I tried to picture Jol chillin' out with a beer on Evan's shambled-down dumpster sofa or eating dinner in Evan's tiny flat. Some new executive lived in the Edwardian mansion that had been their home. But no matter how hard I tried, nothing came to me. That canvas stayed blank.

"Evan's been messaging me. He wants us to work for him. He'll pay us salaries. The money is better than what we made at Lusty's," I said to Sonia. She agreed to see what Evan and Jol had to offer.

When Sonia and I crossed the threshold of the old Rain Dogs, I was thunderstruck. Nothing was upcycled, overstuffed, or even soft here. The shop had been transformed into a sleek and colorful place. Chairs were molded in sunflower yellow plastic, and the desks were slick runways of seafoam tinted glass. Brand new vMacs dotted the continuous countertop. Did Evan and Jol have a staff now? Who were these workstations for?

Clearly, Evan and Jol had left HERE with a tidy severance. I guess remodeling the grungy bookstore was a small expense for them. Jol's style seamlessly blended with the new surroundings. She wore an all-white skirt-suit paired with puffy hoop earrings so huge they could keep her afloat at sea. Her colorful, vintage bakelite bangles rattled together as she rushed to the door to welcome us in.

Evan stepped out of the old break room when he heard the commotion of our arrival. Welcomes and hugs flew. So much about him had changed. Long gone was the oily-haired, hoodie-shrouded comic book geek. This Evan seemed to step out of the society pages in his summer wool slacks, a soft linen shirt, and Burberry loafers. When he spoke, the spell was broken. He still had his playful, boyish mannerisms. I missed him.

"So, are you going to the wedding?" I asked to break the ice.

"Yes. Are you and Sonia coming?" Evan answered with a gentle smile.

"Yes, we are." I surprised myself with the sudden certainty of my answer.

"Good! I told you Jol. Lydia is stronger than anyone I know," Evan said.

"You are a powerful woman," Jol said. She leaned in to wrap her arms around me and give me a quick kiss on the top of my head. When she rejoined Evan, they looked perfect together. I pushed away a covetous thought. Why jealousy bubbled up, I didn't know. I loved my beautiful Sonia. She was my hero. And I was happy for Evan and Jol.

"So, what do you think of the remodel?" Evan asked, sweeping his hand across the new mid-century space.

"We call ourselves the Octagon now," Jol interjected.

"Yeah! The sign just got delivered. You know, it's the type that hangs over the street," Evan said, excited. "Come look, it's in the break room.

I almost didn't want to see the change to my old home away from home. The memory of it was an imaginary place in my mind's eye where I'd retreat to when things got really bad. Dismayed, I realized my wheelchair would not fit through the narrow Victorian door. My cheeks reddened with embarrassment. I could see that Evan shared my mortification.

"Oh, Lydia, I'm so sorry. I didn't consider the door's width. I tried so hard to keep this one spot the same, I didn't even think! I'll get contractors in tomorrow morning to make the whole place 100% accessible," Evan said.

Evan was having a deer-in-the-headlights moment, but Jol stepped up.

"Here, honey, take my hand. Sonia, help me move her." Jol said. Having two absolutely stunning women support me on either side swept away any shame. I was a regal queen. I smiled at Evan as they set me down gently in Leo's old favorite armchair.

"Look, I didn't change a thing! I made a deal with Jol, she could do anything she wanted with the main space as long as I could keep this room as-is," Evan said with pride, his anxiety about the narrow door evaporated.

Tears welled in my eyes. Here was the sofa I slept on so many times. The shitty mini-fridge covered in stickers. The Kit-Kat Klock I bought for Evan. Essentially, this was a fossil set in time.

"I hate it," Jol said with a huge laugh. "But I also totally get it. This is ground zero. The beginning of everything."

"Oh, and look, here's the new sign." Evan slid a laser-etched glass rectangle out of a cardboard sleeve. Thick and blue, it was the kind of tech glass that glowed iridescent from within. The word Octagon seemed to float both inside and outside of its boundaries.

"I love it," I said.

"Me too," Sonia said.

"So, tell me. What are we doing with the Order?" I asked.

"Let's go sit in the front office to talk about that. We wouldn't want to make Jol uncomfortable," Evan said with a wink.

"I agree. This room is not the place for business," Jol said with mild distaste.

She asked for Sonja's help to move me as if it were nothing. I wondered if she had cared for someone like me before. Back in my wheelchair, I joined Sonia, Evan, and Jol in a circle in the middle of the primary-colored space. To me, it looked like a kindergarten room set up for story hour.

Evan started. It felt like a presentation. A lot had changed about him.

"Here's the deal. We are not going to try to claim the Chaos Order. Leo started that. It will still exist. And I'm happy to leave the legacy of the Order to the more extreme radicals. About a quarter of the originals still identify with Leo's mission and stay in touch with him or live on Cara's and Herb's farm. Instead, I hope the four of us will form a new organization that enriches the spirit of boundless possibility. We will create theatrical happenings to get our message across. No violence. No destruction of property. No trespassing. Our goal is to be a hundred percent inclusive. Metamodern. Irony and sincerity combine to reveal the absurdity of life and society. Not to destroy anything, just to lighten the mood.

Our events may seem watered down compared to what came before, but if they want destructive anarchy, let them follow the path that Leo laid down independent of us," Evan said.

I liked the concept. For the movement to mean anything, and to grow, it would take a lot of shaping and a lot of work.

"It is a paradox, for sure," I said. "How to form an organization against organizations? Leaderless and followerless. I mean, how do you make money on something that's anti-consumerist? How do you reveal the flaws by showcasing the system that perpetuates flaws?"

The circle nodded, but I was on a roll. "And permits? How do you get permits for disruption? It will take hard work to figure this all out. It will take connections too."

"Evan was completely right when he said you would make a perfect leader, Lydia," Jol said. I could tell she was impressed and a little surprised. A jolt of energy surged through my body.

"Well, let's get started then," I said.

"Exactly! Action is the name of the game," Evan said, "I want to plan a major disruption. An old-school culture jam. Something based on Cacophony history. We'll see what goes right and what goes wrong, and then adjust. Jol and I have enough runway from our severance to get us through the start up. Eventually, we will need to monetize. But for now, let's do something crazy! Sky's the limit!"

§

THE CORE MEMBERS of the Octagon gathered at Embarcadero Plaza long before the parade was scheduled to start. *Will anyone show,* I wondered. Evan held a megaphone at his side. That was Leo's prop of choice, and it was damn sexy in Evan's hand.

My grey granny wig itched. I looked down at my wheelchair turned rocking chair. A giant teacup rested in my lap. The wonderfully Dadaist concoctions had been whipped up by a group of warehouse artists in Emeryville. Sonia was a chubby pink teapot on a doily, her sexuality hidden away. We were a matching set. She tipped her spout to me in a dainty curtsy. I felt more deeply in love with her every day.

"Here comes the band!" Jol said. She looked intimidating in camel colored jodhpurs and a chocolate-brown top hat.

"I love a parade," Evan sang.

A tuba and its player emerged from the BART station followed by a majorette, batons whirling like propellers. The buzz of kazoos filled the air. My fear of a mass no-show was completely unfounded. Hundreds of people had been involved in planning the event. Outrageous floats and art cars had been built. Of course, everyone would be here. More and more Octagon members, who now called themselves Eights, arrive in costumes from store-bought to extravagantly homemade. Clowns, Dalmatians, stilt walkers, Mummenschanz, robots, Satan and his entourage of hellish hosts. I hugged myself in anticipation. At 11 am, Evan, as the anonymous master of ceremonies, had the crowd raise their right hands and recite the semi-ancient credo of Bishop Joey.

I pledge allegiance to the illusion, and to the pyramid scheme for which it stands. One species, in denial, with error and excess, by all.

We didn't have to wait long. A cheer rose as the floats came into view from around the ferry building—a giant chicken, a neon squid, and Santa's sleigh complete with reindeer. Once assembled, the procession began. Like a Borg ship, the Eights assimilated innocent passersby through handing out party blowers, whistles, birthday hats, and cryptic flyers promising everlasting life or telepathic powers to those who joined in the procession.

"Happy unbirthday to you," we danced and sang.

A vague deja vu could be seen in the eyes of the old men playing chess on the sidewalk. One called out, "That's the way he would have wanted it!"

Three-hundred or four-hundred strong, through the Financial District, we moved in a disorganized jumble. The matching band played The Alphabet Song and we shouted along, "A. B. C. D. E. F. G." Next up, Jaunte Alouette. I loved Jaunte Alouette.

Leo's events had been angry revenge for the marginalized. His art felt more like attacks. Punishment for those who flocked together in the safety of convention. This was different—a joyful parade that included anyone who dared step over the lines of the status quo by simply stepping off the sidewalk and into the flow of chaos; it didn't matter if it was for a day or for a lifetime. All were invited.

"Join us. Join us. Join the parade," we yelled to the curious workers who poked their heads out windows or tentatively stepped out of the front doors of their office buildings.

"If you don't want to have fun, quit gawking, and get back to work!" We scolded playfully.

At Washington Square, the Eights sat in each other's laps or plopped down on any available surface, including in the middle of the street. Hot dogs and lemonade were served courtesy of Evan and Jol. Sunburned and happy, I ate, enjoying every bite. The lemonade was from the gods. Fool and queen. Inside man, and part of the tide. It all felt good.

Older journalists understood this was history repeating itself. That it was no accident. Leo's admiration for the Suicide Club and Cacophony Society was the catalyst for everything he had done, and by extension, what the Octagon did. Leo may have shed fear, but he hadn't been able to shake anger, and that's where it had all gone wrong. At least, in my opinion. The morning after the parade, the Chronicle's cover story read:

THIS PAST WEEKEND, *the underground arts community, the Octagon, revived a long-lost San Francisco tradition formerly hosted by the Church of the Last Laugh. The St. Stupid's Day Parade, now renamed The Spud Boy Parade, was held on September 1st.*

Although the name and date of the parade have changed, many of the traditions of the original event are alive and well. Evan Bouchard, founder of the Octagon, and grand marshal had revelers recite the pledge of Bishop Joey at the Embarcadero, in honor of the former maker of mischief.

The parade was a brilliant display of public silliness and included floats, wild and original costumes, flash mob choreography, and a hosted lunch served picnic style. In honor of its St. Stupid's Day Parade inspiration, the Stations of Stupid were observed, including the Tomb of Stupid, the Statue of the Bare Butt Mechanic, the Sunken Plaza of Slack, the Banker's Heart, and the Station of the End.

Octagon leaders claim there is much more to come. Expect upcoming events that are completely new and innovative, others, tributes to the original Cacophony Society, Billboard Liberation Front, Survival Research Labs, Cyclocide, and its ilk. To sign up for the Octagon newsletter and receive a schedule of secret and public events, visit the Octagon in person at 1800 Church Street. Electronic inquiries will be ignored. Request for membership must be filed in person.

SET ON SIMMER, Evan, Jol, Sonia and I bubbled with new ideas. We circled the yellow chairs each day. Our mission was to allow people to manifest their dreams in creative ways that could be shared publicly. We were in the business of revealing hidden possibilities and new ways of thinking—to let go of the reins and make the city a playground of free expression again. Our work seeped through the boundaries of experience and into the creative works of others. Worthy of a cover story, yes, but more than that, the parade had a positive effect. The mess I had made of my life before was selfish in comparison. I had passion and purpose now.

37

WEDDING

Sonia sprawled naked on Command Central, our name for the adjustable bed in the middle of my living room, now our home office. A vision from an erotic fairytale laid bare, she kicked at the clutter of outfits I had thrown at her feet. Unfettered by my disability, I transferred from the chair to the bed in one easy swing. Stripping as a profession had done wonders for my strength. I didn't regret my time at Lusty's for a minute. What would be the use in that? It had granted me easy comfort with my body.

"I love you, Baby," I said.

"Love you too."

I nuzzled into her side. Curls of wild red hair licked up to her navel.

"You should start getting ready. Jol and Evan will be here in about an hour.

"Yeah, I'm not frettin' it."

I lied. I had been picturing what I would wear and how I would seem to Leo for weeks. I wanted to appear confident, successful, beautiful, tough, and unobtainable. Getting over Leo entirely took top billing in the theater of my mind, and that was the problem. I was self-aware enough to realize that wanting to seem unfazed by Leo meant that I would most definitely be fazed by him.

"I think I'm going with a butch look. You know, for power," I said.

"You'd be herculean in pink bows. But, yes. We need armor. You and I."

I kissed her. I was absolved by her. I didn't have to confess that I was looking for something from Leo, some resolution or atonement; she would have accepted my thoughts as natural regardless of whether they were spoken aloud or not.

Evan rented the latest Tesla for our Marin weekend. I hadn't been over the Golden Gate Bridge since before the accident. As we threaded under the eternal spires and swooping cables, I traced the line of the seawall along the base of the city, looking for the place where Leo had rescued me from the waves, nearly two years ago.

If I could, would I undo that night? If it had never happened, would I be with my beautiful Sonia? She, stunning in her soft, sunset dress, looking out to sea. Would there be a wheelchair folded up behind my seat? Would I even know Jol? Would Evan be the man he is today? Or would he be an unsure boy hiding among his comic books and cowering in the shadow of his family?

Past the colorful houseboat community of the

Sausalito salt marshes and up the rolling hills of the north we climbed. The sky was a deep, vivid blue, filled with puffy tufts. Just past the Skywalker Ranch, we pulled into a dirt lot canopied by dusty Coulter pines. Across forested acres, weathered wooden structures from barns, to cottages, to greenhouses dotted Cara's farm. Permaculture poked through every nook. Stone fruit trees by every porch. Beanstalks grew up walls. Corn sprouted in irregular patches. And all varieties of lettuce skirted the buildings like green tutus. I even saw a row of banana trees in the shade of more pines.

"Come on. Don't sit there gawking. Let's go see the bride and groom." Sonia said.

She helped me into my chair and wheeled me over the ruts and holes in the mudpack lot. It felt like holding hands.

Cara handed out cabin assignments and informed the guests that the refrigerators were fully stocked with beer and food.

"Help yourselves to anything," she said cheerfully. "While you're here, this is your home."

Evan, Jol, and Sonia backtracked to the car to get the bags and get settled in our assigned cottage. I excused myself from the task and resolved to find a spot for us on the grass for the ceremony. My wheels kicked up a symphony of green, earthy smells on the winding path that led to the mown meadow. In the shade next to a string trio, Herb's bouncer and biker friends had set up camp. They waved, smiled, and beckoned me over.

I'm by the wedding arch with Herb's crew. Can't miss us.

Just look for the big guys, I texted Sonia. She texted back, *See you in twenty. Unpacking. The cottage is UwU!*

I looked up. I couldn't help myself. Leo's presence came over me like a storm cloud. He interrupted the atmosphere. Dark. Cold. A rope attached to my heart and pulled with black, barbed needles. The confidence I had hoped for did not come. Instead, I felt exposed, vulnerable, ridiculous in my platform boots, and bowler hat. I had dressed for him, to show him something. But what? My independence? My attractiveness? My obsession?

Why, I asked myself, *why does he make me feel this way?*

Leo smiled his dead smile and raised his glass. Excusing himself from his crowd of adorers, he strode across the open lawn.

Please, Sonia, appear. Please, please, Sonia, appear, I thought frantically.

"Hey," he said. "It's been a while." His words were smooth and easy.

What should I do, make small talk, or say what's on my mind?

"I trusted you, Leo. Why did you do this to me," is what came out of my mouth.

Why can't I walk? Why did you abandon me? Why did you assault me? Did you use us for your own gain? Did you lose control? Or was it all part of some master plan? I thought, but I held back my rant.

"Yes—" he said. "Well, I saw something in you and I saw something in Evan. The seeds of greatness. That's all that really matters, at least to me. Fulfilling one potential.

Not world peace, or love, or kindness. But survival of the creative. The ones who have something to add to the corpus of unique human expression. Those who see beyond their simple needs and the stupidity of the masses. I only introduced chaos into the world to make sure people like you, and Evan, and maybe some of these others reach their potential." He swept his hand like sowing seeds across the farm. "Ultimately, I made you a leader. I made you free. I made you better."

"Free? But I'm crippled! A junkie and a prostitute. Pain is what you made! You made me hate you. That's not better!"

Those in earshot moved away to give us privacy. Strangers might have intervened, but everyone here knew our story. Most did, anyway. Herb's guys honored the need for this conversation to happen.

"What did you want from me, Lydia? A white picket fence? Two and a half kids? Is that what you had in mind? You are a masterpiece the way you are now. Evan too. Without me, you would have ended up simpering scared nothings, doomed to live and die without making a mark," Leo said.

"Would normal have been so bad? Married with kids. Evan, running his comic book shop. Would that be a tragedy?"

"It would be boring. So, yes, a tragedy. The greatest of tragedies. You would have been less than a blip. More insignificant than we already are. Like you never existed. But not all lives need to be meaningless, though most are. That parade you and Evan pulled off, who can say how many people you inspired? What the chain reaction will be? That creative spark! Truth! That's all that matters. And I expect much more from you in the future."

"What about you, Leo? What happened to you?"

"Me? I got lost for a while. It's a side effect. It happens. But insanity can serve a purpose too. Now, I live here in this commune among a lot of people. Some have potential like you. Here, I can be the catalyst for the right minds. If I ended up in prison, it wouldn't have mattered. There are great minds in prison too. The incarcerated don't follow the rules. Fertile ground. I must admit, this farm is more comfortable than a cell," he laughed and looked around the lawn at the colorful people. "You, me, us, we shape a new culture. I'm here with a whole new batch of clay to work with. Who knows what will come of it?"

"But what about me, Leo, was I just clay? What do I do now?" I didn't try to hide the tears that rolled down my cheeks.

"Remove the rest of your fear. It is a limitation. It puts on the brakes. Your attachment to me is still strong. Clear it away. It's useless. You need to notice when you are being small and reactionary. Like now. It's fine. Just see it and let it go. You have the potential to see the infinite. Not everyone does. You are one of the special ones."

"God, Leo, what does that all mean? You sound like a goddamn, fucked up guru. After all we've been through, how can I take advice from you?"

"Forget the messenger and see the truth of the message. Listen carefully, I'm going to tell you exactly what to do to take the last step. Most people don't get an offer like that."

Leo's cryptic map etched itself into my brain. He walked away. I didn't notice. When Sonia finally found me. She said I looked like I had seen a ghost. In a way, I had.

38

ZONE TRIP

Evan

I understood why this was called the loneliest road in America. All scrub and sky and beautiful emptiness. The air buzzed. Things scurried. Millions of years ago, I'm sure this place looked exactly as it does now.

Lydia smiled at me from the open door of the rented bus. She watched as I unfolded her wheelchair and set it in the dust.

"This isn't it, but we're close," Lydia said.

"I know. We've been driving for hours. Get some air."

"You mean stretch my legs," Lydia quipped without regret or malice.

She was so light in my arms. Like the desert heat itself.

By the time I set Lydia in her chair Jol had already climbed halfway up a powder-fine dune that reached to the sky. The heat felt cleansing as I emptied my bladder.

"We need a blank canvas. Oblivion. It's supposed to be out here." Lydia said to no one in particular.

"I know. We'll find it." I leaned in and kissed Lydia's sun-warmed head. She smelled like buttered toast. Windblown wisps of hair tickled my nose.

Sonia, atop a tall boulder, looked out across the desert. She jumped down with a thud. Two plumes whirled out from under her combat boots. Unceremoniously, she pulled up her pink vintage satin slip dress and squatted against the rock. The dust between her boots darkened to a wet grey.

"We're close," she confirmed, "There's a ghost town out that way." Sonia pointed at a 45-degree angle away from the line of the highway. "Jol will have a better view of the place from up on the dune."

"Jol, what do you see up there?" I hollered.

She turned and started down the slope with giant strides. Each footfall, an avalanche.

"There's a couple of little towns. The closest one is abandoned. It's just up the road. I can see it clearly. I'd say we have a little less than ten miles to go."

We loaded back up in the bus and drove on. Signs unreadable, scoured clean by dust storms and pot shots, dotted the roadside. Crumbling white-washed mining buildings still clung to the side of a quarry long since closed. Below the pale cliffs of gypsum, a gas station and mini-mart stood boarded up. The streak of a small animal dashed across the road.

Back in the city, the Octagon was flourishing, but since the wedding, Lydia had become sullen and unfocused. What Leo told her wasn't useful, she claimed. Gibberish. Delusions of grandeur. Regardless, her conversations gravitated to the place in the desert where Leo told her to go. An unchanged place. I could tell she believed going there was important, even if she didn't want to admit it to us or herself.

"Enlightenment is not a straight path. You need to backtrack, clear ties, retreat, advance, because what is inflexible goes against the laws of chaos, and existence is chaotic and absurd. If we hadn't had our misfortunes, would we be better off? Would we be closer to the truth? That's what Leo asked me to answer for myself," she said.

Leo had told her she needed to make this final pilgrimage to fully understand his message. Many had made the trip, but most failed to see the point. It's a forgotten place now, he had told her.

Ironically, it was nearly impossible to find a bus that was gas-powered and had a steering wheel. The grid would not allow autonomous vehicles to go off road and cross the Nevada desert. Intentionally or not, the public grid enforced a system of boundaries. According to the Uber maps, the Black Rock Desert was completely off-road. The range stopped outside of a town called Gerlach. I finally found an under the radar outfit run out of a junkyard that rented sub-legal vehicles.

After the abandoned mining town, we crossed into a small patch of habitation. The wide spot in the road, really. It had two bars, a restaurant, a post office, a firehouse, and a small school. Rusting sculpture dotted the landscape, now unrecognizable, crumbling into metallic sand. I thought towns like this were extinct. Nothing but the decaying art betrayed the aesthetic of the West. I turned the bus into a diner sided in weathered wooden planks.

From the outside, I would never have never guessed that this place served Italian food. It was seat-yourself, so we claimed the long soda fountain with stools like giant nails pounded into yellowing linoleum tiles. The floor had been persevered with layers of floor wax decades deep. Garlic and the tang of rich tomato sauce filled the air. A waitress with deeply tanned skin and shoulder-length hair the color of dirty windows slid oversized menus across the Formica, set down utensils rolled in paper napkins, and took our drink orders. She could have been thirty or fifty. It was hard to tell.

"What will it be today?" The waitress said to the four of us with her ticket pad and pen in hand. I ordered bolognese and a salad with blue cheese. Jol, Sonia, and Lydia ordered a pizza to share.

"All right. I still don't totally understand. What did Leo say we're looking for out here?" I asked.

"He said I'd find what I needed. Not what my anxiety drives me to do, but what my heart desires—the reality of who I really am. He said I was ready. That I had suffered enough. He told me the desert will show me how I betray myself and I'd learn to be free. I reckon you'll find the same thing, whatever that is."

The waitress arrived with the pizza and spaghetti.

"Anything else? Wine?" She asked.

As I answered yes, wine all around, an Einstein shock of crazy grey hair attached to a man pushed through the door. He eyed our group with mild hostility and squeezed into a red Naugahyde booth within earshot.

"Seeker's, huh?" The man said in a voice as crunchy as 40-grit sandpaper. "You know, there used to be a lot of y'all that'd come through here. Not much anymore."

"I'm Lydia, and this is Sonia, Jol, and this is Evan," Lydia said.

"You're a peach and I'm crusty. Wanna make a pie?" He said with a low, rumbling laugh, eyeing the girls.

The stranger looked at me with calculating appraisal while picking his teeth. He wore a once black t-shirt, its fading image so pale from wear and washing, it looked like a crop circle against a field of grey. His jeans were impregnated with dust and dirt, and his work boots left flakes of mud in their wake. Our waitress strafed the old man's table, depositing a glass of water on her way to the main dining room.

"Be right back, Hon," She said to the old-timer.

"Where should we turn off and camp?" Lydia said, ignoring the crass but colorful innuendo of a moment ago.

The stranger stared and continued to suck on his toothpick. When we were about to give up, he exhaled loudly and started speaking again. "Nope, there's no particular place to camp. You'll see. It's all as blank as a fresh canvas. Well, at first it is. Once your mind settles down, you'll see a whole world out there. You have to feel it out for yourself. Who told you to come out here, by the way?"

"Blank. Leo described this place in the same way," Lydia whispered so the stranger couldn't hear her.

"Some asshole. Name's Leo. You wouldn't know him," I replied.

"HA! Wouldn't know him, my ass. That snakey conman is the source of most of our pests, I mean *guests*. Leo's one of the last real fuckernauts. People find different stuff when they spend time out on the desert. Each of us is hardwired with our own interpretation. You can't change what you'll experience. Only thing you can do is uncover it. The difference between Leo and me is he thinks he can direct the chaos. He hangs on to some illusion of control, and that makes him an angry, little man. At least that's the way he was last time he was here. Me? I just surf the waves."

"Why do you stay in this town, then?" Lydia asked.

"For sweet treats like you. And to act as cruise director for snowflakes. Someone's got to do it." He laughed with a cackle.

The waitress swung by and set the bill down by my wine glass.

"I see you've met the Mayor," she said.

The dinner rush had started. Unkempt men and women, who looked a lot like the stranger, filled the place.

The waitress set a beer on the Mayor's table and hurried off to a beckoning patron.

§

A few miles past the town, over the scrubby berm of the low shoulder, the desert opened white and vast with a swipe of black mountains beyond.

"We're close! This is it. What Leo described," Lydia said.

It looked like no destination at all. Leo had given Lydia practical road directions that stopped at Gerlach. After that, the instructions became weird and vague. He told us to drive about twelve miles past the town and look for access to the playa along the shoulder. Which path, it didn't matter. No path is the best path. That is your gate, he had told Lydia. No gate. It's as if he told us to jump into the ocean, but it wasn't an ocean, instead it was nothing. Sheer nothing. Intimidating and utterly serene. Unchanged since the days long before man.

Dust devils whipped the surface of the featureless distance into funnels that towered to the cloudless lavender of the sky, then collapsed as quickly as they formed. A simmering haze hung over a lake of quicksilver. There were no landmarks. I had to trust in Lydia, because I didn't trust Leo. And I was afraid.

"Are you sure you want to go out there?" I asked.

"Yes." Lydia responded.

"It's pretty weird. I don't know. This seems pointless," Jol said.

Despite our fear, I eased the bus through ruts and sagebrush. Friction soon passed away and we seemed to skate. Acceleration was tentative at first, then we picked up speed. After a while, my sense of direction was lost and I drove at random. We flew. An occasional rock would appear to float on the sunset. Fata morgana. A floating effect, like a mirage, but not the same. Lydia peered out the window eagerly.

"We stop soon," she said, "When all civilization, other than us, disappears. A mental shedding."

A final flame of green sparked under a dome of ultraviolet as the sun sank below the ribbon of mountains. Outside the bus, it was cold, dry, and utterly alien. We had packed food, water, fire wood, warm clothes, and sleeping bags. Even though it was September and the desert was our destination, temperature could drop into the low 40s at night.

Patches of hard-packed ground cracked and curled like the back of some great reptile. Over a circle of white that faded into tarnish, then black, the firmament unfolded as the last of the day's light extinguished. It was a wonder. Millions of stars filled the sky. The Milky Way, nearly as white as the alkali desert under us. Above and below, united in the sea of sameness. Meteorites streaked great arches. So many of them, I lost count.

Jol was scared. She pleaded that we stay in the bus, that we go back to town, but I wanted to share the experience that Leo told Lydia to find more than anything in my life. What could be out here? Why had he sent us?

Was I ready in the way he said Lydia was? Or was this another one of his tricks?

Lydia rolled into the darkness. Sonia chose her own path. Scattering. Aloneness was part of the map.

"Don't go," Jol said, panic in her voice.

"I have to go. If you don't want to come, be our home base. Come on out and build a fire for us. It's beautiful and safe. There's nothing to be afraid of."

I walked into solitude. I didn't turn back to see if she got out of the bus or not. In the living darkness, I walked. The only sound was the wind. No one here. An uneasy disorientation came over me. *Lydia! Sonia! I'm lost!* I thought, but no distress call passed my lips. My muscles tensed and my mouth went dry. Was this a punishment? A joke? Leo's final kick in the nuts. But no, the threat was created by my own mind. I thought of Leo. All we had been through.

As my mind stilled, the universe set itself in motion. Bats passed overhead, barely there. The sky moved, seething with distant life. I heard a coyote howl. Thoughts unfolded and rippled across the dust.

"My family!" I shouted to the sky. Run to them, the sky shouted back. Run to Jol, and to Lydia, and to Sonia. I flew back, light as a spirit, unburdened with all I had believed I wanted and thought I needed to achieve. None of it was true. It was all an illusion, a dream of life.

"Jol!" I shouted as I raced toward the bus. "Jol! I love you!"

She rushed toward me and we collided in an embrace.

"Oh, Evan. We thought you were lost. You've been gone so long. Hours! I was so scared," Jol said in a rush of words.

"I can't live without you, Jol. Marry me!"

"I will," she said. She covered me in kisses.

Lydia and Sonia sat quietly by a small campfire. Lydia's wheelchair sat empty a few feet away.

"Come over here," Sonia called.

My arm around Jol's shoulder, we joined Lydia and Sonia at the fire. Lydia had been absorbed by the desert, here, but gone. Our dreams mingled together. Only Lydia's liberation had been fully granted. Leo saw she had been close to freedom all along. Me? I held my ties. My career. I saw a marriage and children before me. A promise. The effort and distraction of these choices would hold me in the world of industry and ambition. But the knowledge that I could let go was something to carry like a precious diamond.

"Lay me on the earth with me and Sonia," Lydia said.

She took my hand and I sank down to lie beside her on the bone-colored, hard-packed dust. Jol joined us under an infinity of stars above. Earth and sky. Me, us, them. All the same. A sense of utter absurdity washed over me, filling me with a profound sense of contentment.

ACKNOWLEDGMENTS

I am grateful to my mother, Donna-Marie Pearson; my husband, Kelly Turner; my son, Buckaroo St John; and my sister Elizabeth Walther for giving me the love and space to follow my passion. I'd like to thank my writing coach, Suzy Vitello; my editor, Kieran Devaney; cover designer Richard Ljoenes; and business partner Corrine Casanova for their tremendous help in bringing Zone Trip into the world. Carol Smith's support and Laura Magee's friendship deserve special mention for giving me the strength to persevere. To the many other friends, family, and mentors who helped along the way, please accept my anonymous thanks. Finally, I want to acknowledge all the amazing teachers at LitReactor.

PRAISE FOR ZONE TRIP

"I love your voice, the themes, and the characters. It's an incredible feat, and I know this book will delight readers."

Suzy Vitello, Author of Faultland and The Empress Chronicles

"Zone Trip is a haunting story that just breaks my heart. The immersive setting, colorful characters, sense of loss, and transcendence at the end? What a ride. It's Tom Robbins, Ken Kesey, and Max Barry filtered through a Chuck Palahniuk lens."

Richard Thomas, author of Spontaneous Human Combustion, a Bram Stoker Award finalist

"Active, urgent, and evocative."

Francesca Lia Block, Author of Weetzie Bat

"Your link between anarchism and absurdism is well-established. Leo seems to be a true anarchist in that his goal is the absurdity, the subversion of expectations, and the dismantling of the system in the name of free artistic expression."

Daniel DeCillis, Ph.D. of Philosophy

ABOUT THE AUTHOR

Kitty Turner's circus and showgirl career spanned five years. Until 2017, she toured the Caribbean casino and resort circuit along the Antilles chain with her husband and a rotating cast of international circus performers aboard a 47 ft. sailboat.

Before moving to the Caribbean in 2007, Kitty co-owned the award-winning nightclub 12 Galaxies in the Mission District of San Francisco. After hurricanes Irma and Maria destroyed her sailboat home, Kitty relocated to the Reno area and founded the book marketing company Daily House Media. Visit https://www.kittyturner.media/ for more.

facebook.com/kittyturner.author
twitter.com/dailyhousemedia
instagram.com/zonetripkitty
amazon.com/author/kittyturner

CPSIA information can be obtained
at www.ICGtesting.com
Printed in the USA
JSHW081024050423
39931JS00002B/150

9 781733 668736